I0622321

Twenty Forty-Eight

A NOVEL BY

Richard Lawrance

Warning: This novel is not written in publishese. It contains writing some readers may find individual or even idiosyncractic.

Acknowledgements

The author wishes to acknowledge an intellectual debt to Richard Tawney's *Religion and the Rise of Capitalism*, on which sections in Chapter 5 draw. Professor Tawney's book was first published in 1926, then by Pelican Books in 1938. There have been many reprints since. To the best of the author's knowledge, the real life Richard Tawney did not die by being shot whilst delivering a public lecture in a large cathedral somewhere in the UK.

The excerpt from T.S.Eliot's "The Hollow Men" in Chapter Eighteen was downloaded from the internet website http://poetry.poetryx.com/poems/784/ on 30 January 2008. The poem was first published in 1925.

My thanks as always to the support and advice of Julian Hafner, Christine Johnson and Greg Vickas and, of course, my parents.

National Library of Australia Cataloguing-in-Publication entry
Author: Lawrance, Richard.
Title: Twenty forty-eight / Richard Lawrance.
ISBN: 9780980857504 (pbk.)
Dewey Number: A823.4

For Norma and Ian

Chapter One

Howard Smithson Johns sat on the veranda of his twenty fourth floor apartment idly sipping scotch as the clock struck twenty seven in the old town square nearby. He clanked the ice around the spacious tumbler from time to time, for the sound of it more than the effect. He liked to do this when he travelled to the larger cities of old. The CBDs of Old Sydney and Old Melbourne used to look like fairylands at this time of night. Most of their offices were empty, the pre-dawn cleaners yet to arrive, but still entire floors of office space were bathed in light.

There was just this hour between the last train of one timetable and the first train of the next, when just the occasional cab ventured through the city streets. Despite almost twenty years of the thirty six hour day, that dead time between twenty seven and twenty eight hours, (or fifteen and sixteen hours depending on which cycle of the 36 hour day you were in) still seemed to hold. The trains still stopped. The streets still emptied. Even though a third of the population were shopping somewhere, and another 33% were just three hours into their work shift, and everyone officially believed that there was no day or night in the Shopping World, in a 'bureaucracy town' like Canberra somehow this magic hour in the darkness of night still exerted a vestige of a previous world order.

Howard could remember the arguments early in his political career. The unions were at the last barricade. Workplace reform had successively removed one layer of workers' rights after another. All that was left was the thirty six hour week. It was ironic that, in all the world, it was the country in which trade unionism had reached its zenith that it also met its nemesis: Smithson Adams. For just as it seemed the few remaining unions would hold sway with public opinion, it was the aging Adams who came back out of the woodwork with the slogan: Choice is All, and All have Choice.

Why argue for a 36 hour week, he reasoned on chat shows across the nation. Why not a 36 hour day? Now that the world was clearly in the fourth phase of progress, the developed nations had the perfect opportunity to lead the way. In a 36 hour day, everyone would still have eight hours of sleep, but they would have 16 hours of leisure. Or ten hours of sleep and 14 hours of leisure. Whatever combination one chose. The weekend was outmoded. Shopping Worlds could be open all hours. The consumer would have complete choice.

The trick was, of course, that every 12 hours a new working day started for a third of the working population. The eight hour day would give way to the round temporal dozen. Governments of the so-called 'developed nations' immediately saw the benefit. In a global movement of materialist catch-up amongst the developing nations, led by China and India, there was not long to go for the economies of the old "West" – the former US, Canada, Old Europe and Australasia. The once-cheap goods from the developing nations would soon cost the same as those produced locally, as the wage gap producing them closed. Here was an opportunity for the "West' to generate a temporary competitive advantage, both in accelerated production and in consumption. The end result would be the same, but at least New Prosperity, as Adams called is, would give the old "West" a competitive edge for a while longer.

And so the thirty six hour day, and the thirty six hour clock (itself a market revolution), was introduced. A third of the nation worked 12 hours while a third of the nation slept and a third shopped. It was the bureaucrats and administrators running transport and utilities infrastructure who couldn't let go of the 'changeover hour', as they called it. The Public Sector Association in Australia argued that they needed just one uniform period in which to check the lines, check the cyber circuitry nationwide, check the road and rail grids. And the public sector organised its 12 hour shifts so that there was still a 'dark' three hours in the middle of the traditional 'night' to work around this magic hour of national quality assurance and quality control.

So it was, twenty years later, that in Canberra – a former public service town - the blues and reds of corporate neons still in this hour alone imbued the silent skyline with the concrete cogency of the dormant office towers whose identity they telegraphed. And between the tall office and hotel towers, streetlights and worklights splashed pavements, kerbsides and side alleys into orange or lavender blue watercolour relief. Occasionally an unidentifiable figure walked from wash to wash. Later that day, someone would want to know what the activity their Consumer Choice Chip would register meant at that hour.

Here the CBD had never amounted to more than a couple of blocks, and since the collapse of federalism the former national capital had fallen, at least on the surface, into relative disuse. These days the city just represented the northern border of VIC. The former Albury-Wodonga was developing strongly as the new Melbourne, and was the seat of VIC government. But Canberra was the centre of Howard Johns' seat in the VIC parliament, so it was here Howard spent much of his time when parliament was not sitting.

Although parliament *was* in fact sitting at the moment. There had been a smear campaign against him, targeting excessive travel claims while he was visiting his mother on Philip Island in the nation state's south. Howard had been given clear intelligence there would also be insinuations about sexual proclivities associated with his 'Philip Island jaunts'.

That these were untrue is not what bothered Howard Johns. That was not why, just 24 hours earlier, he had tried to commit suicide. If anything, it was the acute shame and embarrassment his mother would have to endure that caused him pain. He loved his mother, and would stay alive at all costs just to make sure she could rest assured.

It was true he'd inflated a few travel claims, but only to ensure she was not out-of-pocket herself. The reality was that sometimes, when he was supposedly visiting his mum, he was in fact a guest of one transcorporation or another, doing the back door work up for a government deal. But of course Howard couldn't say that in public response to the so-called scandal. Government was not supposed to be doing 'deals' with business.

However, the scandal's impending escalation was by no means responsible for his actions yesterday. It was true he had 'absconded' from a parliamentary sitting to avoid being in the firing line, but only at the request of the leader of his Chamber. He certainly wouldn't have taken his immediate political situation seriously enough to end his life over it.

As he clinked the ice around in his tumbler and stared mutely out over the near vacant CBD, Howard was still puzzling over his actions. He knew he had been depressed for some time. He found the parry and thrust of parliamentary conflict emotionally exhausting, and was not enough of an egotist to find that it justified the small gains achieved on the basis of principle.

It was principle that had motivated Howard to follow his father into politics. It was a commitment to the desire to pursue social change on the basis he had inherited from both of his parents. While he was committed to the party, and the ideology it represented, fundamentally he was interested in results that mattered to society. And in this, pragmatic as he was, Howard Smithson Johns felt he was an anachronism in the world of contemporary politics. In New Prosperity, principle was a thin fibre that existed in some distant vacuum, suspended all by itself, vibrant but friendless. When push came to shove, ideology just fell away from the main game like banknotes from a gaming table, only to appear again in the next round in another's hand.

It was endless. And in it, Howard had no emotional support of his own. There was no love. No lover. Not even a former partner or a good friend in the Party. Just the loneliness of returning home after endless dinner meetings, evening engagements, strategy planning sessions, press briefings; home to perhaps further phone calls, or simply half a bottle of scotch and sleep. To be up at the fifth hour 'next day' for his near-pathologically driven zip through the back streets of whichever city he happened to be in to begin it all over again.

He was not sure he had even intended suicide when he ran the bath. He just wanted to relax, soak himself away from it all. He was already three quarters of the way through the bottle. He idly took the Wüsthof paring knife his mum had given him for Christmas – his latest culinary plaything – more out of interest in its beauty than any serious commitment to self-harm.

As he undressed to step into the deep, iron, claw-foot antique, he was aware that his sexual ambivalence was an unsettling feature of his current self-doubt. He had not had a relationship with a woman for over two years now. Had undertaken the exemplary two marriages and was, frankly, beyond the effort. And while he was aware he was probably bisexual, he had simply never met a man with whom he had felt capable of exploring anything beyond what passed for casual stereotypical heterosexual male contact. Certainly no intimacy, even less sexually so.

There was just a general sense of emptiness that went to the very core of his self, compounded by the meaninglessness of the political life he led, and he wanted a genuine break from it. So the idea of opening the length of his veins and watching his life slip quietly away into the bath came to him as something of a curiosity. He simply finished the bottle of scotch and executed the surgery with his rather exquisite example of kitchen steel, uncharacteristically without further analysis.

Unfortunately, what Howard had never known about himself until this point was that the sight of his own blood made him nauseous. He had no idea know how he had escaped confrontation with his own haemorrhaging life fluid before now, but the sight of the length of the first forearm leaking red into the warm water brought his scotch and whatever else was left in his stomach up in violent waves. He didn't even make it to the veins of the second wrist.

8

Another factor that probably saved his life was the irrational fact that, as he slit his right forearm from the elbow down towards the wrist, he realised that he would most probably dislodge his Consumer Choice Chip. While Howard was not opposed to the Chip in principle, he did resent the more subversive uses to which its capabilities were put. He agreed with the money-free state that the Chip, with its simple point-of-purchase reading, facilitated. The carriage of health records and other personal data for in-wrist updating also added to personal mobility and individual control over one's information. He agreed that the Chip's capacity to read vital signs and initiate automatic paramedic retrieval in emergencies was a life saver. Its remote interface with the individual's PIMS[1] had transformed individual productivity and sense of security.

But as a politician, Howard was privy to some of the other uses to which the Chip was applied: monitoring all bodily activity, for instance, to provide data for commercial product research and development. Sexual activity and eating were of particular interest to commercial providers. Adverse health status, such as cardiovascular irregularity, was used to automatically adjust insurance and debt repayment risk assessments. Its GPS capability, Howard knew, was used to track movements both for commercial market research purposes but also for security and intelligence monitoring. And he was also aware the Chip had, unknown to the general populace, listening and, in some models, radarvision capabilities.

All of these functions wedded the wearer to the transcorp that produced the model, because the market and R&D data that users unwittingly provided to their transcorp of choice afforded constant competitive advantage. So there was a principle in play here that would have seen Howard perfectly happy to see the Chip sliced from his wrist. And yet he baulked at the final fence. Faltered before the instrument was completely adrift. Perhaps it was because subconsciously he did not want the sudden cessation in his vital signs to instigate an emergency retrieval. Perhaps his deeper mind

[1] personal information management system

9

realised the mistake he was making, and the implications it would have for his career if he survived by unsolicited emergency rescue.

Perhaps an even deeper, more calculating intelligence – the sort that always comes into play during the actual experience of trauma – told him that he had already found a way to retrace his tracks: the vomiting is what would be primarily read and transmitted by the Chip, not the blood loss.

Whatever mental processes worked on his ontology's behalf in those few brief moments, successive waves of emetic convulsions drove Howard Johns from his bath. As he grappled with a confusion of water-and-blood-slopped ceramic surfaces, however, he fumbled with the knife in his left hand, caught it with the blood-bathed right, and inadvertently slashed his left wrist anyway. Luckily this was a transverse cut rather than the more studied lengthwise vein-slit of his right. Otherwise he would never have survived. Nevertheless, the blood now started to flow also from his left wrist as well.

Suddenly intensely alert, he grabbed towels in which he attempted to wrap his haemorrhaging arms whilst he continued to vomit raucously into the bath. He felt dizzy and faint, yet his mind was racing faster than it did during Question Time in the Chamber.

The towels were filling with blood. He was not staunching the bleeding. Between emetic bouts, he had to grab fresh towels from the hall closet and re-bind his arms, tightening them into a tourniquet effect with his teeth. Eventually, once the vomiting subsided, he instinctively threw himself upon his arms on the bathroom floor in order to use his entire body in the application of pressure to the leaking wounds.

Eventually he passed out, to awaken hours later naked and shivering. The unwelcoming light of the next day was fully evident in the apartment beyond the open bathroom door. Howard was horribly, and disappointingly, alive. He spent the rest of the day trying to patch up his wounds without having to go out to make purchases, and to wash the blood out of his towels and his bathroom without unduly registering suspicious activity on the still-implanted CCC.

Mid-afternoon he had finally found sleep. It was dark before he awoke again. He dressed, with no intention of going anywhere but this veranda, and was still here as the darkness drifted into the early hours before daylight, observing restless thoughts move inchoate through his mind, still unable to make sense of his unintentional suicide attempt. He had thought himself desolate, but it was difficult to believe that his life lacked such meaning that he would deem it worthy of ending. It simply didn't make sense.

He would have appreciated the coming days free of responsibilities in the Chamber to further reflect on his state of mind, the health of his self, as it were. And to give his wounds time to heal, as they would show up in the various arrays of security screens through which he routinely passed in his day's work. Unfortunately there was a message on his netface from the Leader of the Chamber that there seemed to have been a reprieve on the campaign against him, for the moment at least, and he was needed back in the Chamber to progress the Water bill. There were, apparently, 'developments'.

He was on downtime at the end of his formal 36 hour cycle, and should really be going to bed. But felt little need of sleep. No fairies for me tonight, he thought. And his eyes rested for a while on the giant monochrome face of Smithson Adams, pasted on the base of the tower block opposite, with its omnipresent text: CONSUMER CHOICE – ALWAYS WITH YOU. And, taking another sip from the clinking tumbler, he dwelt with no small irony on the impact consumer choice had made upon his life just twenty eight hours before.

11

Chapter Two

"Been unwell, have we sir?" asked Greaves pointedly. Obviously intelligence of Howard Smithson Johns' bilious attack 48 hours earlier had reached the Security Service of VIC's Parliament House.

"Yes, overdid the culinary delights, I'm afraid," Howard replied, making sure his shirt cuff did not reveal his bandaged wrists as he proffered his CCC for checking.

"Tough scotch fillet was it, sir?" Greaves enquired with that non-committal archness of the officious, confirming yet again Howard's misgivings about the sensory powers of his Consumer Choice Chip. It was amazing that Parliamentary security forces felt so little need to conceal the full extent of the surveillance reach of the world's number one symbol of consumer choice. Nevertheless the inner doors of the Members entrance slid open and Johns was admitted to his place of work.

After fitful turns between sleep and wakefulness, Johns had mentally paced his way through his official 'sleep' time during the daylight hours of yesterday into today. He had been sure to rise as darkness fell and engage in 'normal' pre-work activities through the early darkness hours. He had then driven the last hours of darkness through the northern country towns of VIC to New Melbourne. It never ceased to amaze Howard the alacrity with which the former Albury Wodonga was spreading north of the Murrumbidgee. There were predictions New Melbourne would reach Wagga Wagga by 2075. And it did seem that, every time he actually did the drive, another kilometre of construction prefab had gone up.

Howard rarely drove, even though it took just four hours from Canberra to VIC Parliament. But on this occasion he knew the airport screening would pick up the fresh scarring on his arms. And in the dark hours the road was usually quieter, and the uninterrupted kilometres of tarmac under headlight could be quite relaxing.

During sunlight hours the drive was an entirely different prospect. Howard could not avoid seeing the speed limit signs every hundred metres or so. Most drivers these days ignored them, but the regularity with which they randomly changed speed limits simply irked the son of Menzies Johns. Howard's father could remember a time when the police had to physically stop a vehicle that they had tracked speeding, and make a professional judgement as to whether the law required application on this occasion – a charge, a fine, or a caution. Nowadays the limit on the signs changed arbitrarily, and the camera mounted on its departing side automatically snapped the number plate of the passing vehicle and instantly added the inevitable fine to the registered owner's lawdebt.

On any average day in the suburbs, 75% of the country's car owners went further into lawdebt by hundreds of dollars. On a rural run, the figure could be thousands. No wonder rural Australia was only for the rich these days.

Howard had inherited his father's utter dismay at this total abrogation of responsibility for the law. Law and debt – that the two should be so synonymous was an abhorrence to a man whose first profession was as a legal counsel. "Law should be about the public interest!" Menzies would rail to his son over one too many a red. "It should be about protecting the majority from harm, protecting them from the minority who would wrong them. It should be about fairness and justice, not this rampant exercise in back-pocket taxation. How can the public be expected to have respect for the law any more? Let alone for those who supposedly enforce it!"

But by that time Menzies Johns was already an old man, and nearing death. The public were already insouciant to the law's role as legitimised extortion, and lawdebt was a fact of life. These days, parents simply accepted the fact that they would hand on impossible debt to their children when they died. The money was only on the books. But, as the pragmatist in Howard well knew, the nation state still had it in their balance sheets, and could use the debt equity to attract future investment from the transcorps.

Nevertheless, it depressed him to drive through the endless kilometres of them, watching the irrelevant signs flip to some new unmeasurable calibration of speed before his very eyes, knowing the dollars simply flowed down the line to some silicon repository deep in the heart of his future. Whereas in the dark hours, they were designed not to be seen, and he could pretend he lived in a time when human judgement had purpose and professions entailed an identity and some sense of social obligation and belonging.

Perhaps, he thought, it was this irksome sense that there was a real difference between right and wrong, that fairness and equity had meaning, that had led to his suicide attempt? Perhaps he felt he was unable to escape his tendency to care – a behaviour so many of his peers seemed to avoid with such ease.

He walked through the pristine halls of VIC Parliament – with its marble floors donated by Transnational, its web-like solar-power-generating water-reticulated roof built at considerable discount by Transglobal, and its grand columns of Papua New Guinea and Amazonian timber veneered for free by Pancontinental. Parliamentary staff ferried visiting lobbyists and dignitaries this way and that. Men and women in suits greeted each other with handshakes after stepping audibly across diplomatic expanses of democratic space. People spoke into cell cards in corners or behind pillars. Bells rang ostentatiously when a decision was called for in one Chamber or another.

It all looked so busy and purposeful. Today the buzz would all be about the Choice Renewal Rate, the latest calculation of which was due. Everyone would have their own prediction of the increase, and its causes. But everybody here knew it was just for show. The only power democracy had these days was either in micro-regulation to keep one step ahead of capital or in legislating for one transcorp a momentary advantage over the others. For all the show of care, no-one really did. Not in these halls, anyway. Most of the lobbying for VIC Parliament was actually done in the offices of the transcorps themselves, or on nominated 'neutral territory' which was constantly moved to avoid premature detection by the opposition. And most of the bureaucratic work of parliamentary staff was done by accountants and IT experts, working out the next development in the world of finance they could manipulate with legislation in order to attract the investment of a transcorp in their nation state's regulatory power.

When senior transcorp figures did visit VIC Parliament, it was purely as a courtesy, to maintain the public front that parliament was indeed the heart of power in the great VIC democracy; which was why people should choose to live and work and spend in VIC, as opposed to NSW or QLD or WA or NT or SA or NZ – or, indeed, PNG or Indonesia or Malaysia or any of the other nation states that populated the geographical region of South Asia, in which the Australasian archipelago represented the Europacific "boot".

The transcorps always tried to send the same people, to give the impression that these were companies with genuinely human faces, interested in and respectful of the democratic workings of government. It was thus no surprise to see O'Brien enter the Seventh Hall in time for the Two Minute Vision.

Howard quite enjoyed the Two Minute Vision. It was a classic exercise in indoctrination. No sooner had the working day started for a particular twelve-hour shift than everyone stopped for this moment to imagine their dreams. Wherever they were, whatever they were supposed to be doing, they stopped work and gathered before the public vision screens as the ever-present image of Smithson Adams crackled into life. He must have aged by now, or even died, but he always seemed the same sprightly and distinguished sixty-year-old who had introduced New Prosperity in the 2030s. His pleasure-lined face creased beneficently into a smile, and myriad mood music moved through multi-layered tones and key shifts out into ambient space.

"Relax for a moment," the same sixty-year old mid-Australian voice suggested. "Still your busy mind. We all work hard, but what is it for?"

Images now of glittering products, the latest technological purchases on the market, relaxing tropical resorts, luxurious hotel-like air travel, and happy, smiling families in comfortable homes drifted across the screen, across Smithson's face, which faded but remained visible in all its screen-filling well-meaning.

"If you had a choice, how would you spend your hard-won earnings? Imagine now. Imagine. For you DO have a choice. You have perfect choice. If it's one thing we have learnt this century, one truth that is true for all, it is that All have Choice, and Choice is All. Close your eyes for a moment."

The music now dipped through its multiple layerings to develop both high variations and deep, sonic base, inviting the imagination to swim into the tonal space between.

"Close your eyes and imagine what you would choose. What would you choose to spend your earnings on? Imagine it, in all its detail. Bask in its beauty and desirability, confident that if you can imagine it, you CAN purchase it, CAN consume it, CAN enjoy it as your own.

"Take your time now. Savour the moment. Savour your own sense of confidence and security. For remember, democracy is freedom, freedom is choice, and choice is the consumer's.

"Democracy is freedom, freedom is choice, and choice is the consumer's," the voice repeated.

"Democracy is freedom, freedom is choice, and choice is the consumer's" it said one last time, more softly, more tenderly, disappearing into a homey ether.

The music then swirled into a sea-like series of strophes and counter-strophes and washed out of the space's ambience like a departing tide. The screen return to its permanent 'still' of the never-aging

Smithson Adams, and people slowly opened their eyes, smiled at each other with silent satisfaction, and went about their business.

As he turned to leave, slightly ahead of the rest, not wishing really to make eye contact with anyone nearby – for he had thoughts of his own that had little to do with consumerism – Johns noticed that O'Brien was looking directly at him, from the rear of the hall. She looked away almost immediately, but not quickly. Rather, she moved her gaze leisurely, demurely, with elegance, as if purpose was hers' and he but one minor object in it.

Although Katharine O'Brien was a senior executive with Transglobal, and he just a lowly not-even-minister, this was not the first time Howard had chanced across her gaze to the point of eye-contact. There was something about her with which he felt a kindred spirit. Something he could not pinpoint.

It was certainly not attraction. She was beautiful enough. Deeply so. But she had that deliberation of feature, an almost sculptural voluminosity that rendered her aesthetic beyond mere sexuality. She carried herself with practised and effortless poise. Her expansive mouth sprang into the handsomest of smiles as she engaged in a handshake or an introduction. But an intelligence always sat well behind the ever-forward eyes, observing the event unfolding before them.

At least, that was how it seemed to Howard. He longed for the opportunity to meet her formally, hear her talk at first hand, to see if his assessment was accurate, or even close. But he was now in Water, and Transglobal did their water deals with another nation state altogether. O'Brien was already moving off, as Howard was himself, when an inattentive figure to one side crashed directly into him.

He was one of those spindly, tight-suited youths that seemed to be forever muttering something into a cell card, a mind locked into a LAN or WAN link with the cybernet, immune to the possibility of human connection in the immediate vicinity. This one bore the tell-tale horns of a genomorph – one of the many mild clone throwbacks that seemed to be increasingly emerging from the combined side effects of genetic engineering and global warming. The general consumer was supposed to accept them as peers, and governments legislated affirmative action for them around the globe. Nonetheless, they were covertly shunned. Although Howard found the horns on this one quite alluring. It was terribly degagé to find genomorphs alluring these days.

The youth did not apologise. On the contrary, his hands came up instantly, motioning Howard to a stand-off position into which he himself stepped back, bracing his cell card protectively between small finger and thumb, forefingers alert like a spider in defence. He looked directly but mutely into Howard's eyes, and Howard noticed the blue band around his CCC wrist – signifying the pride with which he wore his Consumer Choice Chip; the pride that identified him as a member of the Consumer Choice League.

"Consumer Choice," he said nervously, "Always with you."

"Always with you," replied Howard, confirming the normality of today's standard conformist greeting.

The youth snapped his card into the palm of a closed hand and moved on, without another word.

Howard was suspicious of the Consumer Choice League. If consumer choice was everything, where was the need for the fanaticism of a league for it? He guessed that the nation states had to find the fodder for their Sandwich Wars somewhere. A little bit of fanaticism could, perhaps, go a long way.

Anyway, he had a long day ahead of him. Water laws were the main item of the Seventh Chamber that day, and he had twelve long hours of meaningless debate and ridicule across the floor, for in the end the numbers would carry the day – again, and again, and again. Water laws were very big business in Australasia. And as he headed back to his office, he wondered whether this – the futility of his role in the larger political machine – was in fact the reason he had attempted to take his life. He had passed over the idea perhaps too easily the night before but resolved now to test the hypothesis against the progress of the day, on the hour, each hour, to see if it stood the passage of time. There had to be some reason. A real reason. Didn't there.

Chapter Three

Howard Smithson Johns' opportunity to meet Katharine O'Brien was destined to come sooner than he had imagined. After 6 hours in the Chamber, he took a scheduled meal break and went to the VICCaf, the VIC Parliament's sole eatery for staff and the general consumer. There was a private dining room for Members of the Chamber, but for Howard that was harder work than the relative anonymity of the cafeteria-sized VICCaf. Down here he might also chance upon useful back-room intelligence from the bureaucrats themselves.

Today he found a table with two longstanding informants, one of whom worked in Journalese and Brandgrab, the other on legislature in Water. Simpkins and Bishop never usually got on. Simpkins was an out-and-out cynic. A tall, beady-eyed man with a harrowed face and a hawk-like nose, he was the sort of human being who would find it hard to blend into the crowd. In addition, his keen intelligence and lateral thinking placed him well left of the field. In the average business setting, Simpkins would have most likely been a genius at branding and promotion. But it was so unlikely he would put up with the doctrinaire teamspeak and performance dogma of the commercial world, he would not last one campaign.

Bishop, on the other hand, at thirty five already cherub-like in his corpulent proportions, was a genuine consumer choice enthusiast. The ideals of consumer choice simply bounded out of him. He doted on his kids, and simply did not know how to say no to them. By his own heartrendingly devoted report, endless demands for the latest this or that were greeted with enthusiastic support by their father, including the full lexicon of consumerspeak: praising them for their creative vision, reminding them that democracy is freedom, freedom is choice, and choice is the consumers, encouraging them to pursue their goals and brook no compromise. If they could imagine it, they could have it.

Meanwhile he was flat stony broke himself most of the time, because he gave everything he earnt over to his family. His wife was a pinched, sallow looking woman with blousy edges, who ate too much starch-based food because it filled her up and was cheap. Bishop's work clothes were always out of fashion and threadbare at the elbows. He only ever entered and left VIC Parliament House by the staff tunnels. But he was happy.

Two more unlikely lunch companions were difficult to imagine. It could only be a compelling work discussion that brought them together, not only eating at the same table but actively engaged in conversation. Howard made a few healthy-looking meal purchases –he still had no appetite, but wanted to at least look like he was eating normally – and made his way to their table.

"Hi, mind if I join you?"

"Goodness, a Member! We are graced," quipped Simpkins, with a wink at Bishop, who beamed back without understanding.

"Hi Mr John- Howard," Bishop corrected himself. "You see? I remembered this time."

"You certainly did Bruce, and good on you for it."

"Always with you, Howard."

"Always with you, Bruce."

"Always out to lunch, the both of you," rejoined Simpkins.

"After only six hours on, Cedric. It's been a long day in the Chamber already."

"Have you heard the latest Choice Renewal Rate? Fresh off The Market! And call me Simpkins, for money's sake. You know I can't stand this matey ideo-speak first name garbage."

"Well I think a first name basis helps us all to identify with each other as being on the same team," Bishop defended the Member of Chamber.

"That's right, Bruce. Small government is good government, isn't it."

"Exactly."

"So the rate's out, Cedric?" Howard asked the writer with just the hint of a smirk.

"Unlike you, Howie." Simpkins knew Bishop was far too naïve to get the innuendo.

"I've had my two exemplary marriages," Howard defended himself nevertheless.

"So you have. When are you going to do the right thing, Bishop?"

Bishop blushed. The application of consumerist principles to marriage itself was one ideological leap he was too dependent on his own font of emotion to make. Secretly, he loved his wife beyond all, even his children. He could not bear the thought of ever being parted from her. But this was, of course, never a sentiment he would admit to in public.

"Just can't afford it, chaps," he bluffed. "We already have an insurmountable education pre-debt for the kids, and even though I take public transport we still seem to accrue massive lawdebt. As long as Social Safety payments remain structured so that the investment component is all up-front, I just can't afford to make any major changes until I'm forty, and can actually draw on SS to cover the alimony."

"Excuses, excuses," Simpkins dismissed. "You just love your wife, don't you?"

Bishop searched for some appropriate response, but even Simpkins was not cruel enough to leave him in such misery.

"So Howie, the renewal rate," he said, reverting to the opening topic. Howard looked askance at him, taking the cue.

"Twenty three percent! Four year high!" Simpkins volunteered.

Howard nodded appreciatively.

"I can remember when it was called planned obsolescence," Simpkins bemoaned, undermining his own sense of triumph.

Howard knew this was unlikely. Planned obsolescence was a historical concept from the late twentieth century, before Simpkins was even a twinkle in his parents' eye. Indeed, most probably before his parents were the same in theirs'. But Bishop was too easily drawn.

"Now that is a little too cynical, Cedric, even if I do say so. Consumer choice is-"

"All! We *all* know, Bishop!" Simpkins was impatient of another lecture.

"But the more regularly products are renewed, the more choice the consumer-"

"Speaking of renewal, Bishop, tell Howie here what you were telling me," Simpkins interrupted.

"Ah, well, it's not ready for the Chamber yet. We're still mining the legislation," Bishop prevaricated, with genuine concern for the proprieties of his work.

"Yes, but Howard's in Water – Parliamentary Secretary isn't it?"

"One of five, yes."

"So you're just providing him with some initial briefing, to seek pre-emptive feedback, shall we call it." Simpkins was actively goading Bishop now.

"Well, perhaps…" Bishop was still dubious. So Simpkins took the initiative for him.

"Bishop was telling me that there is a chance VIC has legislative rights to greater flows from the Murrumbidgee. Because NSW has extended its Lake Leichhardt storage facilities into the Simpson, they are drawing off more from the Georges River System downflow than was originally agreed."

"But why would we want to stop that? Where's the competitive advantage?" asked Howard, immediately understanding where the conversation was going.

The river argument was a bit of a red herring really, because anyone even mildly informed of the science knew that it was the enclosed pipe systems that brought the seasonal water down from the North into enclosed storage systems that actually provided the more cost-effective water services. The river systems, no matter how much they were connected up through inland canals to keep them from outflow to the sea, were still massively subject to evaporation, and thus less of a commercial proposition.

But rivers had symbolism and, therefore, greater brandgrab power. The transcorps were always going to be attracted to them for the corporate profiling alone.

"There would have to be a trade off," Simpkins explained quickly. "We'd secure greater downflows for ourselves and build a similar storage facility. But we'd use it to reclaim more arable land. Remember, we have less desert than NSW, and more land that's tameable with even the most modest salinity plant in a region."

"Which transcorp is going to be attracted to agriculture?"

"One that needs carbon credits, to offset increased emissions from an existing plant elsewhere."

"Transglobal," Howard divined. Simpkins nodded with an impish grin. Transglobal were one transcorp that had built its capital base on water-based power solutions, leaving solar and geothermal to the other two major players on the planet, Transnational and Pancontinental.

"So we get them to invest in VIC water developments, with agricultural and salinity conversion as value-add, while NSW pays with increased Transglobal industrial emissions."

"Got it in one, son. I think we are even including a water power generating component, aren't we Bishop?"

"The aim is simply to assert our legislative right," Bishop interjected with some misgivings. "There would be no intent of increasing overall emissions in Australasia, or contributing in any negative way to NSW's carbon burden. What's essential is that the overall balance is maintained and global reduction targets met. It's just that legislation is a legitimate method by which we can meet our global aims from a local perspective."

"Unless we happen to be involved in a Sandwich War," Simpkins said, goading Bishop once more. "In which case, anything goes."

"Well, Sandwich War is not a term yet recognised in the legislature - " protested Bishop, sensing a dangerous shift in context.

"Yes, but it is in Journalese, and we write the information briefs, sunshine."

"We don't even know that they exist for sure."

"Yet we hear about them every day in The Market, don't we?"

"There are some who say that fourth phase progress is still incomplete," Bishop persisted, finding his feet again. "We are in an historical process. Minor conflicts and confrontations over borders are still likely to occur in a world in which geographical and state boundaries are resolving along lines of choice.

"These are not necessarily on the scale of war. The supremacy of the logic of choice will see that, in the end, the right choices are made. People will not wittingly make choices that are against their own interests. Especially not in the Australasian region, where stability is greater."

"Bishop, I write the infobriefs. You don't need to feed my own spin back to me. The contrary view we also feed out there is that Sandwich Wars are due to emerging nation states who were slow to embrace New Prosperity and now resent a neighbour who has succeeded in securing major contracts in transcorp supply and demand chains and are, as a result, better able to embrace full consumer choice. And it's these recalcitrant states who engage in the Sandwich Wars – wars which the World Government steps in and controls, while benevolent transcorps assist the recalcitrant government in getting up to choicespeed."

Bishop shook his head, smiling grimly, refusing to believe what he was hearing.

"You try me every time, Cedric. You try me every time, but you won't fool me! I know you are a joker!"

Bishop rallied himself before Simpkins, wagging his finger in mock-reproach.

"You are a joker!" he said again with valiant humour.

Simpkins turned to Howard and spread his hands with raised eyebrows as if to say: What can I say? And Howard made a mental note to distance himself from Simpkins. The intelligence he revealed about the political machinery behind the relationship between government, transcorp and emerging nation states would get him into real trouble one day. Even in VICCaf, there were genuine consumers from the real world of choice beyond the walls of VIC Parliament.

"So are we meeting with Transglobal? Or are we still at the research stage?" Howard asked both men.

Bishop looked sheepish.

"Well, I'm writing a script for the Minister for a meeting with senior Transglobal executives tomorrow," Simpkins volunteered. "And you're listed in the introductions, Howie. You and that fabulous stunner of a Transglobal lobbyist, Katharine O'Brien."

Howard Johns' heart did not skip a beat in the conventional sense, but it certainly did experience a fluttering apprehension that its corporeal custodian might entertain an opportunity to explore a potential affinity with a certain objectified female sooner than it had anticipated. It was certainly an anticipation that engaged some of Howard's attention on the long drive home that night. And one that put out of his mind, for a short period at least, his quest for an explanation for his bid for self-destruction.

Chapter Four

Perhaps it was the possibility to meeting Katharine O'Brien, but Howard Smithson Johns was experiencing something resembling hope as he set out for the long drive home. He certainly felt the most positive he had in a number of weeks. Enough even to ignore, for the most part, the ever-changing speed limit signs. Whatever the reason, he found himself absorbed in preparation for a return, when he reached home, to his most recent personal endeavour.

Why this particular pastime needed to be secret had perplexed Howard up until now. In a world in which choice is all, and all have choice, he should be able to choose to do anything he pleased, within moral and legal parameters. Even the legislators agreed that this should be so: the role of government was to facilitate consumer choice, the role of legislation to facilitate the supply of options for choice, through the transcorps.

But there was still rumour and innuendo abroad that all was not as it seemed. The issue of identity displacement, for instance – there were often those who colloqued in trusted circles of individuals with whom they had 'lost touch' once these were awarded during the era of cyber terrorism. Identity displacement then was a security measure to protect the individual's cyber security – and that meant their life's data. In the same way that mass human counter-hacking had emerged as the only way to combat the virus wars, so identity displacement was the best measure against cybernet identity theft. It was merely convenient that, in the age of New Prosperity, the mandatory changing of one's identity had become a choice virtue: consumers now welcomed identity displacement as a prestige act of individual power. Many actively sought it. Indeed, there was a waiting list.

It was only in the interests of equity that the bureaucracy insisted on quarantining the public identity displacement program for all. According to the Market Place, Government had to fight on a regular basis for the modest proportion of IDs scheduled for commercial re-sale.

In government circles, however, one did not have to scratch far below the surface of ideospeak and brandgrab to reveal an understanding of the capacity identity policy gave nation states to control the supply of workforce data to transcorps; and to ensure the supply of workforce that enabled transcorps to meet shifts in demand. Every nation state well understood the value of assisting the transcorp in shifting sites of production to meet shifts in global demand, and the advent of new technology.

It was a fortuitous side-effect of the discourse to be able to promote it to the consumer as choice: the capacity to be free of the identity trappings of a personal name. A new identity meant new opportunities, new vistas of choice for the consumer. It was a state to be aspired to, one of the great benefits of New Prosperity to the individual. Renaming was a symbol of the truly free consumer, of Total Choice.

But was the practice of encouraging identity-shift as positive in outcomes as proponents of New Prosperity had intended? Was it possible that collusion between government and capital to sustain a capitalist growth cycle, with all of its benefits for the individual, involved a less-than-choice agenda?

In the face of the overwhelming spirit of economic optimism of the day, Howard felt decidedly guilty even entertaining such thoughts. He had himself managed to retain his family name by sacrificing his given name, arguing that his role as a Member of Chamber required some continuity of recognition for consumers. But inwardly he knew how reluctant he was to lose his father's name.

There were, however, some like Simpkins who spoke of an entire Real Truth movement which explored thinking and text beyond the realm of Consumer Choice. It was such intimation of a basis for doubt, coupled with his acute awareness of his growing ennui, that had led Howard Johns to the netface with the intent of searching beyond the surface of the information highway – to lift it up at the edges, as it were, and see what lay beneath.

With Simpkins' journalese advice, he had managed to create a cyber journalist who was untraceable to Howard Winston Johns, or any netface he used. This cyber character, whom he named Mick Turition, was to be Howard's secret adventurer in cyberspace; a champion who would boldly step out into the realm of history beyond ideotext to see what realities existed beyond the world of Consumer Choice.

Mick Turition was still in his early stages of construction, but he had undertaken successful trial forays into some of the more readily available inforepositories. He had, for instance, recovered most of the historical eras of the twenty-first century lost to contemporary ideospeak. The Religious Wars of the 2010s, Mick had reminded Howard, were also known as the Oil Wars, which in turn recalled the historical the link between warfare and the interests of capitalism that was denied in contemporary ideobrief. The geographical sites of these wars – the Middle East, Venezuela, Siberia – no longer existed in the modern map, but he could find them in representations of what used to be called 'countries' on geological formations they used to call 'continents' barely fifty years before.

Howard realised he had forgotten much of this history. Knowledge he had painstakingly researched and built up during his second degree had fallen to the ideospeak layerings of memory re-trace. He had forgotten about the Race Wars resulting from the Oil Wars in the 2020s, which led to the collapse of what they then called the Super Governments (the 'United States' and 'China').

There was a potential in this journey of re-discovery that generated a glow in Howard's centre that he had not felt in a while. Howard had become able to rediscover truth. But Mick Turition did not achieve this feat with the banal precision of an information clerk. Mick

Turition wore a black, broad brimmed hat turned up at the back and drawn down over his brow. A white mackintosh flapped around him as he swept through information, belt flailing, large collar turned up to shield his neck from imaginary wind and prying eyes. Mick Turition turned over data with a flick of finger and thumb, the way gamblers flipped coins. When he turned to watch his back, his body continued facing forward, only his hips twisting slightly, his shoulders guarded, his eyes remaining in shadow. Mick Turition had panache.

Tonight, Howard felt it was time to move Mick out of the relative safety of sanctioned inforeps, to see what else he could turn up behind the scenes. For tonight, as he proceeded methodically through of his usual regularising 'back at home' activities – a tumbler of scotch, a snack, an end-day viewing of the latest Law Industry Report to see what latest rorts the legal system had uncovered, and the nation state revenues raised by lawdebt that day - it began to dawn on Howard why he had seen the need to disguise his elicit cyber space activity through the creation of an alter-ego.

Somewhere deep in his sub-conscious, he realised, he had become aware of the depth of the loss of meaning in his life. That was clearly the real cause of his suicide attempt: an ontological despair that went to the very core of his being. Howard was lost in a sea of merging and re-merging discourses of non-meaning. He had, two days ago, literally slipped through the cracks between himself.

Luckily, his sub-conscious had a more inchoate interest in his own survival than his rational mind could muster. It had pre-driven him to create Mick Turition just in time, so that as he came to need him, a cyber champion was at hand to solve Howard Smithson Johns' ontological dilemma: to assist him in the quest for meaning, for Real Truth. And he could do so safely, hidden from the ever-prying technological surveillance of his own Consumer Choice Chip.

For it was not unusual that Howard Johns would go to his netface at this time of day. He was a Member of the Chamber and a parliamentarian. It was perfectly understandable that he would spend this time of night catching up with consumer correspondence, or infobriefing he had not had time to access during the day. And he did indeed intersperse Mick Turition's activities with genuine replies to enquiries and feedback from real live consumers, and the odd plausible infobrief. Anyone monitoring his CCC would see this as 'normal' Howard Johns downtime activity.

It may have aroused the suspicions of an assiduous CCC monitor that Howard used a keyboard rather than VIVO. The fact of the matter was that Voice-In Voice-Out technology, though germane to all netface use these days, would have given away Mick Turition's nefarious net-activities if Howard's CCC had, as he suspected, listening capability.

If anyone asked, Howard could easily justify his preference for the keyboard. Firstly, he used it all the time – not just at home. And secondly, his career prior to politics had been as a writer in lexidevelopment, actually generating the hyper-language programs for VIVO technology. And, of course, he had used a keyboard as the primary driver. He actually typed faster than he could talk as a result.

So it was that Howard Johns sat down at his netface, with the day drawing all too quickly to a close and, after a few quick replies to correspondents, found his way to where Mick Turition was lounging against a virtual lamppost in cyberspace.

One day, Howard hoped, his creation would burst through the saloon doors of ideobrief and throw the architects of Real Truth to the ground in his presence. Howard would interrogate these denizens of the underworld of discourse, de-centre them as subjects and expose them to the alterity of meaning. Then he would …. here Howard was not quite sure what he would actually do next. His profound intent certainly sounded insightful and meaningful, this questioning of meaning, but it felt hollow in the face of an attempted suicide. One did not, after all, die from ennui; not even by accident.

He decided that a first step might be to establish whether Real Truth actually existed. So Howard sent Mick on a program he had been mentally writing on the long drive home – one that would seek a virtual doorway *out* of the sanctioned infobriefs he had visited, *into* a non-sanctioned text that was nevertheless authentic, or what older academics used to call 'historically validated'.

Howard wasn't sure how he would know an infobrief was 'historically validated'. Although his own education occurred while the term 'history' was still in use, he had only a vague memory of what it meant. But his first aim was to find some non-sanctioned text – something that revealed or asserted an alternative to the sanctioned infobrief from which Mick exited, for instance. But it was important that Mick left via a 'rear entrance' – a *back door* as it were – to avoid the trace of his departure, and that any infobrief he found was text-based, so that Howard could read it rather than have to switch on his VIVO and thus risk CCC detection.

Howard was careful to control a growing excitement as he keyed the program in. He was supposed to be tired, and just polishing off a few routine searches or messages. Nevertheless, once Mick Turition started literally 'walking through' his first inforep, as if through a real library with physical volumes on shelves, Howard started to settle into the search, as if in an academic life of his deep past. Although Mick was much less loving and caring in his quest than Howard himself had once been. Moving through particular infobriefs he virtually pulled from the shelves until, in one, he found the 'back door' he was seeking. He looked around virtually behind him to check he was electronically unobserved, turned the virtual handle and stepped through.

The infobrief he had left was on the World Government movement, and its progress from 2018, when it began, to the formation of the New World Order in 2038. The non-sanctioned text in which Mick now found himself began by reiterating the ideospeak of the ideobrief behind which it was hidden.

Poverty targets set by the World Government movement in 2018 had now, for the most part, been met. After the Third Phase of Progress and the collapse of the two Super Governments in 2020 as a result of the Oil Wars, constraints on accelerated industrialisation disappeared.

But that was not how it continued, as Mick pulled the lamp down closer to the faded, yellowing virtual pages and focussed intently.

The transnationals realised that the dependence on larger and larger national governments or coalitions of government to match larger and larger transnational corporations was not the key to ensuring standardisation of infrastructure and services to finesse corporate objectives. Corporate experience with the smaller dictatorships had helped them to understand how much more quickly capital could be developed if one smaller country was pitched against another to develop competitive advantage.

Mick looked up at Howard, an electronic eyebrow raised: Could this be the kind of truth they were seeking? Howard nodded solemnly. This was a claim capital would never make in contemporary ideospeak. Democracy is freedom, and freedom is choice. Capital is the servant of choice, and transcorps are the servant of capital. That was contemporary ideobrief. But this … Mick read on with a mounting excitement Howard strove to constrain in himself.

So the transnationals placed their strategic and material resources behind nationalisation movements in the smaller countries and ethnic topographies of Europe, Russia, India, China and North America, as they had in the Africas and South Americas, and the transnationals themselves took on

34

and made commercial alternative power sources to fossil fuels. ...

The text here became faded and lost. But the paragraph concluded:

> *The transnationals called this policy New Prosperity, opening the poorer nations up to capital growth.*

Interesting! Mick said to Howard without moving lips he didn't have anyway. Contemporary ideobrief attributed the development of nation states to market forces and the consumer logic that led to New Prosperity. But this text claimed it was in fact the interests of capital, perpetrated by transnationals who were, themselves, engaged in the process of developing smaller nations as viable economic competitors with the more developed nations. A strategic conspiracy of capital, no less!

But we will need to authenticate this text, Howard cautioned. Undaunted, Mick drew Howard's attention to the next section as if to say: but wait, take a look at this!

> *If there are broad geographical descriptors in the world of New Prosperity and the New World Order, they are China (the last Super Government), Europacific, and South Asia. Australia is the "boot" of Europacific, even though topographically it is in the South Asia region. But these geographies are, like all geographies, historically produced, rather than rational. They are also largely irrelevant, and used mostly for transcorp strategic planning.*

Even though its dissolution was only twenty years ago, it still surprised Howard to see Australia referred to as the one nation. This with the notion that 'geographies' are 'historically produced' – mindblowing! whistled Mick Turition silently.

> *Nations are no longer defined by national identity and statehood but rather by saleable cultural heritage. These are packaged as slices of the industrial age, or the colonial age, or the information age and such like, preserved in the landscape. This is a major source of employment for nations experiencing boundary shift. Cultural tourism is one of the globe's fastest-growing industries. Teams of dialect coaches are flown in to train locals to mount functioning re-enactments of town life during the colonial era, and the like.*

> *With a boundary shift or an emerging nation, regions zoned for cultural tourism development are initially declared wage-free zones to enable the unemployed to get onto a job pathway. Food and accommodation are provided, as on a film location. But no wages are paid until income is generated. Dialect and technology training are provided on a user (ie. worker) repayment system.*

Again, the notion that it was transcorps who created the geography of the New World Order differed from contemporary ideobrief. And while cultural tourism destinations were commonly promoted by the transcorps, and on The Market, this was the first policy indication Howard had come across – assuming Mick's infodoc verification programming was on target - that their creation was wired into workforce supply strategy. It was a short leap of logic to link such cultural tourism enterprises with the 'disappearance' of mandatory identity displacementees.

Howard was aware that, despite his best efforts, his excitement levels were rising well above normal. He was starting to tap into recall from his second degree, political science, that he had long forgotten. And Mick Turition did nothing to help. He found a back door to yet another long corridor of library shelving. Mick's fingers deftly flicked through lines of stand-up file boxes packed with manila folders and suddenly slipped one out, flicked out a loose monograph and flung the text before Howard. It was one of his own infobriefs, from barely ten years earlier. For overseas consumption, by the looks. But he could not remember who for, or why.

In Australasia, 1984 marked the first year the federation of Australia opened its doors to the global economy, following the deregulation of the banks in 1983. The irony of the fact that a supposedly Labor government was responsible for this innovation has not been lost on history. From this time on, Australasia has been dependent on global investment patterns, and locked into the capitalist growth spiral that would inevitably require the continent's economy to accommodate the entry of its near neighbours into developed nation status – third phase progress.

The Labor government attempted to pre-empt the inevitability of this regional encroachment into their economic superiority with Keynesian strategies, sinking taxpayers funds into the aggressive development and marketing of Australian education and IT services in the South Asian and Chinese regions. These initiatives floundered during the last decade of the century, however, when the tight fiscal policy of a conservative government simply turned the Australian economy over to global market forces. Without the realisation by capital itself that alternative energy sources to fossil fuel could actually be profitable, the Australasian 'boot' of Europacific would have simply folded economically into South Asia.

And this:

The power and water innovations of the 2010s, in concert with the unrelenting progress of global warming - rising seas levels, or more the threat thereof - led the population towards the centre of the continent, and the relocation of the centres of wealth to WA, NT and QLD. Capital encouraged the States to increase their power by supporting interstate competition for major capital development, at the expense of national federalism.

The boundaries of SA pushed north to take in the Alice and west to absorb Perth and the south east of the continent, to capitalise on its pastoral capacity and draw on the water from the north. NSW pushed north to the Brisbane line and west to give them access to the Lake Eyre and Artesian Basins. VIC pushed its boundary north to grab as much of the Murrumbidgee it could, and Canberra, and absorbed the island state of Tasmania to its south, with the aim of securing its pastoral and wine producing capacity.

All basically wanted either to secure their existing water resources, or access a slice of the Centre, where the power innovations and water technology drawing on seasonal rains in the north were creating an agricultural as well as technological basis for New Prosperity. Even the capital cities started to move inland, away from the rising sea level – Melbourne to Albury Wodonga, Adelaide to Alice, Perth to Kalgoorlie and Broome, Sydney to Dubbo, and QLD developed Mt Isa as well as Townsville, Cairns and Rockhampton. All to be declared Nation States in 2050 – plans well in hand.

Plans well in hand? Mick mused, sardonically regarding Howard with one eyebrow raised (virtually, again). And Howard knew what his cyber champion meant. They were all operating as independent nation states already. Admittedly the celebrations were still scheduled for 2050, but that was more for the marketing value these days. Even back then, it seemed, he well understood the agency of capital in creating the nation states at the expense of federalism. Small Government is Good Government.

How could he have forgotten this stuff? He, the son of Menzies Johns, last champion of federalism! The virulence of memory re-trace was disturbing, and further cause for Howard to suspect meaninglessness as the root of his so very recent disregard for his own life. It was too much for Howard Winston Johns. Mick Turition leant back against the tall stack of filing shelves and lit a cigarette. You've done well enough, Mick, for one night, Howard told his alter ego. But now it's time for bed.

Not for me, pal, Mick Turition replied, flicked the dead match in his right hand towards Howard, took the cigarette out of his mouth with the other, turned and disappeared down the long line of shelves, tails of white mackintosh flapping in his wake.

He's not supposed to do that, Howard thought to himself as he closed down his netface for the night.

Chapter Five

The meeting with Transglobal was itself uneventful. As Simpkins had predicted, it was a bit of a fishing expedition. Transglobal were, by holding a formal meeting on VIC Parliament premises, signifying an interest in doing business. Bishop was there with the Minister, holding armfuls of superfluous legislative briefing material – because of course everyone would in reality access the infobrief they needed on VIVO in the privacy of their own offices. And the meeting was held symbolically in the cavernous Seventh Hall, with its marble floor and timber-veneered columns, both donated by transcorps and both showing to best effect the solar-powered water-reticulated roofing subsidised by Transglobal. Nobody sat. All stood in the centre of the space so that they could be seen to be in 'informal' discussion, but obviously one well-supported by infobrief. The genomorph with the horns and blue Consumer Choice League wristband stood a little way off for, Howard presumed, cyber security purposes.

Katharine O'Brien wore a fabulous full-length mustard-coloured light woollen coat, even though it was summer outside. The coat fell loosely open to reveal a shortish skirt and light, knitted top, both black, beneath which knee-length black boots supported the executive's luxurious thighs. She did not do much of the talking, but stood slightly back, allowing the two suited men to take the front running. Her role had clearly been to establish the groundwork. Similarly, the Minister was supported by a Member slightly senior to Howard. Howard himself stood to one side, also in a supporting role.

Clearly, the Minister was saying, VIC Parliament was confident it had found a legislative basis for Transglobal investment in a portfolio of VIC water initiatives the government would appreciate the opportunity to explore with Transglobal at some length. The Transglobal executives in their turn talked about the global shifts in climate, and that any investment proposition would depend on the infrastructural logic of such factors. And the Minister nodded of course of courses.

*

Everyone knew the story. El Nino and La Nina's dance with the ice age governed the movement of much transcorp production these days. Global warming hadn't gone as predicted by the doomsayers. Neither the predicted micro ice-ages and nor ocean risings had occurred with the uniformity expected. Instead, El Ninos and La Ninas slowly wrapped themselves around the globe in a languorous dance that conformed roughly to a 2 year cycle. Ice caps did not generally melt. They just shifted from one part of the pole to another. Arable land raced around the world to the climate dance.

But what did not appear in today's ideospeak or ideobrief was the knowledge that, to complement the roving fortunes of primary production, the rest of the machinery of Fourth Phase progress also moved into less arable parts of the globe. As the climate tangoed its way around the planet, so transnational developments partnered and mirrored in geographic complementarity. These days, fishing fleets and maritime protection were largely obsolete. Giant fish farms tracked La Nina around the globe and were far more economically effective as a result. Tourism ventures similarly waxed and waned with the climate dance. QLD's own Great Barrier Reef, once a Wonder of the World, came and went in six-monthly cycles.

Although the Age of Order was attributed to the emergence of the New World Order of nation states, in reality climate change control had only been embraced because capital had come to see the economic benefits of it. Transcorps maintained global sustainability by, ironically, maintaining climate sustainability: by trading emissions in specific locations for plant re-locations and new developments. Fourth phase progress was not possible without the global dance of transcorp supply and demand, the two-step and three-step of supply-chain re-locations to maximise new labour catchments and tax-breaks as these emerged.

41

No-one could have predicted that Nature would return to Capital what Capital had given to it. Forecasters could never quite predict in which direction of latitude and longitude the climate dance would move, but the established 2-year cycle gave regional economies the chance to invest in infrastructure in anticipation of an inflow of transnational capital with the same alacrity they once used to prepare for world sports events, in order to make the most of a growth opportunity. Although in the final analysis, the transcorps always held the winning hand.

*

This intelligence was well understood by those on the government side of the discussions in the Grand Hall of VIC Parliament that day. Face-to-face formalities like this were merely symbolic. The genomorph shadowing the meeting inscrutably from its perimeter glanced at Howard nervously from time to time. It was hard to read his face, but Howard thought what he discerned was disdain. Inappropriate in one so evidently his inferior, Howard thought, himself inappropriate in his discomfort.

As the meeting ended, and the Minister led his guests to the highly public front entrance, Howard found himself at last falling into step with Katharine O'Brien. He took the opportunity to open with brandgrab.

"It's a beautiful day outside," he ventured, "Transglobal's contribution to VIC Parliament certainly enables us to appreciate the weather, however it is. All who come here comment on it."

He glanced up significantly, indicating the natural light refracted by the water reticulating through the solar roofing.

"Even though water technology is our main focus, we pride ourselves on our success in combining it with solar resourcing," replied O'Brien, with a respectful incline of the head. But also a curious, half repressed smile. "We try to contribute to the material visibility of all governments with which we have dealings. Mutual prosperity is everything in business, is it not?"

"Indeed," Howard continued smoothly, "And Transglobal will, I am sure, benefit from the legislative opportunities the Minister wishes to discuss. I have seen them myself and, were I in business, I would be quite excited by them."

"Then I am sure Transglobal will be excited too," concluded O'Brien, this time with a full and practised smile.

After a few more steps echoing into the marble silence, Katharine O'Brien spoke again. The Minister and the senior executives were now some steps ahead, and the genomorph and Bishop falling diplomatically behind.

"Are you a religious man, Mr Johns?"

Howard was surprised at this topic, particularly the use of the term 'religious'. It was not common these days, and O'Brien seemed to have placed it deliberately.

"I am not a sectarian," he replied more correctly. "Or, to be more specific, I do not subscribe to any one particular Society Standards Sect. That is not to say I have no personal beliefs. Choice is all."

"So you do not believe in Dogweh?"

This was even more specific, and Howard was entirely unclear where the conversation was leading.

"I have examined the teachings of Dogweh," he lied tactfully, "But also of Yahlah, Braal, and Alhma, and am yet to be convinced of the merits of one over another. They all seem to me of equal merit."

"But not meritorious enough to invest in, even in all four?" O'Brien persisted. The curious half-smile had returned now. "I have observed you during the Two Minutes Vision. You always seem to be a man of conviction. As in, you actually smile during the visioning. Genuinely smile, it seems to me."

Now Howard allowed himself the quirk of an ironic smile.

"Well now, that would suggest that you were yourself not entirely engaged in the visioning exercise, Ms O'Brien."

Katharine O'Brien inclined her head demurely.

"And you have yourself made an investment choice in a sect?" he ventured.

"Well," she averred, "We have reached the entrance. A conversation for another time, perhaps."

She smiled formally as she shook his hand, and did the same with his colleagues. Bishop and the genomorph were now nowhere in sight.

*

Howard had been truthful: he was not a religious man. His parents had not attended any particular church, and left the field for 'religion' blank in his government ID birth record. They had sent him to what used to be known as a 'state school', rather than the plethora of fee-paying religious schools that populated the Australia of his youth.

He had, however, probably one of the largest collections of church bell recordings in VIC – from some 6,000 different churches around the world. Church bells were one of his earliest memories: of lying in a basinet on the veranda of their family apartment in inner city Old Melbourne, hearing the church bells around the city calling the faithful to worship on what must have been Sunday mornings.

Perhaps that was what rooted Howard's concepts of 'belief' or 'faith' in the notion of 'religion' rather than today's Society Standards Sects. Although the commercialisation of religion during the 2020s had developed SSSs on the basis of existing capital infrastructure, audio technology had not favoured the retention of bells. Bell ringing was labour-intensive, and more automated mechanisms for regulating "calls to joint reflection", as they became known, were favoured, with electronic and far more tuneful as well as tonefully precise audio content.

The bells were literally left to rust in their original housings, as competition between SSSs was reflected in the bid to out-do each other in the tunefulness and volume of the "call to joint reflection".

To the teenage Howard Smithson Johns (or Adam Winston Johns as he was still then), Sunday mornings were like living in a neighbourhood of competing hi-fi's. It was a cacophony of audio mediocrity. He was personally relieved when the 36-hour day came in, and the SSSs achieved market individuation by pitching for differential "call to j-flec" slots in the new 252 hour week.

So what impressed Howard about the old twentieth century concept of religion was what inhered within it that produced bells. Which was, he assumed, the same impulse that produced the churches themselves. In the small rural towns in which his mother and father had grown up, the churches had been the focal point of the community. And they had been built by the community. Communities saved income collectively for years in order to afford to have a bell foundered in some distant industrial centre, possibly even overseas, to be transported to their remote geographical location. Both church and bell brought communities together in collective action and consensus.

So it wasn't the content of any one religion that Howard found attractive. He could not, frankly, remember the religions of his youth. He had a vague apprehension of the various stories that underpinned their central tenets, but none of the detail. The Sects of Dogweh, Yahlah, Braal and Alhma - Christuism, Isdaism, Buddjulam and Hindianity respectively – had become such entrenched features of the ideospeak and brandgrab landscapes that it was difficult to recall the original belief systems from which they had been drawn.

Howard wondered, however, whether his quest for Real Truth might lie in that direction – in the belief systems upon which today's SSS's had been constructed. He knew he had committed Mick Turition to the quest for a Real Truth behind the strategic dominance of capital, but something about the corporeality of Katharine O'Brien's allusion to Dogweh, her seemingly intentional placement of the archaic term 'religious' – not that he thought she herself was sending covert messages. But her catching him so off-guard had opened a fissure, as it were, in his self. He had become exposed to … well that was what he couldn't identify. It was so easy to allow the rational mind to set off in pursuit of conspiracies but perhaps this was, after all, what was actually missing at the centre of his life: a belief in meaning beyond the surface construction of Consumer Choice, some source of spiritual truth beyond the ideospeak of Smithson Adams and his New Prosperity, and the New World Order it had spawned.

It had been so long that Howard had even considered the possibility of spirituality, he had quite forgotten its sentient power. The truth was, although Howard visited any and all of the SSSs in any non-sitting period as part of his role as Member for Canberra, he frankly couldn't summarise any of them for anyone with any accuracy. Luckily, before he even left VIC Parliament for the day he could see, across the courtyard and down the generous steps leading up to the main entrance, a Choice Fair unfolding over in Choice Circle. Greaves confirmed Howard's good fortune. The topic for this week's Choice Fair was indeed the Society Standards Sects.

Christuism was the first installation he came to down in the lavish circle of fountains and features that formed the colosseum-like centre of New Melbourne's civic hub. Here, amidst guitar-playing gospel singers and a holographic reconstruction of the resurrection in digital loop, a helpful priest, dressed in Christuism's characteristic dog collared top and ascetic's loin cloth, informed Howard at length of how the monotheistic deity Dogweh gave his three sons, Brahma, Vishnu and Siva, three sisters to marry – Sarasvati, Lakshmi and Parvati. After many instructive adventures and periods of exemplary asceticism, all three are crucified on the Cross for preaching that Democracy is Freedom and Freedom is Choice, to be mourned by their widows and children. And thus the Sect of Christuism is born and marketed by the transcorp, Transglobal.

So, as a Transglobal executive, O'Brien may well have introduced Dogweh to their conversation merely as a return brandgrab. Just polite conversation. There remained, however, still her deliberate placement of the archaic term 'religious'.

Howard thanked the priest with a professional smile and moved on to browse the other Sects. He thought it wise to be better informed when he next met with O'Brien for the mooted 'another time'. Next around the circle came Isdaism. Here he was welcomed by fire-eaters on stilts and acrobats performing feats of remarkable agility. Each Sect, it was clear, was using live performance to appeal directly to the psychomotor level of intelligence, to invite active mental participation and, as a result, buy in. Try it and see. Buy and be saved.

In Isdaism, he was reminded by a helpful visionbrief in which the story was re-enacted in a land far away from VIC, the deity Yahlah revealed the Toran through the Archangel Gabriel to the merchant Muhammed over 23 years. The Toran details how all the religions of the world date from the Sons of Abraham, and the Isdites are the true descendants of Abraham and will inherit the Promised Land, Palestine, to which they were once led by King David. The Toran's central tenet is that Choice is All and All have Choice, and it's precepts are followed to the letter by subscribers.

The exponents of Buddjulam were focussing on the powers of meditation, with incense and colourful powders creating an atmosphere of headiness and relaxation. The exotic sitar and gamelan sounds of South Asia mediated the air between consumers and Buddjulam SSS members, who sat cross legged in saffron robes on firm, exotically woven cushions. A dreamy audio narrative told of the all-seeing and all-powerful Braal who gave the world his only son. After following a life of hedonism as Siddhartha, the son found enlightenment under the Bo tree in Jerusalem and led his twelve disciples to teach the seven-fold way across South Asia and China. As they founded much of their enterprise in today's China and South Asia, it was logical that Pancontinental were the transcorp to market Buddjulam, and that its seven-fold way was based upon the central tenet of Qualsafe: "Why condemn the apple if the fault is found in the juice?"

47

The Qualsafe story was one that Howard privately admired. It led him to harbour a secret desire to join the inner workings of Pancontinental. For it was in pioneering Qualsafe, and the pre-eminence of Qualsafecerts, that Pancontinental made its mark in the world of Consumer Choice. The catchcry, together with Pancontinental's research and development of quality and safety standards, and the supposedly evidence-based Q&SS certificates associated with them, became the mantra for a quality-improvement-based culture that absolved the *origin* of the system of responsibility for itself. Pancontinental's Qualsafecerts, issued with every product or service, placed responsibility in the system itself – that which produces the "juice" in the metaphor - and, more importantly, the individual who finds fault in the first place. If you complain, examine your own values and expectations first – are they 'consonant' with the rest of society? This is, of course, a question to which the individual can never generate sufficient evidence to answer "yes".

The Qualsafecert thus absolves the producer of responsibility for quality, focussing instead the perceiver of fault as the source of improvement. If Choice is All and All have Choice, then the individual in 'All' must take responsibility for the Choices they make. It was ingenious, and the year or so of competitive advantage the introduction of Qualsafecerts gave Pancontinental in the consumer market place, before the other transcorps brandgrabbed the ideospeak, propelled China and South Asia through a quantum leap through Third Phase Progress into the Fourth Phase.

And while this extensive story was not included in the Buddjulam narrative, qualcert merchandising abounded at the Buddjulam choice display.

The final SSS 'sharing' for this Choice Fair was Hindianity. By now Howard's focus was distracted, because he had become aware that he was being shadowed by the genomorph. The little horned man, with his lush fringe of fair hair and tight, four-buttoned suit, made a great display of interest in the SSS exhibits, but always Howard caught his eyes looking away, as if they had been watching him.

Luckily, mass displays of martial arts juxtaposed with virtuoso performances in the dances available from across South Asia – from the Nation States of the Indian sub-continent to Thailand, Malaysia, Cambodia and Indonesia – enabled Howard to move quickly around the installation. Illogically, he found himself trying to 'lose' the genomorph, as if the Consumer Choice League zealot were a spy on his tail.

This was the most lavish of the displays in Choice Circle that afternoon, and consumers were keen to engage in the free lessons that went with each activity in it. And for the casual observer there were plenty of sect devotees around to explain which section of the Hindianity story each dance or martial art related. Yet Howard could not concentrate specifically on any one part of it, for fear of his security 'tail'.

It would, he cursed inwardly, have made a refreshing change not to have to process information from ideobrief and brandgrab but, rather, have the luxury of allowing narrative to unfold through one aesthetic form after another. Nevertheless, snatching snippets as he went, he pieced together the agitated narrative of the three brothers, Moses, David and Joshua, who marry three sisters, Mary, Ruth and Naomi, to all six of whom the deity Alhma reveals the Sanskrit Scriptures on their wedding night atop Mt Sinai. The three couples found Hindianity in Mecca for the good of All, based on Alhma's word, but are forced by the ruling class to leave Mecca for Medina, where they establish a Hindian community and, after 8 years of war, retake Mecca so that All have Choice, and Choice is Freedom.

In the end, much though Howard enjoyed the Fair, and tasted the foods each of the four Sects specialised in, sipped their special sectarian drinks and enjoyed the carnival atmosphere, he came away merely better briefed for any future discussion with O'Brien, and with the sour taste of a potentially fanatic genomorph in his mouth.

There was nothing here that filled the hole in meaning at his centre, that brought to him a sense of enlightenment or spirituality.

And that, it occurred to him, was what he lacked: a sense of soul. Soul and spirit were concepts that seemed to lurk restlessly in amongst the narrative elements of each of the Society Standards Sects, and perhaps if he were to commit himself to their ceremonies and songs and events he too would find the joy their subscribers did in their devotions. For Howard, however, there was just the trace of something else, of a truth he might once have known, or was yet to apprehend.

So it was that, back at home, during downtime, Howard Smithson Johns again became the cyber journalist Mick Turition and went hunting for more than just ideospeak on the four SSSs marketed by the transcorps these days.

Chapter Six

Howard found Mick Turition in a town of low, ancient, sandstone buildings with open or loose-fitting wooden doorways, windows with only rough cloth coverings, and narrow dusty streets. Donkeys appeared to be the only form of transport, and that for kegs of water or victuals, bundles of ground seed and other ingredients for the making of household breads and meals. People were dark skinned, of South Asian appearance, and wore loose, light-coloured clothing which showed up the grime. Walls and streets alike were soiled, and there appeared no system of drainage or sewage.

Mick seemed to have anticipated Howard's quest for spirituality in the intervening hours since his last mission. As he hurried through the streets, he pulled from the weathered leather satchel he now carried one infobrief after another; each one associated an archaic religion with, if not endorsement of war, acquiescence to it.

"There were only two spiritual movements that seemed not to condone violence or material acquisition, Howard," Mick said, ducking into an alleyway to catch his breath. His characteristic wide-brimmed hat was now brown with dust and stained with sweat. He wore a roughly tied cotton neckerchief that was similarly drenched. The white mack had given way to a light traveller's jacket, also the worse for wear. "Buddhism and Hinduism. And they were both recipes for oppression. Millions of their believers have been slaughtered in successive waves of imperialist conquerors. I don't care how spiritual they are, Howard, what's the point in being spiritual but dead?"

"And look – even here - " Mick thrust a newly arrived unofficial infobrief from his satchel from the turn of the century, documenting the military subjugation of the Hindu Tamils by the Buddhist Sinhalese in emerging nation state of Sri Lanka.

"But I got one more lead," he said, and broke from the shade out into the narrow street.

For Choice's Sake, what are you running from? Howard (virtually) asked his cyber self. But he had already guessed the answer. Every individual Mick Turition passed in the street had the potential to turn out to be a NERA agent. Ever since the virus epidemics of the 2020s, and the resulting reign of Cyber Terrorism nobody talked about anymore, 'shadows' from the Net Enforcement & Regulation Authority roamed the cybernet in search of cyberhacks. And sure enough, just as Mick pressed on down the narrow street two dark-skinned individuals morphed into the black-raincoated black-capped figures characteristic of the NERA 'shadows' so popularised in The Market every time a cyberhack ring was broken.

Mick drip-fed a trail of documents from his satchel, ducked into a doorway, and watched as the NERA took the bait and sped by, bodily absorbing the data trail he had left for them. It would, presumably, take them straight back to source, and away from Mick Turition.

Mick then doubled back down a couple of side alleys and came to what he seemed to have been looking for: A garish poster featuring representations of Brahma, Siva and Vishnu, all labouring up the hill to Calvary bearing the crosses for their crucifixion, their brows mopped by their wives, Sarasvati, Parvati and Lakshmi, with a call to "J-Flec for Dogweh!" splashed across in large capital letters.

"Thought you might find a little salvation in your parent's religion," Mick whispered to Howard as he lifted the poster away from the wall on which it was poorly pasted, to reveal a sizeable hole through which the cyber journalist easily stepped.

Mick pulled the poster back in place behind him. It was now a heavy curtain covering some sort of vestry, and Howard found his cyber champion in the cavernous hall of a large gothic cathedral, clearly of the Christian origin. It was like nothing to be found in VIC, or any neighbouring nation state that Howard was aware of. Its tall columns were the colour of dark granite and arced gracefully into mitre-shaped ceilings that drew the gigantic church into the shape of a cross laid in dramatic relief upon the ground.

There were plain but beautiful stained glass windows representing what Howard could only guess to be the life of the Christian saviour, Jesus, and his followers; for they resembled nothing that endured in the churches co-opted by the Society Standards Sects of today. And, unlike VIC churches, this one had none of those stained, solid, uncomfortable wooden pews he loved so much. Indeed, nowhere to sit at all. The floor was an echoing carapace of carefully positioned flag stones.

In one corner, a man stood on a modest podium, speaking to a small crowd gathered around him.

"In the Middle Ages, class and inequality were seen like parts of an organism," the man was saying. He was straining to make himself heard clearly in the booming space. "Each part had its own function, be it prayer, or duty, or material exchange, or subsistence agriculture. Each whole person had a right to the means only of the combined status of their parts, and no claim to more.

"Within classes equality was required for social balance; for if one person assumed the living of two, another would go short. But between classes, inequality was almost inevitable, for each class to enjoy rights extending from the unique function it performed in society. It is here that the Church lent imbalance to status between classes. For in a class sanctioned by the Church, privilege and power became office and duty, property and wealth became responsibility and right."

He was not a particularly tall man, but he was aging. He wore an old threadbare suit that indicated a certain parsimony of habit underlined by the shirt, tie and fading cardigan it contained. Winged silvering hair gave prominence to a balding pate, and a full moustache lent dignity to an otherwise bulbous chin. He was not dressed as a man of the Age of Order. Nor did he speak as one.

53

"There was, however, a complementary belief that economic interests were subordinate to the meaningful currency of life, which was salvation; for the practice of economic business was one aspect of personal conduct upon which the rules of morality were binding. A man could seek such wealth as was necessary for a livelihood in his status, but to covet more was not entrepreneurial but avarice, and avarice is a deadly sin."

The people in the crowd were not dressed for the 2040s either. They were pale, unhealthy looking people, huddled in heavy coats and hats and sturdy shoes. The stockings worn by the women had seams, and were thicker than any available today. All looked as if they were permanently cold.

"Trade was acceptable: differential natural resources between countries indicated this was intended by Providence. But the individual must be sure that trade is conducted for the public benefit, and that the profits they take are no more than the wages of their labour. Finance was a form of the sin of usury, and usury, as avarice, was at best sordid and at worst disreputable. The unpardonable sin was that of the speculator or the middleman, who achieved private gain by the exploitation of public necessities."

Someone broke from the crowd and seemed to be leaving. But at the last minute, as she approached Mick Turition – who had now found his white mackintosh once more – a shadow morphed from the furs in which the woman was clad. Mick ducked behind a clover-shaped column and let the NERA agent pass. The agent had clearly detected Mick's presence, but not his form. Mick tried to merge in to the rear of the crowd, but people were eyeing him uncomfortably, even suspiciously.

"The ecclesiastical attack on usury probably reached its zenith in the legislation of the Councils of Lyons (1274) and of Vienne (1312), in which anyone declaring that usury was not a sin was to be punished as a heretic, and inquisitors were to 'proceed' against them."

The crowd were, however, clearly not of the era nominated by the speaker in his text. Their dress was far more of the twentieth century at least. Or nineteenth. Howard was unsure when seamed stockings were introduced. The church, however, could easily be of medieval origin. This was the very product of community spirit so admired by Howard. Could this be where Mick intended him to find the source of true spirituality?

"All of this changes with the sixteenth century. The Renaissance was an age of social risk-taking in the same way as the early nineteenth – because it was an age of unprecedented social dislocation. But this dislocation was due to economic influences. The religious revolution of the age, the Reformation, came upon a world heaving with the most dramatic economic crisis Europe had experienced since the fall of Rome.

"Economic power, fomented in the alchemic vessels of the Medici's Italy, was fracturing through a thousand cracks into the geology of Western Europe's social order. With the great 'New World' Discoveries of Columbus and Diaz, the lava flow came on like a king tide. The sixteenth century saw wealth and trade expand as rapidly as the concentration of financial power cooled into the volcano's core. As the landscape of social class rose and fell in plate-like convulsions, the triumph of a new culture and system of ideas found its footing in the emerging landforms. Individualistic, competitive, swept forward by an immense expansion of commerce and finance, this new age offered opportunities of speculative gain on a scale unknown before."

Mick suddenly stepped from the back of the crowd. Three shadows emerged from the overcoats and long trousers of men in the human conglomerate around him. He turned and ran, strewing documents from his satchel this way and that.

"It was logical that in this age of individual enterprise, individualism would also emerge in religion, along with an individualist morality and the ascendance of personal character," continued the speaker, as if neither Mick Turition nor NERA agents were there.

55

"The Reformationists saw the world of business and society as a battlefield, across which character could march with valour. They lost sight of the knowledge that character is social, and society, since it is the expression of character, is spiritual."

The shadows scrabbled around on the great stone flags, clutching at one document after another. They seemed indecisive: trace back to source or pursue the insurgent? Mick took advantage of their uncertainty, running the breadth of the church in a wide circle, his shoes echoing on the flagstones.

"Moreover, the Church was itself already an immense vested interest, implicated to the hilt in the economic fabric, amongst the greatest of landowners."

The shadows clearly couldn't hear Mick. One went off towards the exit as if chasing him. Another disappeared through the vestry curtain through which Mick had arrived. Another began to circle slowly, treading carefully, as if 'listening' for Mick to betray his presence.

Mick trod as softly as he could, rejoining the crowd on its furthest side. He could see the shadow resume its coat, trousers, scarf and hat in the crowd, but at a slight distance, scanning for the suspected cyberhack.

"From the failure of the Usury Bill of 1571 onward, the usurer disappears from Episcopal charges. Even amongst the Reformationists of the 16th and 17th centuries, the most vigorous opponents of the usury and avarice of finance, the groundwork for the endorsement of capitalism was laid."

Howard, unlike Mick, was now fully concentrated on the speaker's text, as the rest of the crowd seemed to be. They clearly lived in an age before vision, in which people were used to listening to discourse of some complexity unfold. An era of listeners.

"Calvin's treatment of capital, for instance, was to approach the ethics of money-lending not as a question of usury but as a specific example of the social complexity of a Christian community. In this light, he assumed credit to be a normal and inevitable incident in the life of society.

"If preachers of this time did not overtly separate trade from religion in the mind of the congregation, they implied a collusion between them by their very silence on the subject. Capital, religion and the state became society's new geological plates, shifting to share the same geography.

"Where in the Middle Ages the Church had been the authority on questions of morality enforced by the State, in the sixteenth century the Church became the ecclesiastical department of the State, and religion was used to lend a moral sanction to secular social policy.

"The characteristic doctrine became one which left little room for religious teaching as to economic morality, and in so doing anticipated the theorising of capital later epitomized by Adam Smith."

At this point, a lone individual broke from the front of the crowd, yelled in an old accent, "Professor Tawney, you are a heretic!" and shot the speaker. As the latter staggered back, clutching his chest, two more shadows emerged from the rear of the crowd along with the man in the hat and closed in on Mick Turition. Mick took the opportunity of the shooting to himself draw his Webley and fire at all three NERA agents. The crowd seemed not to notice, rushing forward to grapple the real gunman to the ground and support the fallen speaker.

There were many gasps and other exclamations of concern and horror. But none for Mick Turition, as he dashed and wove between the gothic columns of the church, loosing his remaining three shots on his pursuers. One fell clutching his leg, and disappeared. Another Mick appeared to wing in the shoulder. He collapsed into a column, dissolving as he went. The third seemed literally to slam head-first into a column as he ducked to avoid Mick's sixth and last shot. He staggered back, holding his nose, but did not disappear. Two further

NERA agents now ran into the church from outside. Mick strode up the stairs to the great church's only pulpit and jumped, feet first, through an ancient stained glass window.

He landed in a cybernet posting from a church in central Old Sydney, St James, which New Prosperity and the Society Standards Sects movement seemed to have missed. It was still practicing the Christian religion and proudly using its original, nineteenth century bell.

"So," he said, turning easily to Howard and adjusting his hat, "Not what you'd hoped for. No spirituality, Howard. Just capitalism. Just materialism. Just consumerism. Just choice."

Howard felt emotionally deflated. Any vestige of spirituality he had hoped to find within himself was, it seemed, endemically corrupted by the history of warfare and the ideology of commerce. He could find no conviction in his mind that some inchoate soul had driven him to attempt its release forever. The hole in himself that had led to his near-death experience just seemed to gape wider and wider, like an expanding vortex into a void of meaninglessness.

He was exhausted. It was late, and he should no longer be at his netface. His flagging endorphins would register on his CCC. But he could not bear to waste the hard-won fruits of his end-of-day labour. So he opted to test Mick Turition's powers as a cyber journalist by marketing a quick story on the church bell ringers of St James, keeping the labouring tradition of manual bell ringing alive.

It was only a handful of pars, and took just minutes to write, and seconds for Mick Turition to pitch across The Market. If anything, Howard hoped in the last dregs of wakefulness that the story might draw out other seekers of Real Truth, attracted by the beyond-ideospeak nature of the topic. Sadly, after returning to his regular netface link as Howard Johns to respond to a few Consumer enquiries of the VIC Chamber Member for Canberra, Howard came back to Mick Turition's netspace to find 3,000 rejections for his version the St James's bell ringers, and 485 placings of copycat stories siting the bell-ringers in SSSs.

Underground cyber journalism was not, it seemed, going to be any easier than the search for Real Truth.

Chapter Seven

Next day the long-awaited attack on the character of Howard Smithson Johns arrived at Chamber Seven of VIC Parliament. Clearly the opposition knew they were getting nowhere against the current swathe of water legislation, which included, Howard now understood, the groundwork for the deal with Transglobal. Obviously running out of filibuster to block the passage of the legislation, the opposition decided to play the trump card they had been holding back for over a week.

As predicted, it involved allegedly false travel and accommodation claims by the Member for Canberra made while staying with his mother on Philip Island during visits to Old Melbourne. Everybody knew the attacks were baseless, and that Howard had actually been negotiating with Transnational for the solar developments between the outback towns of Ivanhoe and Cobar that would pay for the VICgov re-irrigation projects around the upper Murray River.

He was, it also had to be admitted, attempting to help his mum out. Her husband's superannuation had been gutted with the bureaucratic and fiscal evisceration of the national government. Every year another 'recalculation' of her Social Safety debt revealed yet another and even more outrageous 'overpayment' that, as part of yet another 'nationwide campaign', improved the government's balance sheet enough for a momentary debt equity advantage in a transcorp negotiation, plunged pensioners like Ruth Johns deeper than ever into their entanglement with the Social Safety 'net'.

The psychological pressure on Howard's mother was enormous. Ruth John's generation had been raised with a concept of self-respect deeply rooted in financial independence, and being able to 'pay one's way'. Dependence on government welfare was shunned, accessed as a last resort. In the era of Consumer Choice, Social Safety was pre-paid or provided on a repayment scheme at a modest interest - the complete reverse of the old 'welfare' principle. Howard had been pre-paying Social Safety since his early twenties and thought no more of it, but people of his mother's era had no such capacity, and the idea that they were constantly running up unrepayable debt was beyond their ethical tolerance. To make matters worse, Ruth had invested in further Open University education, using her senior's concession and, whilst she had as a result accessed some consultancy work in transnational organisational culture with the transcorps, this work was yet to repay the cost of her Masters degree.

She thus fretted at the size of both education and social safety debts she was passing on to her only son. If she learnt of the current beat up, she would fret even more; especially at the meretricious insinuations in the Chamber as to where Howard did stay on those occasions when, it had been identified, he was not actually staying with his mother. Although the opposition would themselves readily enjoy similar transcorp hospitality at the drop of a hat, they were happy to raise questions about the Member for Canberra's sexual predilections for the momentary advantage it afforded them on the floor of the Chamber.

Howard knew these imputations would enrage his mother, and cause her distress in case they were true. She would not care if he was homosexual, but would still hold the old belief that such information, if made public, could damage a politician's career for life. She did not understand that these days sexuality was just another object of commodification. 'Coming out', as it was still called, might in fact give him a modest electoral advantage.

Nevertheless, Howard lost no time in checking with Simpkins the impact of the story in The Market, in case he needed to forewarn his mum. The initial duration of the story was impressive – a full five minutes on the front page of the VIC section of The Market for the Australasian region. By comparison, Simpkins pointed out, a major market advantage for Pancontinential, resulting from the resolution of multiple border disputes between the nation states of PNG, Indonesia, Aceh and Timor which saw control of supply-side industry sites for Pancontinental rotating from one labour source to another, lasted only two minutes on screen one.

Ruth would need to be mining The Market for stories on her son after that. Simpkins called a colleague in cyber security to run a check on her netface account, and she had not been online at the time. Howard remained concerned, however.

As luck would have it, the Leader of the House was keen to get him out of town so that they could get the raft of water legislation through. Howard was thus to travel to Old Melbourne to further discussions with Transglobal over the deal on offer. Bishop would accompany him, and somebody from cyber security so that they could secure communications with respective head offices as necessary.

Howard thought it unlikely that he would further encounter O'Brien during these meetings. The Transglobal executive seemed largely based in New Melbourne as the transcorp's public interface with VIC Parliament. She was there again that day during the Two Minutes Vision, for instance. And Howard could not resist sneaking a glimpse of her during the visioning. She did indeed have her eyes closed, but opened one in time to catch him looking. When he looked back, she had that curious half-smile on her face again.

He also noticed the horned genomorph again, this time positioned between himself and O'Brien. The diminutive figure also seemed deeply engrossed in the visioning, but at the end of the broadcast, when his eyes opened, they looked directly at Howard with, he discerned once more, stark disapprobation. Howard found himself hoping that this was not the official in cyber security with whom Simpkins had checked on his mother's netface activity.

It was certainly with concern that Howard spotted the genomorph seated with Bishop a few seats back from him on the 28:00 hrs shuttle out of New Melbourne that evening. And with a level of excitement that he found himself seated next to Katharine O'Brien.

Chapter Eight

"So do you believe in Dogweh?"

This time it was Howard Smithson Johns' turn to ask the question.

He and O'Brien had dispensed the routine exchanges of brandgrab and a polite discussion on the impact on Transglobal of Pancontinental's border-shift coup that day in South Asia. So Howard sought to move the conversation onto less ideocorrect ground, through a safe brandgrab.

O'Brien smiled her half-smile and gazed out of the shuttle's window.

"Well, I would be disloyal to my organisation if I said I didn't," she replied. "You have been reading up?" She looked back at him, the smile fading.

"Well, I wanted to be sure of my facts, in case the subject came up again in conversation. Discussion in relation to Society Standards Sects is, after all, commonplace. Particularly amongst my constituents."

"Consumers, surely?" checked O'Brien, but with mild irony.

"Exactly. Which reminds me, I noted your use of the term 'religious' with interest yesterday," said Howard, taking irony as a cue. O'Brien, however, raised both eyebrows to him in inquiry.

"When you asked me if I was a religious man."

"An absent-minded slip of the tongue, I should imagine," she responded dismissively. "I expect you and I are of a similar age. We were brought up in a time when religions were still linguistic currency."

O'Brien seemed unable to maintain the mask of indifference for long, however. Her half-smile quickly returned as she ventured;

"I caught you checking me out during the visioning this morning."

Howard had no quick response, and so smiled to himself.

"You don't believe?" It was a cloaked question.

"Of course I believe," Howard replied congenially and quickly, "But being in government, I am interested in strategy, and an interest in strategy impels me to seek the heart of ideospeak, its source, so that I can find the shortest intellectual route by which to effect government goals and objectives. And I hope both you and I need not disagree that the heart of ideospeak does not lie with government."

"I would've thought government's goals were very much aligned with those of the transcorporations, wouldn't you? We both believe that progress is the way to preserve the pre-eminence of consumer choice as both the economy's and society's primary driver." O'Brien was resorting to ideospeak now. Howard decided to tackle it head on, calling upon the intelligence revealed by Mick Turition's 'back door' cybernet findings just two days previous.

"But surely you don't imagine government is the source of ideospeak for Consumer Choice do you? Capital invented that. It came with New Prosperity, and the brandgrab of Smithson Adams."

"But isn't the New World Order the global champion of New Prosperity and Consumer Choice?" O'Brien came back quickly.

"Believe me, government has been my longest career to date, and I can assure you that while government shares with capital the ideospeak of New Prosperity in the interests of progress, the language of government is one of legislation and regulation. That is where we are creative. Even democratic representation is a hard concept for government's bureaucrats to get their mouths around. Fiscal accountability is much closer to their hearts."

"Perhaps it is time for your next career," O'Brien suggested, but absently. And Howard immediately wondered whether that was the affinity he was reading in her: a head-hunt. Certainly an opportunity he would not discount. There was no indication he would progress in government much beyond his current Ministerial Secretary status.

But he was reluctant to surrender his current agenda in this conversation entirely.

"Indeed, particularly if it were to lead me closer to a strategic role."

"That's the second time you have linked strategy to the commercial sector," O'Brien observed.

"My experience indicates that is where its source lies."

And even as he uttered the idea, it began to occur to Howard that perhaps this was after all where the 'hole' in his sense of meaningfulness lay; perhaps this was the truly gnawing sense of unease that had led to his suicide attempt, had worked within him from a seed of doubt into a festering and spreading ulcer of subconscious self-distrust: the suspicion that real meaning lay beyond the surface construction of Consumer Choice, some source of truth beyond the ideospeak of Smithson Adams and his New Prosperity, and the New World Order it had spawned.

It was so obvious now that he came to think about it. The idea that consumers were in some sort of control was simply a massive feint perpetuated by transcorps in order to maintain the capital growth spiral on which their sustainability depended. The recent forays of Mick Turition into twenty first century history had only served to demonstrate this fact. If Real Truth was to be found anywhere, Howard reasoned, surely it was in the ideological centre of power – at the heart of the transcorps themselves. Not in any underworld or organised counter-revolution, nor in any spiritual centre to the human soul. Perhaps this was something Katharine O'Brien understood. Perhaps this was the joint apprehension that linked them, attracted their interest in each other. (If indeed, he had to remind himself, they were actually interested *in each other*.)

"So if your experience indicates that it does not lie with government, the corollary would be that it does not lie in some other organisational entity either, wouldn't it? Why would you assume that one organisational system does it better – or more strategically, in your terms – than another? You confess not to believe in Dogweh over any other deity, ie. no one deity, no one source of human perfectibility has primacy for you, and yet you believe in a perfectibility of organisations? Of systems?"

Perhaps they did not share the same understanding after all. But Howard was not to be daunted.

"Isn't competition the basis of commerce, of business? Isn't competition based on the concept of perfectibility?" He was fishing now.

"Better than. Can you go one better? Can we do better than? It's a comparative, not a superlative."

"But the superlative is implied. Excellence. We want to be the best, sell the best product, provide the best service. Best practice." "But surely best practice, benchmarking, the entire practice of quality improvement is comparative Mr Johns? I think the parlance of "best" is one of journalese. I agree that in the last century it took commerce almost fifty years from Demming and Juran to understand that it was conflating two contrasting concepts – the one comparative and the other superlative. Business and commerce still came into this century spouting an ideospeak that assumed the perfectibility of 'the best', mercilessly linked to the concept of the 'winner' and the 'loser'.

"But that sporting mythology was never the conceptualisation of transnational commerce. We came into this century without "playing the game", without needing to "get ahead of the field" or remain "in front of the pack". The sporting superlative was always the preserve of small business and corporate hacks and, as history has shown, neither had the mental fortitude to embrace the creativity required even for effective Third Phase Progress, let alone Fourth Phase.

"I don't believe there is any global conspiracy in the rise of the transcorps, or of Fourth Phase Progress, Mr Johns - "

"No, I'm not implying - "

"I know it is not conventional ideospeak to speak of historicity, but nevertheless the emergence of the transcorps *is* purely historical. It is, literally, how it has turned out. And I would contend that the intellectual agency that gave the transcorps the capacity to establish their current place in global economy is the clarity they were able to develop in relation to precisely this topic.

"The successful ideospeak of excellence has proved to be one that is comparative rather than ontological or metaphorical. Business, commerce today, does not think of excellence as being a state in itself or a point of perfection embodied by some "other" of ultimate power and authority, a state of being that only one or two individuals can achieve through their own "winning" entrepreneurial persistence.

"Charismatic leadership is something for The Market alone, Mr Johns. Excellence for today's transcorp is a transitory point of comparison in order to provide the basis for understanding the next improvement, the next innovation, and how that can be achieved."

"But not achieved towards an idea of perfection," Howard ventured rhetorically. He felt hopelessly outclassed. O'Brien was able to stride through an ideological landscape that left him trying to follow like an innocent in the foothills. She wielded concepts that did not even enter into the daily discourse of his world or appear in contemporary ideobrief. It was a confounding conversation. And Howard was wondering whether he would have been safer sticking to the quest for spiritual transcendence.

"This has been an interesting conversation, Mr Johns," she said, closing the discussion with just an edge of condescension, as the shuttle had commenced its descent into Old Melbourne. "I hope our discussions regarding you water proposals over the next few days prove to be equally as stimulating."

The couple sat in silence for the brief remainder of the flight. And Howard's attention drifted to the couple of businessmen in the seats behind him who, he realised, had not stopped talking about domestic shuttle routes, and the marvel that they had achieved such seats on frequent flyer bonuses, since they boarded.

There was an entire generation of these men and women who spent most of their lives in shuttle queues and offloads, doing business over their cell cards wherever they stood or sat, did deals from one meeting as they tried to get on a flight to the next. The constantly moving fayre of air shuttle schedules was forever at the periphery of their mind's eye, commanding the fevered attention of near-autonomic neurones. Perhaps Katherine O'Brien was right, but how else but through a strategic centre could organisation emerge from such chaos of commerce?

Chapter Nine

Discussions over the next couple of days were not stimulating. They were laborious, and necessarily so. It took a long time for Bishop and Howard to lay out the legislative opportunity VIC Parliament was offering, for in it also lay the detail of the proposed commercial activities they hoped Transglobal would deem attractive and timely enough to invest in.

This was a tightrope presentation because, on one hand, it needed to have the structure and narrative flow of a highly attractive 'pitch' or 'sell' while, on the other, ensuring the full complexity of VIC's analysis of the legislation and market environment was well understood. It was in this level of detail that the superiority and full ingenuity of their pitch lay.

Transglobal were, fortunately, open to the approach. They were used to dealing with governments, often from nation states with social protocols far less amenable to direct negotiation than those found in the Australasian archipelago. O'Brien was in fact leading these early discussions for Transglobal, and she guided Howard's presentation through the intricacies of Transglobal's own needs and expectations with practiced patience and diplomacy.

Their exchanges, however, were professional and task-focussed, with frequent breaks in which Howard and Bishop, with the aid of the genomorph, whose name appeared to be simply Nihils, worked by wireless from their respective rooms, mining global data and legislative comparators to support the next component of their presentation. In the end Transglobal would withdraw to make their own decisions, so the VIC government team needed to do as much of the data and document spade-work as possible to ensure their pitch was to its utmost competitive advantage. If Transglobal bought in at this stage, the rest of the negotiation would depend not on new information but on the info-mining Howard, Bishop and Nihils did now.

Howard's team were put up in fairly smart accommodation, but in separate locations around the Old Melbourne CBD. These locations were very much like the rooms in which they met with the Transglobal team – custom-renovated apartments and offices in the old two- or three-storey Nineteenth Century terraces that once housed, presumably, the business class of urban Victoria, as the nation-state was formerly known. Although Transglobal had a brand new high office tower in New Sydney, in fact most of their main operations were still from the now fairly run-down office tower they had built in Old Melbourne in the second decade of the century.

In the team's one visit to the old Transglobal Tower in Bourke Street, the electric doors appeared sluggish, the vestibule lights flickered, and the lifts threatened to seize any second and had old touch-button technology that often failed to light up. This was the sort of building condemned thirty years ago as a fire trap and a catacombs of electronic failure. Being trapped in a lift failure was the least of one's concern.

But Howard guessed the old electrics were actually backed up by extraordinarily new technology, and the pretence of age and deterioration was a 'feint' to put off the casual observer. Housing the transcorp's VIC operations in this older, seemingly tumbledown premises in a near-deserted CBD was part of the same feint. As was the extensive use of internally refurbished older inner city residential dwellings. It was a vestige of the Internet Terrorism of the 2020s that neither transcorps nor government had ever really recovered from.

As the hackers had taken over the old World Wide Web, and viruses became a second by second occurrence, the only way any sizeable infosystem maintained security was by investing massively in their own counter-hackers, and in keeping their systems physically as well as electronically so continually on the move that only the system managers knew what access codes were current and where at any one moment. The faster their programmers developed software to counter the viruses, the faster the hackers broke them down. Cyber technicians like the genomorph, Nihils, became a vital part of any organisation's survival, for by 2020 all Fourth Phase organisations depended entirely on the electronic medium for their logistic, administrative and financial operations. Without effective microsecond control over its infosystems, an organisation could haemorrhage finances or other valuable information in a moment.

Obviously over time, the transcorps had gained the upper hand and developed technological as well as software controls that kept the hackers at bay. But the need to conceal the physical location of their most important networks had led them to re-wire and rebuild from the inside these discrete constellations of locations around the older CBDs whilst, on the surface, building 'new' 'more sophisticated' centres in the new metropolises inland.

So that where, under Second and Third Phase Progress, keeping members of a bidding team in separate apartments was a competitive tactic to reduce their negotiation strength, in the New Prosperity of Fourth Phase Progress it was, conversely, a way of supporting them as a team by providing them with a relatively unassailable netface access. Nihils' role, as well as facilitating their info-mining endeavours, was to maintain the security of their netface connection, which he did by switching their connection codes every couple of minutes. This meant that Howard's and Bishop's work was frustrated by constant changes in font type and formatting commands, as well as the demands of the information management itself. If any of them had depended on VIVO rather than their keyboards, they would have been at sea.

After three days of such intensive activity, sleep became an arbitrary measure of the passing of time. This was calibrated instead by face-to-face meetings, and the periods agreed between them to enable the necessary preparation by Howard's team. At the end of the pitch, Howard was glad to finalise the closing formalities with O'Brien and her team, and see his duo head off for the shuttle home while he took 36 hours off to visit his mother.

This was not just to create the accommodation 'alibi' that was causing him so much strife in VIC Parliament currently (and which the party whip had advised him to keep up). He also wanted to re-assure himself that she had heard no news of the campaign against him in the Chamber, or her implication in it. He had phoned her briefly on his way from the airport, but only long enough to engage in "How are you?" soundings which yielded little except that she was "fine". He had intended to follow-up with further calls, but the schedule had been prohibitive.

He believed he owed his mother more than he could ever repay, because he had entered and continued to work in the profession that had cost her her husband. For Menzies Johns should have been a great man, a historical statesman, a political hero. He had sacrificed so many principles, made so many concessions in order to hold together the ethos of federalism, and a national government. Howard had been studying double politics and IT at university at the time, and could still remember, as research for his final thesis, attending the last Republican Forum in 2025. He remembered watching his father literally move from delegate to delegate, regardless of party alignment or political persuasion, individually trying to solicit commitment to a consensus from each one. And behind him, Howard could see the wave of eyebrows and cross-floor looks, leanings over and notes passed and strolls across the floor that eventually folded in around his father to strand him as the solitary island of federal principle in a sea of disagreement and counter-deals.

By the end of the week, whilst there was a commitment to a further twenty five years of federalism, in effect the state governments had decided to work towards nation state status. Within five years, federalism was dead. Its official dissolution, and the joint inauguration of the nation states, was scheduled for 2050, but any form of meaningful national governance had been void now for twenty years. And its collapse broke Menzies Johns' heart. For a man who had been unusual amongst federal politicians in his honesty and integrity, a man who should have retired to a healthy superannuation and a fulfilling life, Howard's father had limped from heart attack to heart attack into death, as historical account after account heaped responsibility for the collapse of the national government he had loved at his feet.

And Howard's mum had supported her husband through it all with unflinching stoicism. Even now, in her eighties, she attempted to remember the good times and search for the positives in the bad. The last thing Howard wanted on her doorstep was an unsightly, small minded and mean-spirited scandal implicating her son.

The hire car was one of the new solar and electric hybrids – no oil-based fuel at all. It was the first time Howard had driven one and he was unimpressed. Snappy acceleration in the city, but once on the open road and at speed the response was sluggish. It was also fitted with automatic speed limit control, so once on the highway to Philip Island he was constantly jolting from one speed to another every hundred metres or so, as the limits changed randomly around him. By the time he reached his mother's house in Cowes, he was a frustrated and unhappy man, grateful to enter familiar and comforting surroundings.

Ruth Johns looked considerably older than when he had seen her last, a matter of months before. The shadows under her eyes had deepened, her laugh lines faded, and her mouth turned further down. It was still easy to see that she had been a beautiful woman in her prime, and had aged well, but she was aging faster now.

This alarmed Howard. His mum was all the family he had left. His uncles, aunts and cousins had long gone the way of mandatory identity displacement. His mother had vigorously resisted a similar fate to date – rejected the offer of a CCC, depended on her seniors card for credit transactions, using what "real money" she still had hoarded away when she could find a vendor willing to accept it, refused to validate new transaction cards that arrived with any name change on them. She had an old fashioned filing cabinet full of VIC

73

Government's attempts to manoeuvre her into one new identity bracket after another. Howard had himself pulled rank in order to preserve her historical identity.

The result, however, was a reduced access to both WIPs[2] and SAPs[3]. Appointments with health services involving physical attention were hard to secure, phone or internet health advice was limited, and discount purchases were dependent on presentation of her concession card at point of purchase. And at eighty three, she was no longer finding it easy to make her way even to local convenience stores, let alone to Cowes' spectacular Shopping World. She had also never adjusted to the 36-hour day, preferring to sleep and wake with nightfall and sunrise, and so found the perpetual daytime of Shopping Worlds disorienting in every way.

Her 24-hour clock also affected his visits. Sometimes he would arrive at the end of a working day just as the sun was rising, and his mother with it for the start of her day. And he would be getting up at 4.00 hrs the next day ready for breakfast as his mum was preparing for an evening meal and a glass of sherry at sunset. On this occasion, however, he had timed his visit to coincide with her 24-hour clock so that the morning of his arrival was, indeed, also morning for his mother.

"You're looking well Mum," he lied, as she disappeared into her small cottage kitchen to make tea.

"Keeping body and soul together, Adam," she said without looking back. "Keeping body and soul together."

"You're supposed to call me Howard, Mum," he stirred. "That was the price for your last transaction card rejection, remember?"

"Oh Adam, no-one can hear us in here," she grumbled dismissively from the kitchen.

---

[2] Welfare and Infrastructure Provision
[3] Social Access Provision

Howard wanted to say that he was not so sure about that, but knew it was not worth going into the range of ways in which he knew any well resourced transcorp could find their way into one's audiospace.

"How's Yvonne?" she called, referring to Howard's first wife.

"Long gone," Howard replied whilst idly scrutinising the mantelpiece, crammed as it was with the gathered ornaments of years. There were a few he remembered buying her himself.

"I tried ringing her a couple of weeks back. Someone else answered. Tried directory assistance. Couldn't find her. Couldn't even find directory assistance."

"Did you use VIVO Mum?"

"Oh Adam, I don't even know what – oh wait a minute. Yes, I spoke into the phone. I asked for her name. But they said there was no-one on their records by that name. So I asked for directory assistance. And they kept asking me for the director of what? Or the director to who? We couldn't understand each other at all."

The absence of dust was comforting – at least she was still looking after the house. And the whistle of her old kettle on the gas stove and methodical clink of china lent a similar impression of competence in the kitchen.

"You're supposed to wait, Mum. The phone service will ask you how they can help you next. You just have to use common language. How can I find so-and-so – that sort of thing. Then it will understand what you want and be able to respond."

"Oh Adam, I know you're an expert on computer programs, but honestly they don't work for ordinary folk like me."

"You're not ordinary folk, Mum. You're a biochemist and a professional historian with a PhD on the collapse of the union movement. And you have a Masters in Organisational Culture."

She was bringing in the tea on a tray – the same old brown enamel teapot, wire tea-strainer with faded yellow plastic handle, sitting in its little alloy drip catcher, and the two floral bone china teacups, with two biscuits on a matching plate. But she found it difficult to manage the weight and, though he knew she would say no, he promised himself he would carry the tray in next time. It was too easy to accept her assurances of independence.

"Well, Adam, all I can say is that today's computers are just beyond me, I'm afraid."

"So you haven't been on the netface then?"

"Oh yes, I get on there alright. Just can't do much once I'm on it. Managed to find out about your dubious sexual peccadilloes, though, and your bludging off the government and blaming it on me. Shameful behaviour. Shameful."

Howard was crestfallen. She had already found out.

"I'm sorry, Mum. I would've warned you earlier, but I understood – well, I was hoping you hadn't found out."

"Yes, it only lasted 5 minutes on the news, didn't it. I suppose you had one of your security chaps monitoring my internet usage, and they said I hadn't been online at the time. Well, more fool them. I found the archive of the item, didn't I. With a search. You see? Some of my old internet skills still work on this – what do they call it again now?"

"Netface."

"And the shame's on them Adam, not on you dear. Oppositions are all the same, aren't they? They'll try anything. I hope you haven't been worrying about me, Adam. It'd take more than some stupid Opposition ploy to block the passage of your water legislation through the House to bother me, son."

"Chamber, Mum. They're called Chambers now. And yes, I thought you might be upset about being involved in the scandal."
"Well, it's not much of a scandal is it? A son gives his mum a couple of dollars to cover the price of a cup of tea and the washing powder,

and every man and his dog's supposed to be up in arms about it? I don't think so."

"Well ... I'm relieved."

"So what's happened to Yvonne, do you think?" she said, returning to the subject of familiar interest. Howard knew his mother fretted that he had no stable life partner.

"I don't know Mum. I really don't keep in touch. I don't care that much, I'm afraid."

"Yes, but I do son. I liked her."

"Well, I could get a trace done, I suppose. If you're keen."

"It would be nice. I suspect she's had one of those mandatory name change orders."

"I wouldn't be surprised. But she'll still be traceable through our records, at government level."

"It would be nice to know she's still alive."

"They're all still alive, Mum. It's just a name displacement."

"Yes, but you can never find them again. Not us ordinary folk, Adam. It's just like the Disappeared of South America and Africa during the last century, you know. And the Jews in Germany."

"That's old history, Mum."

"That's right, Adam. What I'm supposed to be good at, remember?"

She had a point. He would run a check on his former wife for her.

"Do you still get out, Mum?" His turn to change the subject.

"Not the way I used to, Adam. As you know, I used to adore my beach walks. I understand that climate change has not proceeded in exactly the manner anticipated but, believe me, these days it has to be a really low tide to reveal even the narrowest strip of sand. The re-gen has provided a useful barrier and keeps the high tides back but you can't walk through it these days. It's just not the same. But I get out to…" - she seemed to search for the term – "…local events from time to time. Probably once a week."

"Well that's good. At least you can be with other people."

"Exactly."

The clock on the mantelpiece chimed ten as they sipped their tea. It was a beautiful old timepiece: an original wind-up action set in a wooden casement shaped in a wide, sweeping arch, designed to stand squarely in the centre of the mantelpieces of Nineteenth and early Twentieth century houses. The chime itself was a narrow strip of iron coiled in on itself like a butterfly's proboscis. A small mechanical hammer struck the spiralled iron every quarter hour, and the number of hours was presented on the hour. As a child, Howard used to turn the clock around, open the little door at its rear, and spend ages watching the mechanism gathering itself up for each chime.

"Still keeping good time?" he asked, nodding towards the clock.

"As far as I know. I don't keep any other time, Adam."

"Do you remember the church bells in Old Melbourne? On a Sunday morning. I was thinking about them the other day."

"You mean in the city?"

"Yes. It was one of my earliest memories. Being out on a veranda on what I presume was a Sunday morning, hearing the bells."

"That must have been when we were in the apartment in South Melbourne. It didn't have a veranda though. And I don't remember being able to hear the bells. But I might have put your bassinet near an open window, for the fresh air. I used to prepare a Sunday lunch for your Dad. He used to like a Sunday lunch. Meant we could have the Sunday evening together. You'd be asleep by then."

Howard complimented his mother on the biscuits and helped her wash up. But while he was putting the pot away he came across the box the biscuits came in. It was quite a large one.

78

"I hope you're eating more than biscuits, Mum," he observed, then looked more closely at the box.

"Of course I am, dear. We're having a nice bit of brisket for dinner."

"These biscuits are packed locally. See? The box says it's packed here in Cowes."

"Made locally too. Some of them by me."

"Are you doing charity work, Mum? Didn't think you approved of charity."

"I don't, Howard. This is a collective. Based on exchange rather than money."

Now the penny dropped. This was what his mother had meant by 'local events'.

"A Money Free Exchange? You want to watch that, Mum. The tax collectors will be onto you. And the free trade authorities."

He was not serious, but she took the bait anyway.

"No money changes hands, Adam, so what is there to tax?"

"Restriction on trade then, isn't it? Anti-competitive, because you are excluding competitors from the consumer credit system."

This part was true. MFEs were still demonised in The Market, and the tax sharks who hunted them down were today's infobrief heroes.

"Adam, in the last few decades of the Twentieth century non-monetarism was a serious alternative to the pandemic ascent of transglobal capitalism. The subsumption of the cash economy into New Prosperity's consumer credit system just co-opted the term, making a mockery of the practice in the process. And they used their 'superior' non-cash system to make money-free collectives the scapegoat for all that went wrong, just as they did with the internet terrorists. And don't think I don't know when you're winding me up, son."

Howard smiled. And his mother snapped shut the cupboard containing the offending biscuit box. Non-monetarism had gone hand in hand with the demise of the union movement, and had been central to Ruth Johns' PhD thesis. But the mention of MFEs had given Howard an idea for Mick Turition's next assignment.

If there was, as Katharine O'Brien had implied during their conversation on the shuttle, no great strategic conspiracy to transglobal capital, perhaps he could test the hypothesis in the logical positivist paradigm, by trying to prove the opposite: that Real Truth did after all lie with some revolutionary underclass. It could, for instance, be found in these Money Free Exchangers. If this were the case, then the tax sharks were sure to be onto the insurrectionists. Track down the tax sharks, and Howard would find the revolutionary cells of MFEs. Track down the cells of MFEs via the tax sharks, and O'Brien would be proved right. No MFE's hunted by tax sharks; no strategic chaos.

It seemed a good enough thesis at the time. That night, after their brisket dinner and a nightcap saw Ruth Johns off to bed at around 21.00 hrs, Howard used her netface to access Mick Turition. Mick was chatting up a couple of cyber hackers from the nation state of Hainan in a virtual bar in Shanghai. Howard promptly sent him off into existing ideobriefs on Money Free Exchanges to see if he could draw out the tax sharks.

"This is not exactly fun, Howie," Mick commented drily as he threaded his way through one expected position on non-monetary production and exchange after another. "Such participants are, nevertheless, producers of products and services which *should* be available for all consumers. The Money Free Exchange is as much economic activity as the existing consumer credit system, and should thus be subject to tax for the benefit of all. I mean, who believes this stuff?"

"Well, the majority of the population, Mick, who are very happy in their right to spend their earnings on their choice of products and services. They don't give a damn that tax security is granted unlimited netface power."

It wasn't long before Mick spotted a team of tax sharks mounting a surveillance operation on an isolated hacker dismantling a matrix of security barriers around an Electronic Data Transfer system in a major credit facility. The tax sharks were themselves hiding behind large accounts, and moving through algorithms of netface security to avoid detection by the hacker. They were even feeding the hacker false leads and pass codes.

Once Mick had identified one tax shark, he quickly learnt to identify others. It was not long before he was himself shadowing these shadows of the nation state economy, and found those among them who were in search of Money Free Exchangers.

"You should see these guys," Mick marvelled. "They're hell bent on nabbing the market gardeners, the backyard chicken coupers, back alley snail racers, cake bakers and jam makers, quilters and home dress-makers, bric-a-brac marketeers and thrift exchanges – they talk to each other about them the whole time, as if they are some sort of serious threat to society, like criminals. I mean, these people are harmless, surely?"

"Not according to The Market, Mick. They are a serious underworld. If there truly is no strategic centre to capital, then The Market would be correct: the MFEs would form a serious and organised counter-insurgency," Howard said electronically to his virtual alter-ego. "They would be the source of Real Truth."

"I love it when you talk dirty," said Mick, who was now virtually leaping over the 'back fences' of the netface security systems to get a look at the MFEers the tax sharks were stalking. But he could only identify the actual subjects of surveillance from the electronic conversations between the tax sharks themselves. He did not have the tax shark's licence to slip behind the netface to identify its user.

"We need to break the codes, Mick. We need live Money Free Exchangers to interview if we are going to get to any truth there is to it. We could expose this issue if we could get to them, you know."

"Of course I know, Mr Smart Arse. I'm a version of you. But this is going to take time. And you might have exposed your mum's netface enough for one night. You better leave this with me."

Mick was right. Howard had already been on the netface for two hours, and that was a long enough period of relatively untraceable cybernet activity to arouse suspicion. So he programmed Mick to pursue the codes while Howard was himself offline, and left Mick Turition for the day.

As Mick headed off to the further electronic catacombs of the cybernet, however, Howard could not help but notice that his own Cyber Champion was being followed. By whom, he could not tell, for the shadow was only brief. But it was enough of a glimpse to cause Howard Johns no small alarm.

Chapter Ten

By 24:00 hrs it was time for Howard to be heading back for New Melbourne. He was feeling relaxed on the drive back to Old Melbourne airport, despite the forced speed-limit shunting of his hire vehicle. Time with his mum usually did that for Howard. Despite his concern for her health and well being, she was a mentally active and intelligent woman as well as a loving mother, and after all of these years he still enjoyed her company and felt relieved of some of the burden of responsibility identity constantly loaded him with. It was nice, once in a while, to feel 'at home' in the way children do; that sense of 'being looked after'. In the world of adult life, it happened so seldom. The individual is all. Even in the more collective cultures found in the nation states of the China and South Asia regions, individual responsibility for others just added to the burden of responsibility for oneself.

He was making good time as he approached the West Gate Bridge, taking the southern ring route to the airport. There, however, he had to slow through a chicanery of diversions as the aging road system was force-fed through its fifth or sixth iteration. To his right he could see one of Old Melbourne's now rare Shopping Worlds. This would once have been one of the first of the new generation of New Prosperity Shopping Worlds, but it was now showing its age both in design and maintenance.

He didn't know quite what impulse led him to exit the constricted freeway. Part of his mind was rationalising: well this is still VIC, and I represent all of VIC in the parliament, not just my own constituency. Another lobe of his thinking was rueing the fact that he never went into Shopping Worlds except for brandgrab campaigns and elections. In yet another neuronic convolution of his frontal lobe he was associating the deterioration and age of the giant shopping complex with the age and clutter of his mother's house. Then there was that inveterate handful of cells inwardly accusing him of

83

missing a vital turn or road sign. The reality, of course, was that it was over thirty five years since road systems has routinely been reengineered to make it almost possible to avoid driving into these cornucopias of consumer choice. He was, thus, inevitably unaware of making any actual decision when he found himself on the slip road off the freeway descending towards the Shopping World's maze of entrances, exits and car parks.

He was aware, however, that it never ceased to amaze him how effectively shopping complexes were designed to trap the consumer. Little entrances of varying shapes and sizes were designed to lead them by a complex of lanes and rows, columns and ramps to an eventual parking space they would never find again. And even if they made an assiduous note of the level and location, once they were absorbed into the mood music, mind-numbing artificial lighting and endless malls, halls and moving walkways of the consumer complex itself, it was impossible to find one's way out again. People just spent hours roaming from one level to another, buying things for which they had no real use long after they had satisfied the actual need that brought them in the first place. But, of course, they were happy.

And this had been one of the community development aims of the Shopping World movement. Howard could clearly remember the epidemic of suicides that accompanied the reduction of human social traffic to the individual's home, working by computer through the old WANs and LANs and, later, WorldWideWeb and eClouds. So many individuals forced out of social discourse into conducting their existence 'online', including their shopping. Then came the Internet Wars, and they found their credit disappearing, their bank accounts dissolving, and their identities eviscerated by the hacking plague.

It was one of the aspects of New Prosperity that Howard actually felt some ideological alignment with at the time; that the creation and mass-media promotion of the Shopping Worlds managed to extract people from their hermit-like slavery to the computer screen, to come out into society and actually walk amongst others of their kind.

Social engineering perhaps, but also a life saver for those introjected by the LCD screen onto the inevitable unsustainability of their own minds without actual social contact. And so the Shopping World became, in the age of Consumer Choice, the embodiment of social optimism as well as the apex of material aspiration. It was the sublime. Or at least, it was once, for this particular vestige of former retail glory.

And so Howard found himself wandering with a slightly aimless nostalgia (and a more directional one hour limit, for he had to catch the 30:00 shuttle) through yellow-lit malls of specialty shops with the inevitable grocerymart or domestic goods chain open-mouthed at the end. The consumers in this complex were few, and dressed in the cheapest clothes. They looked generally pale and unhealthy, hair frequently unkempt, teeth visibly poor, eyes hollowed and red-rimmed. With the general migration inland, only the waged poor and debt-laden remained in Old Melbourne, particularly down here near the waterline. Howard was glad he did not have to campaign in an electorate like this.

After half an hour he had seen enough and started to seek signs that might lead him back to his vehicle. In the more modern Shopping Worlds there were VIVO points with chip recognition that at least gave you a nominal chance of finding your way back to your vehicle. But this complex was both pre-CCC and pre-VIVO, and had caught up with neither in any subsequent re-fit. Walking from sign to sign, site map to site map, seeking a way back to his vehicle, Howard soon started chancing short cuts through the internal catacombs leading to central amenities, picking up his pace.

He began to feel the edge of panic of someone lost, trapped in a bad dream, driven by his need to make his next scheduled engagement with time, the shuttle. When he finally reached a narrow corridor leading off a long shopping concourse in an older section of the complex, he thought he had finally found the exit from the short-cut he had charted in the last store guide. But as he strode purposefully down it and burst through the fire door, he found himself in the open air.

The early light of dawn was just beginning to stretch up into the sky. He had emerged from the Shopping World onto the suburb's original high street. It was a classic. Wide enough for two horse-drawn carriages to pass. The later tram lines still scoring the centre of the cambered roadway, although presumably disused today. Even in old Old Melbourne the brown-coal-power-greedy trams must have died long ago. Pavements raised above the rut- and mud-line of the original pre-tarmac street with cut-stone kerbs. And lined on either side with individual specialty shops. In the pale blue lamplight he could see no-one in either direction, and many of the shopfronts appeared either empty or boarded up. It was such a desolate precinct for one so crowded with structure and past.

To his immediate right, however, one shop appeared to be open. It was very ill-lit from deep within – an old wire-and-halogen bulb, by the looks. Howard could not imagine where the proprietor sourced such supplies any more. The heavy, wood-framed shop door opened easily, ringing a little bell coiled above it in the process. A moustachioed man with a balding head of thin, greying hair behind a counter at the far end of the shop looked up, but did not smile. He wore thick, heavy-framed glasses – a rarity in these days of corneal laser surgery and intra-temporal lobe chip enhancement – which concealed any expression in and around his eyes.

Howard took only as much initial notice of the contents of the shop as needed to negotiate the jumbled display tables and shelves to reach the shop's counter. It appeared, however, to sell mostly bric-a-brac – a 'dead product' enterprise not favoured under New Prosperity, which probably explained why the proprietor was in the location he was.

"Excuse me," enquired Howard reaching the man behind the counter, "But I'm looking for Level 1 C36."

The man looked blankly at him.

86

"In the Shopping World? A car parking bay?"

"Of course, sir," the man blinked visibly behind his thick lenses, "It took me a moment to ... It is just one level up, sir. You are in the right geographical location, but one level too low."

"Great, thanks. Looking for my car!"

Howard turned to leave but was distracted by a handbell sitting on the counter. He half-turned back.

"May I?" he asked the man behind the counter.

"Be my guest," the man gestured the bell.

Howard picked up the bell and held it tentatively to his ear. He gently tweaked the handgrip so that the hammer sounded against the bell internally, and was impressed at the clarity, truth and length of the tone.

"It's very good," he said approvingly to the man he presumed to be the shop's proprietor. "Are they still making these? It's Dalai Lama, I assume. Or not?"

Howard was aware that the nation state of Tibet had accelerated its passage through Third Phase Progress by mass-producing artefacts of the religion that had made it famous, championed by its leader, the Dalai Lama. And with the loss of the old religions to the Society Standards Sects, Dalai Lama had become the brand name for the industry. Many other nation states now competed with replicas and copies of Dalai Lama products, but none could reproduce the meditative ring tone of the originals. This one was superb.

"It precedes Dalai Lama, sir." The shop proprietor had a clipped accent that sounded not quite Australasian. It could have been New Zealand. Or from one of the South Asian nation states in the Indian sub-continent. "It is an antique."

"But a mass-produced one, presumably. I mean, it wouldn't be last century even, would it?"

"Early last century, I believe," the man behind the counter confirmed.

"Wow," exclaimed Howard artlessly. For if the proprietor was to be believed this was indeed an original, a genuine Tibetan prayer bell. "Is it for sale?"

"Everything is for sale, sir," the man said, spreading his hands and affording a small smile beneath his grey, brush-like moustache.

"I'll take it," Howard said hurriedly, conscious of the time.

"Do you not want to know how much, sir?" the man asked, beginning to wrap it anyway.

"I supposed I should, but I don't care really. Until it appears in my credit statement, I suppose," Howard joked.

"I am afraid it will not be doing that, sir," the man replied.

Howard looked at him askance.

"I do not give credit, sir," the man explained.

"So, er, I mean, how will I pay?"

"Well, you could try money, sir."

"You mean, cash money?"

"That would be a good start, yes sir."

Howard had nothing on him even to barter with, let alone real money.

"Well, I'm sorry, but I..." Howard proffered his CCC wrist, to complete his explanation.

The man stopped wrapping the handbell.

"I am sorry sir. I do not have the facilities. I will take an appropriate exchange."

Howard slapped his pockets in search of currency he knew was not there. Even the cake his mother had left for him to take was in the hire car one level above in the shopping complex behind the shop.

"Look, I've got a cake up one level, in my car... It's home made?"

The impassive look of the shop proprietor was unyielding.

"I'm sorry. I have to go."

He half-hesitated, half-grimaced, then left the shop in a hurry.

From the street he could now make out in the strengthening dawn the name of the shop above its awning: "Cross Antiques". The aging Shopping World towered like a monolith into the sky behind it, dwarfing the shop and those like it along the old high street. The image was surreal in the pearly light. But it was one on which Howard could not dwell. He raced back into the shopping complex, strode quickly up two moving walkways to the level above, and back the way he had come to find, as promised, the fire door leading to Level 1 and on it, Parking Bay C36 in which, his hire car.

He lost no time in finding the nearest exit and, once out on the street, working his way back onto the freeway and on to Old Melbourne Airport.

89

Chapter Eleven

Howard was unable to stop thinking about the Tibetan Prayer Handbell. He dreamt about it that night, back in his Canberra apartment. Woke up imagining its tone in his ears. Wishing he had had something with him that might have persuaded the shop proprietor to part with it. The likelihood of him finding even the shopping world again was remote, let alone the exit from it to the old high street that led to Cross Antiques. But then, he rationalised, there was no certainty the shop owner was telling the truth. It could just as easily been one of the thousands of copies of such handbells now manufactured and sold around the world. But then there was that tone....

He did not go in to VIC Parliament that day, as Chamber Seven was not sitting. Instead he filed his report on the negotiations with Transglobal to find, to his pleasure, that Transglobal had already communicated to the party whip their acceptance of the pitch he and his team had devoted so much effort in delivering in Old Melbourne. There was netmail from the Minister himself congratulating Howard and his team on their work.

This was a big win for Howard, and he hoped that it might signal to the party that he was ready to actually go in to bat on a negotiation. Up until now he had become one of the party's main anchors at the pitch stage, but had never seen a pitch through to negotiation and closure.

There was also netmail from Katharine O'Brien, thanking him for 'taking the time to meet with our team', and congratulating him on the 'quality of your presentation' which was 'thoroughly researched and apposite'. It was a formal communication, but it was from her personal netmail address. He wasn't sure if this meant anything, but replied thanking her in return, and hoping that their paths would cross in the future. He thought about adding a tongue-in-cheek suggestion that this might be at the next Christuism service in the VIC Parliament Reflection Centre, but thought better of it.

His latest PIMS[4] report was also in, and he was pleased to note that his suicide attempt was indeed recorded as an 'emetic attack' with an associated rise in blood pressure. The PIMS had put him on retrieval alert, but only for a few minutes. He also noted that his drive to New Melbourne the following day had added ten-and-a-half thousand dollars to his lawdebt in speeding fines.

He then tackled a backlog of consumer enquiries from constituents, between which he 'borrowed' moments to check on Mick Turition's progress with the MFE communication codes. Mick was not doing well. He did not have the programs to crack the codes and, like Howard, had become aware that he was himself being shadowed. He had tried to throw his shadow by moving through a number of contrasting stories. He happened across an old VIC vintner, for instance, who had managed to sustain some 30-year old vine shiraz through the last flash freeze – but by the time he got to the source, 38 other journalists had been and gone and the vintner had sold his stock and vineyard three times over and closed his site.

He went off sniffing for a student unrest story instead. There were still a few pockets of resistance to pre-paid education - students who issued statements about the incomprehensibility of education debt that no-one could afford to repay in a lifetime, particularly when re-education for a next career was expected at least twice in any lifetime. Perhaps, he reasoned virtually on his creator's behalf, this was where the Real Truth underworld might be found. He followed two or three leads but each time, even using back door routes, by the time he got to the story it had already been written up, with responses from both government and opposition spokespeople, by at least a dozen other cyber journos and posted on The Market by the first in. In one, the students had even been bought off with

---

4 personal information management system

scholarships for other nation states with lower education fees, notably the Philippines and PNG. It was like an online instalott[5].

As a last resort, he tried pursuing a couple of the latest Family Values Schemes, to see if he could come up with an angle on one of the market segments within the family and their product package use within a particular Shopping World. The Market loved these 'good news' stories about how magnificently consumers in their family groupings took up consumer packages, because the transcorps depended on such schemes to keep up market circulation. A desperate ploy, because even if Mick could show such stories were a sham, individual family economic failure did not prove that there was a global strategic centre to capital. And in any case, every lead Mick picked up had already been and gone on The Market.

Howard reproved Mick for is caprice, reminding him that the MFE interview subjects were the scientific opposite to global strategy they were seeking, according to the evidence. But Mick pointed to his shadow.

"If I don't shake this guy," he said with an edge of genuine unease, "We don't get to prove nothin'."

At each venture, he explained, he would use the opportunity to, in electronic terms, 'double back' to see if his shadow had followed him. Mick hoped to actually confront the shadow and unmask them. But each time, though the trace was evident, the shadow was nowhere to be seen.

The danger, of course, was that the shadow was a tax shark, and a tax shark may well be able to trace Mick back to Howard. Howard was beginning to think he needed further advice from Simpkins when, during downtime, Mick was himself surprised by the shadow itself.

He was following a coded communication chain that clearly had tax security's interest and was therefore, he hoped, the intranet of an

---

[5] instant lottery

MFE. Mick almost thought he was getting the hang of the code. There were repeated phrases that were stacking up into a 'language' he might, with Howard's assistance, started to apportion meaning to. But just as he turned an electronic corner, rudimentary phrase book in hand, he literally passed through a cyber shadow that disappeared into the path through which he had just come, leaving a 'note' in his hand. It read, "Do you want sex?"

Howard laughed out loud. Mick Turition's shadow was a commercial vendor, selling sex through the cybernet. Clearly the conventional market avenues were already flooded, so this vendor was prowling less conventional cyber topography for business.

Still, a prescience to be watched. If a smart sex vendor could track Mick Turition, the latter might be easy prey for the tax shark, or even NERA. Howard went to sleep enjoying his amusement, but resolving to seek further advice from Simpkins next day on how to tackle the codes. If he could find a way of phrasing an enquiry that did not reveal too much about his quarry, he might . . .

In VIC parliament the following morning, however, Simpkins was nowhere to be found. He was not responding to his cell card, and his netmail was returning a "no longer at this address" notice. Once Howard started to search further afield, he inevitably attracted the attention of both VIC Parliament security and cyber security. He had to explain what he wanted Simpkins for, and could someone else assist? Then during the Two Minute Vision, Howard noticed the genomorph, Nihils, was observing him from a short distance.

Although the Member of the Chamber had become more familiar with the cyber security operative during their pitch to O'Brien in Old Melbourne and, frankly, been impressed with both his skills and professionalism, Howard still harboured a suspicion that Nihils' indifference and disdain revealed a concerted Consumer Choice League agenda. Or worse, that Nihils had been internally assigned to monitor Howard; although part of Howard's mind still wanted not to imagine why he merited monitoring. This was, after all, a democratic

world in which consumer choice was always with you. As the Two
Minute Vision routinely reminded them all:

DEMOCRACY IS FREEDOM

FREEDOM IS CHOICE

CHOICE IS THE CONSUMER'S

But, as Howard well knew, in the world of politics there was always
more than one fish beneath the surface that could jump up to bite you
without warning. Howard's patrilineal and political heritage was
well known. His mother's politics were perhaps less familiar to those
in power these days, but Howard kept his head down and was
generally as good a boy as he could be. The recent campaign against
him was incidental, and the party knew it. As soon as he entered the
Chamber that morning, the party whip had once again congratulated
him on his success with Transglobal and informed him that, thanks
to his constructive absence, the water legislation had been passed.

Howard was still mulling his way through such thoughts as the Two
Minute Vision came to its end. As he turned absent-mindedly to
leave, for the second time in as many weeks the genomorph bumped
into him. Although this time it was more of a sideways glance.
Nihils did not look at him but, more, grabbed his arm during the
collision, as if using Howard to steady himself enough to continue
his passage. But as Howard vaguely watched the genomorph's
departing back, he realised that a piece of paper – yes, *paper* – had
been crumpled into his hand.

Luckily it was his left hand, leaving his right hand free. For as he left
the Seventh Hall there were a number of 'chance meetings' with
colleagues and stakeholders which required the customary
handshake and some casual conversation. When he reached the
relative privacy of his office, he unfolded the note to read, in block
letters at the top, the question:

"DO YOU WANT SEX?"

Chapter Twelve

It took a moment for the message to sink in. It could be a coincidence, Howard reasoned, but "DO YOU WANT SEX?" was exactly the same message delivered to Mick Turition the day before. Howard refolded the note without apparent haste, and tried not to look around involuntarily for internal optics. There were tell-tale lenses all over VIC Parliament, but although functional these were also for show. It was fibre-optic and infra-red vision that actually captured activity over the entirety of the complex. It was impossible for Howard to know from where in his room he was being remotely observed, even with the most detailed search.

The clandestine nature of the genomorph's approach made Howard intensely suspicious. It replicated itself in a similar impulse towards secrecy in the recipient. Howard produced a smile and a laugh, as if someone had passed him a joke. He smiled and nodded with satisfaction some more, as if appreciating the joke's finer ramifications. Then, with a closing nod and raising of his eyebrows, folded the note up and put it casually in his trouser pocket while something more important caught his attention on the desk before him.

He was not sure quite where to read the rest of the note unobserved. Howard was naturally curious. Was the little horned genomorph seriously approaching him for a sexual liaison? Or, more likely, was the approach some sort of code? If the connection was real, if Nihils was the tail shadowing Mick Turition, then he already knew of Howard's cybernet activities. So why make contact? If Nihils was monitoring Howard for cyber security, he would not have made himself known to Howard so obviously. But of course, the covert nature of the open approach could itself be laying the groundwork for a trap; this was, after all, how the tax sharks went about their work. Nihils could be working for the opposition, trying to set Howard up for another assault in the Chamber.

So if curiosity was not enough of a motivation, necessity was. Howard needed to find out what the genomorph was up to. So back in the Chamber Howard chose the lead-in to question time to surreptitiously retrieve the note whilst extracting his handkerchief to blow his nose, then keeping the note in the palm of his hands. He knew the last speech before question time would be long and boring, from a back bencher like himself who needed to impress her constituents back home. Howard was thus justified in nodding off. As his head dropped into seeming slumber, he lowered his thumb covering the note couched in his lap to quickly read the short remainder of the note.

It was in much smaller writing, fainter, less easy for monitoring optics to pick up in the sizeable Chamber.

"MEET ME AT NEXT 50TH"

It only took a second. Howard covered the text again with the subtlest of movements, and then jerked 'awake' to a pretence of looking around momentarily in case anyone had noticed him 'nodding off'.

The message was a reference to a regular event in Choice Circle, just outside VIC Parliament. Even though every nation state in Australasia was already fully functional in its own right, each was running a long-term promotion campaign to keep the population focussed on the merits of nation statehood, which became 'official' in two years' time.

This took the form of quarterly statewide promotions of the 2050 celebration, which would be a year-long event. Each promotion revealed a new exciting aspect of the celebrations that would bring overwhelming benefits to consumers. At each promotion, the transcorps made sure there were armfuls of free gifts and special deals and packages that also reminded consumers how important nation statehood was for their wealth, health and freedom – for Democracy was Freedom, Freedom was Choice, and Choice was the Consumer's.

The promotions were broadcast in Shopping Worlds throughout the nation state, as well as through the domestic netface services. The live events broadcast in VIC as part of the promotion, however, were always from VIC Parliament's Choice Circle, symbolic meeting place for all of VIC. A chance to be seen on live netspace attracted thousands of consumers to such occasions. The public euphoria of Consumer Choice had a life of its own, and consumers revelled in opportunities like this to reinforce their newfound freedom and prosperity.

One such quarterly promotion had been scheduled for that afternoon, at 20:00 hours. Most employers would either allow an 'early minute' or an extended meal break for consumers to attend the event. The promotion would begin as the sun set, to symbolise the end of one era and birth of a new. As the last rays of the sun withdrew their characteristic pink hues from the buildings around Choice Circle, a spectacular light show would fill the venue and the sky above it, heralding for all the new era born with the Age of Order and New Prosperity. This resolved itself into a graphic and audio presentation about Nation Statehood on the giant screen that dominated Choice Circle, which served as a giant solar power collector during daylight hours. The remainder of the two-hour show was filled with popular performing acts interspersed or, indeed, sometimes combined with the various consumer handouts and deals.

Howard continued to question his attendance at this assignation. But if it was entrapment, he reasoned finally, it was just too clumsy: Nihils had compromised himself with the overtly solicitous nature of the note. Howard could legitimately be engaging in a commercial sexual transaction. It was his choice, after all.

Although clone throwbacks were not uncommon in twenty first century VIC, Howard was hopeful he would be able to spot the modest horns of his correspondent in the crowd. He arrived early, guessing the genomorph would do the same, and from the steps of VIC Parliament it did not take long to spot the cyber security operative in the growing crowd. He did not move in at first so as not to draw attention to either himself or his target. As the crowd grew, however, he gradually worked his way into it until, once the light show spectacular was over and the various product promotions underway, he finally found himself shoulder to shoulder with the genomorph.

Nihils did not look at him, or speak to him. The mere fact that Howard had turned up was confirmation of his interest. Instead Nihils passed another note to him by hand, at their serried shoulders. Nihils then pressed forward into the crowd, feigning enthusiasm for the act then performing. Howard glanced only briefly at the note once Nihils had gone. It was again a folded piece of notepaper on the front of which was written simply "NERA".

This was an interesting coded instruction. It clearly had the assonant meaning: Howard was getting "nearer" to Nihils' purpose. But on the surface, of course, the acronym stood for Net Enforcement and Regulation Authority – one of the few regulatory authorities commerce actually took responsibility for. Transcorps were generally happy for government to bear the burden of civil regulation. Control over cyberspace, however, was of such a premium to capital that business could ill afford the risk of 'outsourcing' responsibility for its security – especially not to government.

The third element of the code was the fact well known in senior government circles that the transcorps used NERA to manage surveillance operations via the satellite systems they had purchased off the super governments at knock down prices during the 2020s and 30s. Nihils would know that Howard would know that a NERA surveillance satellite could read the text on the note in his hands, even in the shadow of the stage presentations before the crowd in which Howard was pinioned.

Howard was thus reminded that this was not the place to open the note. After a suitable pause, he slowly shouldered his way out of the crowd and back to his office, ostensibly to complete his day's work. It was on leaving work, after first turning off his own office light, that in the light spilling in from the corridor he quickly read the detail of Nihil's second (or third, counting Mick Turition's shadow) note. The text told him to meet Simpkins at an address in an old quarter of New Melbourne at 28:00 that day.

Howard looked at the time signal in the corridor as he closed the office door behind him. It was 28:00 precisely. He would have to be late.

Chapter Thirteen

Howard stood before the plain plywood front door of an old fibro bungalow in what had once been a workers' quarter of New Melbourne. Howard judged this part of town had its origins well back into the previous century, when New Melbourne was still Albury Wodonga and was home to a number of small manufacturing industries. These small fibro dwellings, on their meagre square blocks, were found scattered around the light industrial areas throughout mid-to-late twentieth century Australia. They were poorly made, pokey, and difficult to cool or heat. While many of them remained in the outer suburbs of the coastal capital cities now emptying in the move to the interland, Howard was unsure why this quarter on the Albury side of the Murrumbidgee had survived the redevelopment of the regional river town into the new capital of VIC.

The street was badly lit, and there was no light over the porch, nor any visible means of securing the attention of any occupants. So Howard simply rapped on the hollow door with his bare knuckles. The genomorph answered it and ushered Howard inside. The house was as dimly lit as the street outside, and consisted of a series of small featureless fibro walls. In silence, Nihils led him into what appeared to be the lounge. It was lit by a single lamp which supported an elliptical column in which oleaginous orange blobs rose and descended like deformed jellyfish or crippled egg yolks – Howard wasn't sure which. The walls of the room were hung with South Asian batik clothes, and large cushions around the walls provided the only seating.

Nihils went to what appeared to be an old hi-fi system in one corner, turned up the sound and fiddled with a couple of small black plastic knobs to achieve a desired setting. They made no difference to the sound, which was a neither pleasant nor unpleasant drifty sort of rock music, again from before Howard was born. Howard wondered where the genomorph found this stuff. But once he seemed to have satisfied himself with the setting, he turned to Howard and spoke. It was the first time Howard had really heard his voice.

"I've just tuned out any cybernet signal to this house, including CCC reception. Instead, I've tuned into a program in this box that has recorded your CCC on arrival and will just transmit that through a series of routine activities until I turn it off. So now nobody who may be monitoring you through your CCC can either hear you, or detect your physiological activity. But conversely, you can't use your CCC for anything. You are, by all accounts, offline, with a replacement pattern feeding into your PIMS modelled on your signal upon entry.

"Luckily we're in a fairly low reception area here anyway. Nobody in these houses would be worth much to the transcorps by way of CCC. They aren't major clients for netface purchase either. So not much attention comes this way. Which is why I live here. Simpkins has been subjected to a mandatory name displacement order. I think it was because he was stepping too far out of his box."

The genomorph moved so smoothly from his introductory explanation to the purpose of the meeting that Howard found the news hard to take in.

"So he's not here."

"Obviously. But you have been making enquiries, Mr Johns. And they have been noticed."

"By you?"

Nihils simply nodded.

"It's my job. But those for whom I work were interested, as you might expect."

There was a pause.

"So does he have a new name?" Howard asked suddenly. "I mean, do we know where he is?"

"How much does that matter?"

The voice was quite high, now that Howard gave it his attention; mellifluous and dulcet in tone. Soothing, in spite of its currently alarming content.

Howard shrugged. It seemed like a stupid question now. "I've seen the netmail and cell card records. But if you want to know, he's gone. Not sure where to yet. I can find out. But it depends on how much you want to risk detection. When consumers try to track identity displacements, they are just given the conventional ultra-customer-focussed run around. But if I start to dig, NERA will know, cyber security at VIC Parliament will know, so you will need to have a reason as to what it is you need from Simpkins that you can't get from someone else in Journalese and Brandgrab. Is it *your* Cyber Shadow?"

"Mick?"

"Yes, weird name. Mick Turition. Sounds like something out of the last century. A private dick or some such. Speaking of which, shall we get into it?"

"Into what?"

"Well, do you want sex or not? Guaranteed CCC-free time, no optics, no internal audio except that generated by my hi-fi, and of course us. Best not to waste it."

"Well, I'm not sure I..."

But Nihils was already passing him out of the little lounge room, across the narrow hallway and into what was an equally dimly-lit bedroom. Howard noticed for the first time that he was wearing a sort-of martial arts costume, with the trousers on the wrong way round so that, through the tie, a little arrow-headed tail poked out. Howard almost laughed. But as Nihils slipped the ties, dropped his trousers and lay spreadeagled across a futon, Howard found the way the tail set off the pert curves of the genomorph's buttocks disturbingly alluring. His penis was already swelling uncomfortably between his loins.

"Of course you do," Nihils was saying as he went. "We've already monitored the heightening of your CCC anxiety readings when the opposition went onto the alternative accommodation you could have been accessing while supposedly at your mum's, particularly when they cast aspersions against your sexuality. Dead give-away, Mr Johns. Dead give-away."

"But I've never ..."

"First time for everything. I've showered. Perfectly clean. As clean as you need me to be, anyway. Don't worry, no-one needs to know."

"But how do I know I can-"

"Trust me? Well I'm lying here naked before you for a start. Apart, of course, from my designer Consumer Choice League wristband. I don't do that for just anyone you know. I've fancied you for ages. But if you make a start, I'll fill you in on the some of the rest. Like how to crack the codes your Cyber Sleuth is tracking, for instance."

There seemed to be no reason not to accept the invitation, apart of course from the Consumer Choice League wristband. For Nihils had indeed now removed his martial arts top and was lying naked, in all his pale sinewy smallness, before the Member of the Chamber. And somehow, with such a prospect before him, the Consumer Choice League wristband somewhat paled in its significance. So Howard dropped his own trousers and underpants, left his own shirt behind him, and took his erection to the rear end of the cyber security operative.

"Just work some of this in first, Mr Johns," said Nihils, handing him a water-based lubricant. "You can use a condom if you like but, as I've said, I'm perfectly clean."

Howard felt an electric pleasure at having permission to massage lubricant into the crevasse between the beautiful buttocks of a young male, albeit one with a small sprightly tail at its coccyx. He could barely catch his breath for a while. Pressing the lubricant into the anus was even more exhilarating.

"Right in," Nihils encouraged. "You can massage it right in. It's fairly elastic, you'll find."

And so it was. Howard never thought he would actually find himself lubricating his own penis and climbing onto the back of a fellow male. It was an act he had long dismissed for himself, even though he was aware of his own bisexuality. Not only because he had never met a man he actually found attractive enough, but also because he simply didn't want the complication at this stage in his life. Homosexuality was not frowned upon under New Prosperity. It had an entire sales and service industry associated with it, and was quite a vibrant sector in and of itself. But The Market still throve on the changeover when someone formerly considered of one sexual orientation suddenly 'came out', batting for the other side, to use an old cricketing metaphor, and while this could be to his electoral favour, it also might not. Yet here he was, in no time at all, fucking a near complete stranger stupid.

And as he did so, Nihils talked him through the program he would need to write to give Mick Turition access to the codes of the MFEs. Howard had the presence of mind to ask him about the connection with NERA on the note. Nihils explained that most cyber security operatives were subcontracted from NERA. The transcorps wouldn't have it any other way. Needed government under their cyber-thumbs, not the other way round. Nihils himself had once undergone mandatory name displacement, drafted off to work as manual labour on one of the water pipelines from the north to the interland. They had him on a gene improvement program at the same time.

"Why?" Howard puffed.

"Because I had started to make cybernet searches for information on the Tie-cutters. You might've heard of them. Or not. Before my time. They were males who turned their backs on traditional male roles during the first couple of decades of this century. They literally cut their ties, refused to accept the patriarchal winners-and-losers control-and-manage ideology of commerce and capitalism of the time. And of course they had no joy with the moribund bureaucracy of government. So they were outed – lost their jobs many of them, placed on reservations in what used to be known as the Outback, made welfare dependent by government so that they could be demonisation fodder for the media. Many of them joined Aboriginal communities. Stop me if I'm getting beyond you."

Howard rooted on in breathy silence.

"Anyway, definitely no place in the world of New Prosperity. Not the sort of subject a young cyber nerd like me should be investigating. I think they feared I would become part of some revival of Internet Terrorism. I certainly knew how to.

"Anyway, I did a runner. Went bush myself, and located an old tie-cutter's reservation. Hacked my way back into the cybernet, found another name and got myself back into the business – with NERA this time, on a completely re-invented curriculum vitae. I couldn't hide the horns and tail, but by then genomorphs were coming under pro-action schemes, so it helped if anything. Guilty conscience, I reckon. Anyway, when I saw your Mick Turition out on the block, I knew where you were coming from. Speaking of which, how are you doing back there?"

"Fine," Howard's exertions had raised the pitch of his voice as much as the pace of his breathing. "I'm rapidly responding to a bodily agency I had not anticipated, and am in the process redefining my gender orientation with a psychological alacrity previously unknown to me. Nihils, I think I love you."

"Aren't you just fucking me?"

"Yes, that too. It's confusing, isn't it."

At which point Howard Smithson Johns jettisoned the entire seed of his loins into the elastic rectum of the genomorph, Nihils, with a cascade of ecstatic cries that fell away in a series of soft, near-whimpering "ohs".

"Trust me now?" asked Nihils softly.

"Sweet Jesus," Howard exhaled.

"Not a Dogweh man then," cooed Nihils, as Howard drifted into an exhausted doze.

Chapter Fourteen

It surprised Howard Smithson Johns to be standing so soon again in front of the decaying frontage of Cross Antiques. Nihils had 'loaned' him one hundred old Australian dollars, of undisclosed origin. The dream team were back in Old Melbourne again, selected to proceed with the Transglobal water deal negotiations at Katharine O'Brien's request, no less. Negotiations like this could last anything up to three weeks, so Nihils and Howard knew they were, with the dependable Bishop, 'away from home' for a while.

Howard was dying to get back into Nihils' pants, there was no denying it. His quest for Real Truth had found an eminently material diversion in the physiology of sexual gratification. Thoughts of suicide, even unexplained ones, couldn't have been further from his mind. Who cared why he had tried to top himself? He had discovered the joys of anal sex. But for the last seventy two hours they had been separated in outer CBD Transglobal accommodation of the same sort they had stayed in before, communicating by netface and meeting only at scheduled face-to-face appointments with Tranglobal. So while Nihils had with him his CCC/PIMS bypass device, they had not had much of an opportunity to deploy it.

At the end of their third day of negotiations, Howard had taken his customary trip out to spend the night with his mother, and had made the detour back via the Shopping World near the West Gate Bridge. By parking at Level 1 C36, he was able to find his way to the exit onto the old High Street relatively easily – not until after, however, negotiating a violent detour in which a video crew were shooting footage. The noise of gunfire and shouting in conflicting foreign languages filled one entire cul-de-sac in the shopping complex and, through gaps between the floor-to-ceiling barriers, Howard made out military fatigues with the insignias of Thailand, Karen and Myanmar, all in various stages of running battle with each other. Presumably yet another action vision for netface entertainment in which the noble forces of some pro-Fourth Phase nation state battle the niggardly envy of their Third Phase neighbours but are, with the help of some de-identified yet eminently identifiable transnational corporation (there were, after all, only four of them to choose from), victorious.

Such propaganda vision was staple fare for netface entertainment these days. The few customers in the Shopping World largely ignored the commotion, so this was obviously a popular venue for such activity. It was probably all that kept the enterprise from commercial oblivion: being a perfect set for Third Phase Progress nation states.

It was now 9:00 and the sun was already high. In broad daylight, the high street looked even sadder than it did under the eerie blue street lights of night. Dusty, failing concrete facades, collapsing over-pavement awnings, rubbish drifting about the street in minor eddies. Cross Antiques was probably the most presentable shopfront in the street. Even so, paint was shredding from its brickwork and the text announcing its name was badly faded. The shopfront windows were clouded with grime and, without the pale electric bulb illumination from within afforded by night, they were impossible to see through from the outside. In daylight, it was a shop you would simply walk by, thinking it derelict.

Howard could tell by the surprise exhibited by the shop proprietor on his entry that this was certainly the way most consumers treated the premises. The proprietor had so few customers that he immediately recognised Howard.

"Hallo again," he said beneath his thick-lensed glasses as Howard made his way through the bric-a-brac directly to the counter at the shop's rear. "Are you back for the prayer bell?"

"If it's still available," Howard confirmed with a smile.

The man gestured the counter, where the prayer bell stood exactly where Howard had last found it. Howard picked it up again and rang it gently beside his ear. Still the same perfect tone.

"And you say this is pre-Dalai Lama?"

"Well, from before the brand Dalai Lama, yes. It's from the time when such accoutrements were used in the Taoist religion, as practiced in what was then a colonised state of old China, Tibet. The Dalai Lama was actually Tibet's religious leader at the time."

Howard nodded. He privately noted that the shop proprietor used the term "old China" rather than "Communist China". The political term "communist" had never been banned or even officially exorcised, as far as Howard knew. It was just an example of the way the ideological ascendance of New Prosperity saw some terms fall into complete disuse. When Howard entered politics, democracy was still a term associated with government. Now it meant freedom, and freedom meant choice, and choice was the consumer's.

"You sound very knowledgeable about the past."

The man gestured the shop around him with a smile.

"As you see, I surround myself with old things, have my shop in an old version of a Shopping World rather than in the newer version behind me here, and am obviously not a young man myself. Yes, I remember the past."

"I noticed from the street that you have rooms upstairs. Do you live here as well?"

"Alas, with the construction of the new Shopping World in my back yard, I could not stand either the noise or the dust and fumes. And once I saw how the magnificent edifice of progress humbled my modest premises, I could not bear to return. And as you know, we are all waiting for Port Philip Bay to run down the main street here. I live on higher ground."

"Still, I suppose you can use the extra storage anyway," Howard was fishing now.

"Sadly, my business has never been brisk. My room is exactly as I left it. I tried to rent it out for a while but, with the myriad of wireless networks emitting from the Shopping World behind me, no-

110

one could get either an effective cell card or netface signal. It is amazing how important such things are to people, you know."

"Well, they are to me, but I must admit I often come to Old Melbourne on business and, well, I could use somewhere I could, not to put too fine a point on it, get away from it all without having to get *too far* away from it all, if you see what I mean."

The man looked back at him, nonplussed. Howard occupied himself examining the prayer bell once more.

"Surely the coast would be more satisfactory as a getaway," the man suggested eventually.

"Of course. It's just that I could walk to the CBD from here."

"Walk?" the man asked with seeming incredulity. Nobody ventured out onto the streets on foot in this day and age if they could avoid it. The police invented new fineable offences daily, and it was as expensive as driving. The man quickly covered for any offence he, in his turn, might have caused in his rash reaction.

"I mean to say, surely the central business district is dead these days, sir."

"Of course. Silly of me. How much for bell? I have cash."

It was only those who needed to who knew just how much business was actually done in and around the old CBD. As far as the general consumer was concerned, Internet Terrorism and the impact of climate change had seen the 'shop front' offices of most major businesses move to the new interland capitals of Australasia's nation states. None were supposed to suspect that inside the tawdry glass and plastic architecture of the old office buildings, cybertechnology hummed by the planet-load, credit was invented, reinvented and moved around the world from micro-second to micro-second, and the complex economic balance between credit, the consumer, labour and production upon which the growth spiral of capitalism depended was given nano-second attention. And that took a lot of cyberspace.

111

This was just one state of heightened awareness Howard had developed in the short time he had known Nihils, who was a mine of information on all things cyber. He had also, it seemed, perfected the art of getting 'behind' the system for which Howard had attempted to design Mick Turition. In two short days, based on Nihils advice, and with Nihils' own shadow actually in cyberspace to lend a hand, Howard's Cyber Champion had tracked down an MFE network to a small coastal community to the west of Old Melbourne. They had names and addresses, and were in the process of making covert contact. Mick Turition might at last get a story worthy of The Market's attention. And commence the proof of Howard's hypothesis. Or disprove it. In his newfound libidinal fervour, Howard was starting to lose grasp of his original logic.

"I'm just doing this as a favour, mind," Mick had reproved his creator. "I've got plenty of other things to be doing, you know. There's a whole chapter on a conflict called The Cold War I've found my way into in which I've met this really amazing chick called Tatania. Her hair is so black it's almost purple, and you should see her lips! I'd really like to run my fingers over them with machine graphite."

Howard had to remind himself that he had not programmed Mick Turition for the finer points of romance.

Nihils had also enlightened Howard as to the real state of the cybernet's immunity to viruses. Common ideobrief was that the transcorps and NERA had viruses under control but, according to Nihils, NERA had for too long underestimated the virulence of the viruses generated by the Internet Terrorists of the 2020s. Although cyber security operatives like himself were well able to mount effective barriers against virus invasion, in reality, the viruses were mutating daily, even hourly. The need for the size of netface banks housed secretly in the CBDs of the old state capitals was testament to the sheer volume of cybernet security operatives the transcorps needed to keep viruses at bay. It was a pandemic catastrophe just waiting to happen.

"What currency do you have sir?"

"Sorry?"

"What currency is your cash in?"

"Oh, dollars. Australian dollars."

"Thank you. In that case, the price is forty eight dollars."

"Oh, thanks. What would it be in other currency?"

"That would depend on the currency, sir. Clearly, currency from countries in transition from Third Phase Progress to Fourth Phase Progress gives me more ready purchasing power in those countries. But all is relative."

The idea that this lowly shop proprietor with no netface access and no consumer credit billing facility could be trading with overseas nation states was confounding.

"Forty eight it is, then."

Howard handed over half the amount Nihils had given him – a well-worn green-yellow fifty dollar note.

"Alas, sir, I have no change. Can I offer you something else to make up the amount?"

Howard looked briefly around, but could see only an endless conversation of barter in order to identify a product that both agreed equalled two dollars in value. It seemed pointless.

"Make it fifty," he dismissed.

"Thank you, sir," said the man, wrapping the prayer bell in plain paper.

"Although you *could* show me your room. Upstairs," Howard added.

"If you wish, sir. Although it really is quite unprepared."

The room was, indeed, ill-prepared for presentation. Years of dust lay everywhere. But beneath, it was easy to see a rather homey bachelor's flat. A double bed of the wooden slat frame type, with a simple but real wood bedhead, stood against the rear wall to one side of the room, facing one of two windows overlooking the street. It was still made up, ready for use, with plain white sheets and grey woollen blankets. The shop owner explained that he had plenty of spare bed linen.

Above the bed on the wall was a wooden crucifix, bearing a nailed and spread-armed figure Howard recognised to be the old Christian hero, Jesus. It looked antique. Next to the bed, against a side wall, was a wooden chest of drawers, above which was a framed South Asian painting of a multi-armed man and a multi-armed woman riding in profile on an elephant. They look of royal stock. The shop proprietor did not know the exact origin of the picture, but it was from somewhere in the Indian sub-continent, and was of the Hindu deities Shiva and Parvati, gods of dance and destruction in that former belief system.

On the opposite side of the room, which spanned the width of the shop below, was a modest kitchenette with a gas stove, porcelain sink and wooden draining board, and a wooden table with matching chairs Howard also dated from the previous century. In the centre of the table stood a brass candelabra with many candle holders, all fanning out in the one plane from a central stem. It was blackened with age, and quite beautiful. The shop owner professed ignorance of its origins.

On the rear wall of this side of the room, over the sink, was a framed illumination of another South Asian deity the shop proprietor identified as Buddha. On the wall above the dining table on the far side of the room, caught now in the slanting light of the climbing sun through the room's other window, was another illumination, but this one consisting of mostly Cyrillic text – a form of writing not seen much these days in the context of global communication. It came,

114

Howard was informed, from one of the eastern Europacific nation states, but the proprietor was unsure where. It was also very old.

A small shower and toilet was off to one side of the room, at the rear of a landing which served as the entrance to the room. This was at the front of the side wall nearest the bed. A set of old wooden stairs descended from the front of this landing, and doubled back half-way down to a separate doorway onto the high street, adjacent to the shop. The shop next door had a mirroring set of stairs which backed onto these with a shared wall, leading to its back yard, but these were apparently never used.

There was a tremendous sense of peace and stillness about the room, despite the incessant hum of the Shopping World behind. It seemed to Howard a perfect space for he and Nihils to share some clandestine time together. With the confounding plethora of wireless network signals from the Shopping World immediately behind them, Nihils' CCC/PIMS bypass would work a treat.

He asked if he could rent the room for a short period, stressing the need for discretion. This was to be his 'getaway' while on business in Old Melbourne. The man, who turned out to be the Mr Cross of the antique store's eponymous name, readily agreed both to the letting and the discretion.

"Do I look like a man who has a great many people to confide in?" he asked with a smile.

Howard paid for the room in advance with his remaining fifty dollar note. This was, evidently, enough for a week's rent. Nihils would have to find him some more cash. The currency seemed not to matter to Mr Cross.

Howard left Cross Antiques with a spring in his step and an antique prayer bell wrapped up in his hand. As he ascended through the Shopping World to his car parking bay, the detours and barriers had disappeared and, with them, the various contingents of warring military. Peace had, it seemed, been yet again restored somewhere in

the world, thanks to the pervading common sense of Consumer
Choice.

Chapter Fifteen

For the next three weeks, Nihils and Howard seemed to find at least an hour in every day when they could secrete themselves in the room above Cross Antiques and make love. Liaisons like this were, evidently, something Nihils engaged in quite regularly, Consumer Choice League membership notwithstanding.

"That's just something I do for appearances," Nihils dismissed the blue wristband. "I go along to the meetings and say outlandishly pro-choice things. There's nothing a nation state in need of demonstrable pro-active policies likes better than to have a genomorph who's fanatical about Consumer Choice. It certainly keeps them keeps them off my back, so to speak."

The sex itself never lasted long, no matter how many positions or techniques they tried. Cute though it was, the tail tended to get in the way. And basically both men seemed to have a limited tolerance for the physical acts of amore in any one encounter. The only phenomenon that actually lengthened their intercourse was the type of conversation that had characterised its inception.

It was through such discussions that Howard learnt about the Underclass, and Nihils' involvement in it. Howard had of course read about such a class in his earlier years, but the term had largely disappeared from official ideobrief. It never appeared in The Market. However, he had not been as aware as perhaps he should have been, as an aspiring politician, that the movement began with the introduction of Singing for your Susso campaign in the 2020s – a campaign initiated by artists seeking to convert the Work For Social Safety (or Work for WIPS and SAPS[6] as it was known in some states) into a form of work that contributed to cultural and community development, personal growth, self-esteem and self-actualisation.

---

[6] Welfare Infrastructure Provision and Social Access Provision

"Susso" was apparently the term used in old Australia for the first formal government welfare payment, to relieve abject poverty amongst the unemployed during the Great Depression of the twentieth century. The artists were attempting to summon up the spirit of social responsibility associated historically with the welfare movement, rather than the subjugation of the will of the employee (and, by implication, the employment-less) to the Mutual Responsibility ethic underpinning Work for Social Safety.

Unfortunately, government supported the Singing for your Susso initiative only as long as it took the Mutual Responsibility movement to co-opt it, after which Work for Social Safety conveniently folded into Singing for your Susso and the spirit of the latter was lost for a good ten years, enabling governments to rebrand it under the ideospeak of Consumer Choice in the late 2030s.

The course taken by many artists as a result was, ironically, to refuse to Sing for their Susso, on the grounds of conscience. But the ideological reductionism of Mutual Responsibility made it difficult for them to articulate the basis of their conscientious objection without resorting to quite complex and intellectual argument. In fact, according to Nihils, it was in response to the challenge presented by the dissenting artists that governments around the Third Phase world harmonised the dominance of journalese, brandgrab and the ideobrief. Never again would ideology escape the combined control of capital and government.

As a result, those with the creativity and imagination to provide visionary fuel to alternative thought – the artists – were simply fined for breaching Mutual Responsibility obligations, remanded for not paying their fines and reserved 'for their own protection' in outlands that had no other commercial value.

Reservation in the interests of protection and social safety was so acceptable to the majority that it became a convenient way to deal with most alternatives to the thinking of capital and government. Mutual Responsibility obligations were almost custom-tailored to enable the subjugation of any individual to reservation for abuse of WIPS and SAPS.

Howard could vaguely remember the Singing for your Susso movement, but only as the war cry of the Social Safety WIPS and SAPS. Now that Nihils mentioned them, during a particularly energetic fuck which involved Howard standing up on his knees and rollicking backwards and forwards like a piston thumping Nihils into the bedhead, he could also recall identifying with the artists in his adolescence. But obviously not enough. They had completely vacated his memory since.

In a voice which betrayed the jackhammering percussion only otherwise apparent in the tail at its housing's nethermost rear, wiggling away like some fanatical meteorological device, Nihils went on to explain that Howard's dysfunctional memory was not surprising. With the introduction of mandatory identity displacement in the 2030s, management of dissent became far more sophisticated and systematic. But, according to Nihils, the underclass still existed on reservations around the world, several in each nation state in the Australasian archipelago.

Since the privatisation of correctional services, the reservations had fallen into neglect because no half-decent business could find the willing workforce to staff such remote locations, and governments simply would not pay sufficient Welfare Infrastructure Provision to make them profitable. So, Nihils said as Howard whooped into a steam liner of an orgasm, the reservations became a bit of a law unto themselves, and attracted genomorphs like himself and other dissenters, such as the Tie-cutters.

It had actually been the presentiment of Mick Turition locating and interviewing members of the underclass on such a reservation, along with members of Money-Free Exchange network, that had brought Howard Johns to one of his best orgasms yet. The whole notion that an underclass of 'disappeared' might actually exist after all came upon Howard with all the orgasmic force of an epiphany. It was like re-discovering some deep apprehension long lost. A dim

119

understanding from his past rose through the void in meaning that had inhabited the centre of his pre-suicidal ennui: here was a cause for a social conscience. This was really shaping up as a source of new motivation for him. The existence of a real underclass so clearly the result of a collusion of oppression by capital and government would in fact serve to demonstrate the existence of a strategic centre to capital. That this was contrary to his original thesis, the logic of which continued to unravel in his mind, only served to reinforce for him its cogency.

But as the immensity of the orgasm subsided, so too did the magnitude of Howard's newfound quest for meaning. After sex, Nihils and Howard were generally far less intense in their discourse. They liked to sit up in bed, the top sheet neatly folded across their laps, drinking tea out of a pair of rather pleasant floral tea cups they purchased from Mr Cross downstairs. These, and the pot and milk jug from which they were serviced, reminded Howard of his Mum, and Nihils of a past he had never known.

During such periods of repose, Howard with his slightly paunchy chest and belly, Nihils with his near anorexic rib-and-clavicle torso, both entirely sunlight deprived, engaged in almost whimsical conversation about the finer points of their bare room, the potential spirituality implicit in the pictures adorning the walls around them, and dreams about the lives they would like to lead, together or apart. It was some time before Howard felt confident enough in his newfound companion to be able to ask him more sensitive and personal questions about the relationship between them, such as:

"What made you send me the note, Nihils?"

"You mean the electronic one or the real one?"

"Well, both, I suppose. The second one in particular was a bit of a risk, wasn't it?"

"I guess discovering Mick Turition was the first indication you might be open to it; although, as I said at the outset, we'd been tracking you since your CCC reaction to the suggestion in the Chamber about your activities when you *weren't* staying with your Mum."

"You just always seemed so, well, cold towards me."

"Professional, Howie. Professional, surely. When you look like I do, and do what I do, it's wise to stay dispassionate and indecipherable."

"So how did you make the decision? You must have made a decision."

"Agreed. But isn't it a matter of the type of decision? I can understand, Howard, that coming as you do from a professional sphere in which there is tremendous emphasis on meaning – what this legislation means, what that transcorp decision means, what the Leader of the House said means, what a question in the Chamber means – it's easy to think of decisions as involving meaning and implication, imputation and inference.

"In reality, however, decisions are just that: acts of determination. Our bodies make most of them for us without out even knowing. What separates us, however, from other animals and life forms is sentience: knowing, through the senses in combination with the mind.

"So what's the best arbiter of a decision for us as human beings? A sense? A thought? A rational argument? In reality, Howard, why is any one superior? Especially when most of the time rationality is used to justify a decision we have in fact already made due to an a-rational attention to other factors – sense, ideological orientation, strategic and tactical signposts, a crisis, physical trauma.

"I'm a survivor or torture and trauma, Howard. Before they started to experiment on my genes, they subjected me to physical and psychological horrors you cannot imagine, or have only read about thanks to Mick Turition's back-door peregrinations.

"I'm well beyond believing that there is a logic to decision-making that involves any of the qualities you may value, such as compassion, integrity, honesty, altruism, love, truth. In the end, we really do act fundamentally in our own best interests, and the decisions we make are largely irrelevant in the scheme of things.

"So for me, for every why, there is at least an equal and opposite why not, and probably a whole range of other why nots. I just weigh up the odds, and decide what's in my best interests."

"So you have no feelings for me?"

"Of course I have feelings for you. As I said, I fancied you for ages. But so what? What have the feelings got to do with whether or not we actually have sex? They are just one factor. And one factor at any one moment. You place far too much faith in the temporality of things, Howard; in the linear nature of chronology and narrative. When your head is literally under the pump so long you think you are going to drown, neither time nor reason have much dominion. Especially if someone is kicking you in the balls at the same time so that you are vomiting into your own attempts to breathe."

"I think I'm sorry I asked," reflected Howard.

"Yes, it's not one of our more cheerful conversations, is it? Shall we talk about the cups again?"

Chapter Sixteen

During working hours Nihils and Howard were apart, but even then Nihils managed to create 'dark' periods for them in which the couple could meet in cyberspace as Mick Turition and his Shadow. In these short sojourns, Mick and Shadow made short work of a number of MFE code chains, and managed to track down an existing MFE network operating just west of Old Melbourne, along the coast. Mick actually made contact with a number of operatives, and sought their agreement for an interview.

In cybereality, the Exchangers spoke through thick, closed wooden doors fastened with ancient iron locks. They disguised their netface portals in the electronic equivalent of copses and earthen mounds. Mick's tendency was to blast the locks with his Webley and kick the doors down, but his Shadow retrained him, urging moderation. When they tried moderation, however, it was greeted with intense silence, which just frustrated Mick all the more.

Before his Cyber Champion chucked a virtual wobbly, Howard reasoned to all concerned that the best course was personal contact – for, as the Shadow Nihils had been able to unearth, the same calibre of personal netface portal details must be as available to the tax sharks as they were to Mick and Shadow. They were thus unnecessarily exposed.

"I don't give a rat's arse how exposed we are," snarled Mick churlishly, wielding his pistol. "I'm ready for 'em. Bring it on, I say!"

"Yes but Mick, you are a computer program. Nihils and I are the ones who will actually bear any repercussions of your actions in the real world."

"Him and his bloody poofy shadow," Mick grumbled, kicked some virtual stones and sulked off, his greying white mackintosh flapping haplessly. "One of the fucking bitches from Hainan reckons she's pregnant. Bloody virtual dickhead! What does she think I am, real?"

"Anyway, discovered some fabulous vision from the turn of the century where some guy like me gets to fight endless guys all dressed the same. Shoot one and two spring up in his place. They just keep on coming. Now that's gotta be worth getting into."

And, as Howard wondered momentarily where he had gone wrong with his cyber-muse, Mick was gone.

Nihils could not see the need to personalise the exchange. He reminded Howard of the millimetre accuracy of transcorp satellite vision.

"You're just putting yourself at risk, sentimentalising those old ideals of trust, honesty and a firm handshake you inherited from your father," Nihils accused.

"But surely the era of internet terrorism alerted us all to the total unreliability of cybercommunication," Howard argued back.

"And that's all over," Nihils trotted out the current ideospeak. "Today's consumers have totally cyber-safe choice."

"That's not what you've been telling me."

"And you're fool enough to believe me. So much for human contact…"

Howard thought for a moment of reminding his horned and tailed lover that he was the inventor of VIVO technology, but there was no point arguing with him. But then, there was no changing Howard's inveterate faith in the value of human-to-human contact either.

"Look at our current negotiations," he tried a different tack, "How would we be doing as well as we are without those vital face-to-face meetings in which we deal with the uncertainties that only body language, multisensorial perception and the intelligence of feeling can help us work our ways through?"

"And you don't think O'Brien and her team have done this a thousand times before, and worked through every angle you might present beforehand?"

There was the further difficulty of justifying a trip into the countryside in the midst of negotiations. It could be easily monitored as Nihils has suggested, his little black box notwithstanding. Even if Howard justified the trip on the basis of visiting constituents, it would be constituents of another Member of the Chamber and there would need to be a communication trail that led to a reason for Howard's intervention in a colleague's domain.

"Why do we need to be so worried about being detected anyway?" Howard declared petulantly as they sat up in bed above Cross Antiques. "This is the era of Consumer Choice. Democracy is freedom, freedom is choice, and choice is the consumer's. What are we contemplating that is of threat to anyone? We have choice."

"Exactly," Nihils replied without conviction, "We have choice. You have choice. I have choice. People who have mandatory identity displacement orders have choice. The underclass choose to live the way they do. After all, you meet with the producers of products and services of choice every day, don't you? You work in government, which facilitates the infrastructure vital to the consumer's access to choice. You engage with healthy human contact and communication with all of them, and you know they can be trusted, don't you? You know, for instance, that your Consumer Choice Chip offers exactly and only the services included in the brandinfo that came with your customer qualcert."

"There's no arguing with you when you're like this," Howard complained wistfully.

"Like what: with horns and a tail?"

"You know what I mean."

"Now we've been down the meaning path, Howie, many times. Why don't we just have sex again, eh?"

125

As luck would have it, Howard had no need to construct an elaborate cover for a foray into the VIC south west in his quest for an underclass and MFEs. Katharine O'Brien herself provided the perfect excuse. The Transglobal negotiation team were attempting to introduce a wind variation to the VIC government's water proposal. Howard had gone back to the Party to seek urgent advice and logistic support from his counterpart in the Wind portfolio. In the meantime, he was playing a this-is-a-new-idea-we're-not-sure general-puddling-around game of prevarication.

Transglobal could see immediately that he was playing for time so O'Brien herself intervened to cut the crap.

"Why not come for a ride?" she invited him by cybermail. "See our VIC wind facility for yourself, since we've clearly got a bit of time here. Perhaps you and your team might like to stay on for a day. Enjoy the sea air. While it still lasts."

The last comment was, clearly, a joke. Howard allowed himself to believe that he might be attracting Katharine O'Brien's confidence at last.

So it was in week three of their negotiations that Howard found himself, Nihils and Bishop, heading out of Port Phillip Bay in a sleek, wind and solar powered cruiser for the short voyage up the coast to Warrnambool. It was a perfect winter's day, pale sun and cloudless sky, and the state-of-the-art launch simply slipped through the swell.

"I don't suppose you get out on the water much, living where you do," O'Brien conjectured as the open water of Bass Strait took them fully into its care.

"Certainly not on one of these," Howard replied appreciatively.

A flying sail was released from the foc's'le. It unfurled on a kite-like cable one hundred metres above the vessel, which accelerated like a fast-train clearing the suburbs – silent, swift, deadly. But out here, there was nothing to populate the tracks but water.

The coastal suburb of Geelong soon disappeared behind them, and with it the ungainly urban sprawl of Old Melbourne. Soon the cliffs of the Great Ocean Road reared up from the sea and cut their serrated way along VIC's south western coast. Along them marched the legion lines of giant windmills.

Howard had never seen so many of them together before. Rows upon rows of slender, tapered towers rose ninety metres into the sky, each row allowing alternate access for the giant three-bladed propellers to the full force of the mighty winds of Bass Strait. They looked for all the world like an armada of mega-engines lashed to the southern headland of the continent, droning in unison to haul the mighty land deep into the planet's south. In reality, of course, the effect was precisely the reverse; the winds from the south brought power to the engines of the land.

The wind farm spread along the length of the coast as far as the eye could see. As the launch sailed closer in to shore, the deep whirring of the turbines throbbed out across the waves. Howard could understand why people chose not to live near these harmless, eco-friendly powerhouses. But from any distance, compared to the still cumbersome water technology available for desalination, water transfer from the north, and the re-aquafication of the interland, the elegance and beauty of the wind farm was as impressive as its technological sophistication. Over half of VIC's current domestic and industrial power needs were met by wind resources. The open anal crater of Gippsland's brown coal industry these days fuelled only the still-carbon-hungry growth economies of South Asia and China.

"So you can see why we are reluctant to invest all that heavily in the power-generating capacity of any water resource developments in

VIC," said Katharine O'Brien, observing the quiet awe in Howard's gaze. "We've done water, Howard."

"I don't think it is a mandatory component of our proposal," Howard commented as frankly as he dared. "I imagine you will be happy with the revised plan once we hear back from our Wind and Water boffins."

"Boffins?" O'Brien queried with a sceptical eyebrow. "And you question *my* use of antiquated terms. I've arranged for lunch on board, by the way. Once we moor at Warrnambool. Hope you're hungry."

The sea air made him hungry indeed and an hour later they were dining on a simple picnic of cold chicken, avocado, Tasmanian smoked salmon, caviar, farm-fresh bread and Krug champagne, at anchor in the cultural tourism centre Warrnambool's modest harbour.

"I've arranged overnight accommodation for the three of you in town here, as Transglobal's guests, and a hire car. I thought you might like to drive yourselves back along the Great Ocean Road," said O'Brien as they ate. "The views are quite charming, if you haven't seen them before."

All three men agreed that they had not.

"So you won't be joining us?" asked Howard politely, for the offer was clear.

"Always many business pressures," O'Brien excused herself with equal diplomacy. "I believe I will be working even on the return voyage."

"But I imagine the rewards are equal to the demands," Howard opined.

"Yes, but not as close to the centre of strategy as I think you imagine," replied O'Brien with a seemingly unguarded candour redolent of their recent flight together from New to Old Melbourne. "It's mostly just hard work, believe me."

"But closer to the source of direction, perhaps," Howard ventured. "Strategic direction."

"That's the second time I've heard that conjecture from you, Mr Johns," O'Brien pushed back. "And from a representative of government. I'm surprised you undervalue your central role in our mutual relationship."

Howard smiled without enthusiasm in response, and sipped his champagne. He had engaged in the topic out of habit rather than intent. His current focus was on the underclass rather than their overlords.

"So there is no truth in the Real Truth Movement, then," he said finally. Nihils caught his eye with an impassively impish glint.

Katharine O'Brien made no reply. Instead, she stood up and moved to the stern of the vessel. Howard followed.

"You do realise, don't you Mr Johns, how easy it is to be heard as well as seen, even out here on the water."

"I apologise. Of course I do. We purchase our satellite intelligence from you."

"Exactly," said O'Brien, lifting her gaze from the calm waters beyond the vessel's end to confront his, but only briefly. She then leant the small of her graceful back against the vessel's gunwale and looked back into the open deck.

"Your team are doing very well, Howard. Should you ever consider a career outside government, you should talk to me."

Howard could not resist a smile. His next career move was well overdue.

"Thank you," he said. "You will be the first to know."

"In the meantime, enjoy your well-deserved respite," she said, glancing at him once more before returning to the rest of her guests. "And I think you'll find that the Real Truth movement, where it is to be found in contemporary ideobrief, focuses on an underclass, not an overclass. Although I confess, it's not a topic I have had cause to research much myself."

Howard was embarrassed to find his own confusion reflected back at him, however charmingly. It was as if she could read his mind. He had to clarify in his own mind what he was really interested in: centre of power or underclass? For surely real truth could only be real in one or the other? No, that was rubbish. He could only *believe* in the truth of one or the other. It was a question of ideological commitment. For, in Howard's mind, the two had to be diametrically opposed in meaning. The politician in him was naturally drawn to the centre of power. So what was it in him that wanted to identify with the disempowered? Particularly those amongst the disenfranchised who sought to redress the power imbalance that was their lot.

It was thus in a state of intellectual ambivalence that Howard pursued his plan with Nihils for a foray into the world of the underclass.

Chapter Seventeen

In order to create some pre-downtime space for Nihils and himself later that day, Howard gave Bishop the task of gathering together the Water office's ideo- and infobriefing to prepare a draft plan for the next stage in their negotiations, which the three of them could discuss over breakfast. Bishop's assumption would be that Nihils and Howard were similarly retiring to their respective rooms to prepare their contributions to the same meeting. In reality, however, Nihils and Howard took the hire car and drove to the small township of Timboon inland, in search of the local MFE network Mick and Shadow had uncovered.

As the ordered semi-suburban rows of Warrnambool fell away to the coastal undulations of pastoral South Western VIC, and the hum of the giant wind farms gave way to scattered squares of paddock populated by the occasional weatherboard cottage, it became obvious that the contacts the two netface sleuths had made in cyberspace were unlikely to be the wealthy counter-consumer choice crooks The Market tended to depict. As they approached Timboon, small weatherboard bungalows, originally for local farmworkers, were what defined the town. These days they most probably housed refugees from Old Melbourne, or escapees from the consumer's work treadmill elsewhere. They were understandably cautious about discussing their MFE activities with Mick Turition and his offsider, particularly as neither could produce ID testifying to their attested status as journalists.

The first gentleman they approached clearly had a healthy vegetable garden out the back, with abundance of the same on either side of the short path by which they accessed the house. Nihils said later that he also had the soiled hands of a gardener. But, in his baggy trousers, well-worn green cardigan, collarless shirt and disarray of greying hair, he was instantly suspicious of a pair of well-dressed males knocking on his door; especially at, Howard could see from the dull yellow light spilling over the deserted place at the kitchen table deeper into the house, dinner time. Even with the tousled effect Nihils had worked up with his firm endowment of hair, his boutique horns were still detectable.

The man admitted to being the destination of the cybermail contact by Mick Turition, but claimed his age made his voice difficult for VIVO to decipher which resulted in too many botched communications to make the medium worth bothering with for much longer, and anything the pair could do to correct the matter merited their immediate attention. He had great difficulty in making any cyber purchases – on which he and his wife were dependent in such a remote community – and was forced to live almost totally off what he could produce in his own garden.

In other words, the man was imposing on Howard and Nihils the 'feint' presumption that the reason for their contact was an official role as tax security. Despite a tight manoeuvre of follow-up questions and gambits by 'Mick Turition' and his 'Shadow', the man refused to allow them to escape this characterisation. After a brief exchange, the man excused himself to finish his tea, and closed the door.

The next exchange was even briefer. The house they had identified from Nihils' cyber trace was a similar dwelling, with even lower lighting issuing from within, and the woman who answered the door had the lined complexion of someone twice Howard's age, even though her physique and demeanour suggested she was half it. She was stoned, slouched against the doorframe as if part of it, puffing on the spliff between her long fingers, saying "Wha?" and "Come-agin?" a lot, and constantly looking the pair up and down with a laconic sneer. Finally she slurred "Yer-up-yer-arse mayte" and disappeared into the house. She did not even close the front door. It was not difficult to guess what she contributed to the MFE, or at least bartered from it.

This was obviously not going to be is easy.

132

"How many more addresses have we got?" Howard asked, anxious the fading light would not favour further enquiry. "I'm not sure we're dressed for this, you know."

"Perhaps you should just be up-front, Howie, and ask them for their vote."

Two further houses on the outskirts of Timboon yielded similar suspicion. Clearly the appearance of the two cyber sleuths, and the obviously hired car they drove, was not inspiring sufficient confidence to yield a scoop to undermine The Market.

"Let's try the Tie-cutters while we still have some time," Nihils suggested. "It's just up the coast. And I suspect I might know one or two of them."

It was now well and truly dark, but still a good four hours until the pair's 'official' downtime. So they drove like the clappers – or as alike to the clappers as their hire car's automatic speed control permitted. It was a frustrating journey through a tortuous landscape of minor coastal hills and scrub, and by the time they found the modest spread of vegetation, with its faded signage and tumble-down fencing spilling out into the soaring sand dunes on either side, they had only three hours before downtime.

During the course of the drive, however, Howard was able to quietly and privately overcome his own stupidity in assuming that 'reservations' in 'outlands' should somehow be out in the desert. That was certainly where historically Australians had 'reserved' their Aboriginal populations 'for their own protection', and their 'alien' populations during international hostilities, again 'for their own protection', and refugees who 'jumped' the immigration 'queue' to arrive 'illegally' by boat (pretty much, indeed, as the country's original white population had).

But of course in a period of eco-crisis and climate change, and with the re-aquafication of the continent's centre with seasonal water

133

from the north, it was logical that the threatened coastal regions became the country's new 'outlands'. Here, in amongst the deep drone of the wind turbines, was certainly a fine place to sinecure a selection of the nation state's unwanted.

There was no longer a gate on the entrance to the compound. Nor was their any street lighting within. By carlight, Howard and Nihils picked out a variety of dwellings. Some were no more than the corrugated iron huts government had originally erected on the site for those it committed to 'reservation for their own protection'. Others were more recent constructions, some of quite sophisticated eco-architecture. One could only assume the compound aspired to eco-sufficiency. There was no light to be seen, however, emitting from any building the two sleuths could locate.

"They might know we're here," suggested Nihils.

"Obviously, with two great beams of headlight ranging all over the place," replied Howard testily.

"No, I mean knew we were coming, and closed down. What's the old saying? Battened down the hatches?"

Nihils motioned Howard to stop the car and switch off the engine. He then retrieved his portable CCC and cybernet bypass from the back seat, and his netface, and stepped out of the vehicle.

A little way off, Howard could see the small winking blue light that indicated the CCC bypass was operating and, a short while after, Nihils himself reflected in the backlight from his netface screen. Howard got out of the car to join him.

"If the car has automatic speed control, it's bound to have other electronic intelligence," Nihils explained. "The bypass should work, but it might also seize if it has too much to deal with, and I need to contact them. I'm using a local wireless connection. If anyone's here, they will know we can at least get onto their local area network and get under cyber security controls. They might be more likely to trust us."

"Or less."

"That's the risk. But either way, wouldn't you feel it was a necessary one to take? You need to know what you're enemy's up to, don't you. Anyway, I'm trying a few friendly codes they might recognise. And dropping a few names. These guys appear to have developed their own LAN. Not easy to hack into."

Nihils' fingers flew as he talked. He was faster on the keyboard even than Howard.

"This wasn't the reservation you were on?"

"No. Mine was way north of here. But we were all in touch with each other. Internet terrorism, my dear Member, was never as inchoate in its anarchy as it was depicted in The Market. Eureka!" he cried. "I've found a professor!"

Professors were a rarity in academic circles these days. A side effect of the commercialisation of education was that no-one could afford to sustain a singular line of study long enough to develop the depth of knowledge required for the status of professor. Tertiary education was aimed primarily at preparation for career or career change, and minimising education debt through the shortest curricular route. The result was that around the world the professors were aging and increasingly unlikely to be replaced with meaningful successors. Those who remained were consequently the 'stars' of university brandgrab, photographed in all of their regalia and thrust from the cyberspace brandsites as major symbols of the promise of success. So both Howard and Nihils were naturally curious to find a 'drop out' from a system that was anxious to retain what academic credibility it had left.

A light came on in a dowdy, fibro dwelling on the far side of the compound. Returning stealthily to their car, Howard drove Nihils there as silently as the vehicle allowed, while Nihils continued filleting cyberspace from his keyboard. The man standing expectantly in the open front door was dressed not unlike the MFE gardener in Timboon – aging cardigan, threadbare trousers, plain white shirt with a fraying collar, poorly managed grey hair, but with the one important differentiating feature: the mandatory heavy-rimmed glasses.

"Bit of an affectation," Nihils muttered under his breath, noticing the anomaly immediately. "Couldn't afford laser optics on his salary, eh?"

"Perhaps he's just a sentimentalist," Howard offered.

The pair left the car, Nihils bringing his netface and portable cyberspace bypass with him.

"No need for the blocker here," the old man called as they approached. He had what Nihils would later describe to Howard in bed as a 'creamy sort of voice', not quite consonant with his apparent age. "We make sure we are covered as necessary."

"So I imagined," Nihils said as they approached. "But you can never be sure, can you."

"Yes, best to be safe, I suppose, if you have taken the risk it seems you have to come here. The Shadow, I presume. Enchanting name. Between the idea and the reality, eh? Between the motion and the act. But I didn't quite catch the name of your accomplice."

The man extended his hand towards Howard.

"Mick. Mick Turition," Nihils introduced his companion.

"Ah, even better. Between desire and the spasm. Very inventive."

He shook hands with a loose wrist.

"Come in, my friends. Come in. There is better protection in here."

"I hope you don't mind if I…" Nihils indicated his netface as they sat down on old bentwood chairs in a sparse combined kitchen and living room.

"Please," the professor agreed. "We know you are here, believe me. Your knowledge of the cybernet has impressed us."

"Used to be in Silver City," explained Nihils as his fingers recommenced their lightning application to the keyboard.

"Broken Hill?" confirmed the professor. Nihils nodded without looking up from his netface.

"Are there many of you here?" asked Howard as Mick Turition.

"About forty. We actually have underground dwellings we hope neither government nor the transcorps know about. We keep a number of us up here in the monitored dwellings to keep up appearances. I have asked a friend to come over, if that's alright."

"Of course. We are your guests. But you keep the place dark?"

"It's not an eco-consideration as you might think. Part of our charter of rights is the retention of the 24 hour day. Most of us are actually in bed asleep, Mr Turition."

"Please, call me Mick. Do you have a copy of your charter?"

"It's alright, I've found it," Nihils interjected, eyes still on his screen.

The other two men nodded appreciatively.

"So –er – Shadow here tells me you are a professor."

"Was. Although of course once we attain the title, we retain it for life. Yes, of Medicine."

"Ah."

"Not what you expected."

"No, I thought…"

"The Eliot? A certain benign urbanity more redolent of the humanities perhaps? I'm sorry, I am satirising myself, not you. I still function as one of our community's doctors, but these days I have plenty of time for poetry and literature. There are a group of us here, actually, and we have cultivated a substantial horticultural medicine research and development laboratory. Pancontinental and Transnational purchase our results regularly. So you see, we are not so downtrodden after all."

"As I think I am becoming aware," Nihils commented, still concentrating on his screen.

The professor smiled benignly. Howard did not understand, but figured Nihils would tell him what he needed to know when the time came.

"Surely you could have undertaken that sort of R&D without joining a reservation?" he asked instead.

"Perhaps, but I joined the reservation because I could not abide what was happening to my profession."

"But your status is so highly valued in it."

"Ah, you mean as an academic. Yes, but only symbolically, Mick. As the 'front man', as it were, the masthead. No real power. Not really valued. But no, I meant medicine. It's true that we brought it on ourselves. Twenty first century and the majority of us were still clinging to a biomedical double degree and a small business model of medical practice. Of course the transcorps would move in and clean up with us. None of us wanted to be bothered with the increasing complexities of practice management, tax, insurance and litigation. Even fewer in the emerging generations wanted to buy into practices or enter into partnerships and associateships.

"And of course, once we entered the corporate model, we could see the sense in delegating to the nurses and allied health more effectively so that we could concentrate on what we were trained for – the medicine. But we should have seen that substitution would make more economic sense to the corporates.

138

"Before we knew it, every man and his dog was doing our work, and our wages were pegged at the same level while the physician assistant and bottle washer surpassed them. Then the terms and conditions began to slide.

"By the end of it, I came to truly understand what my fellow educators had been on about all of those years, when they talked about the deprofessionalisation of education. I had stood by and watched the same happen to medicine. It's been the same with the engineers, and the architects. Only the lawyers seem to have survived. Surprise, surprise."

Howard heard the screen door squeak ajar just beyond the back door to the kitchen. There was a soft knock.

"Come in Brad," called the professor gently over his shoulder without turning.

The back door opened to reveal a tall, stout, muscular young man in track pants and a running singlet. Startling blue eyes beamed out from beneath a broad, high, veined forehead with both energy and intensity. He nodded to Howard and eyed Nihils cautiously.

"These are the ones from the LAN intercept," the professor explained.

The newcomer nodded again.

"Brad used to be a footballer," the professor explained. And for once, Nihils' fingers froze. He looked up at the imposing sportsman in recognition.

"Brad Donman," he said simply. The man nodded once more.

"You disappeared."

Another nod. And then a smile, as he gestured his own immanence.

"Must be a bloody miracle, eh?" he said laconically, with that voice sportsmen so often lock inside their Adams apple. "Must've been the doc, eh?" He nodded to the professor. "Modern medicine can do wonders these days."

139

"Sorry," said Howard, excusing his ignorance, "But are we talking about an identity displacement here?"

"A MIDO, yeh. Shoulda known it was comin' once I'd had my five minutes in The Market. Started to pick off the family almost immediately. One after another they went. What was their new name? Where could I find them? Then the sponsorship went. Then the order. Then the knock at the door. Silly bastards – they only sent the one bloke. But the doc here says it's always like that."

"I think they don't expect you to suspect anything unusual," the professor offered. "It's just routine, isn't it?"

Brad laughed with a scoff.

"I gave him routine alright. A routine flat on his back. Didn't see me for dust. Fuckin' bastards. Anyway doc – sorry, pleased to meet youse guys, but somethin's come up."

"What?" asked the professor.

"We've got company," Nihils replied for the sportsman, his eyes and fingers still furiously engaged with the netface. "Coming in pretty much right now. Slaloming through the wind turbines to cover the noise of their rotors, I suspect. But definitely coming in. We have to go, Howie- sorry, Mick."

Nihils closed the lid of his netface with a click and stood up.

"We've got seconds. Sorry professor. Good to meet you. We'll try to make it back."

"Who is it?" asked the professor, beginning to make his own preparations for an invasion.

"Tax Sharks. But they're coming in with Transglobal security forces."

"Security forces? Transglobal?" Howard was genuinely surprised.

"Of course," said Nihils gathering up his portable cyber bypass. "You don't think nation state governments can afford the calibre of

140

firepower necessary to run a sandwich war, do you? Jeezus Howard–Mick. Let's go."

"Sorry, professor," Howard was already on his way out of the door.

"Of course," the professor replied with understanding, himself otherwise engaged.

"Fucking Transglobal! We can't afford to be found here!" Howard swore through gritted teeth as he flipped the ignition, and Nihils closed his door. "This bloody heap'll get us nowhere. They'll probably pick it up and drive us … well, wherever they bloody well want to."

Howard was panicking. Nihils was already working on both his netface and bypass unit once more.

"Try and get us into the dunes. The sand banks will flay the signal. I might be able to bypass them."

Howard had the car moving.

"Kill the lights!" Nihils hissed, irritably leaning across himself to touch the relevant pad.

"But how can I see?"

Nihils turned the lights back on to low beam.

"Alright, but gun it. There – we should be free of the speed control now."

He seemed to have converted his bypass unit into a jammer.

Howard hit the accelerator, and the joint juices of solar and electric power banks unleashed a sudden surge into the night from their hire car's normally moderated engine. The aura of the car's headlights, even on low beam, quickly found the sand dunes beyond the compound, and Howard left what road surfaces there were in the dilapidated reservation and headed straight for the nearest sizeable mound of sand.

The remains of a cyclone fence came up quickly, but Howard just gunned the car straight through it. The withering alloy links easily parted, and Howard found himself slithering and sliding through the soft sand beyond.

"Don't climb. Stay low. Follow the valleys. Look for a hard shoulder, Howard, or we'll get bogged. And for God's sake put it into four wheel drive." For the which act, Nihils once again grabbed the gear shift and applied the drive ratio himself.

It was barely seconds before Howard reached the first 'valley' and, in attempting to swing onto something harder by way of surface, knocked the gear lever into rear wheel drive and spun the car through one hundred and eighty degrees, sand flying from the back wheels. The rear wheels themselves started to spin down into the sand, and Nihils reached across, pulled the ignition and killed the lights in one swift movement, plunging the vehicle into instant stillness and darkness.

"This'll have to do," he said in a hoarse whisper, trying to listen hard beyond the drone of the wind turbines beyond the dunes. He wound down his window hurriedly and lowered the lid of his netface to hide the glow from the screen.

The car was only just concealed between two dunes. From this position they were looking directly into the compound some five hundred metres away. Figures were running between the dwellings in the darkness. There were some urgent voices, but no-one was shouting. Some emerged as if from nowhere. Howard guessed these were concealed entrances to their underground dwellings.

"Here they come," hissed Nihils.

The sound was unmistakable. From beneath the constant hum of the wind farm came the low whine and rotor throb of helicopters. There were just three of them. They swept in over the compound from the east and drew up into a hover at about two hundred feet, each positioning themselves at the point of a triangle that subtended the entire expanse of the reservation.

"They're not big enough for a landing force," Howard observed.

With a sudden, panicked movement Nihils snapped open his netface, glanced at it, said "Shit!", jabbed a key that plunged the whole machine into darkness, and snapped it shut again.

"They're wiping out their LAN!" he explained. "And I suspect wiping their entire electronic network. The tie-cutters here, Howard, are using their own unregistered LAN to jam local consumer chip transmissions and feed false data outputs instead. While to visiting Social Safety and Tax Security officers they dissemble the expected lethargy and ennui of reservationists, underground they are developing bio-diversity modelling programs and products which they plan to launch as their own private enterprise. They are feeding false data to the transcorps while they develop their own competitive advantage, so that they can make enough of a hit on the global bio-diversity market to enable them to return to the society of their choice as wealthy men.

"That's what I was uncovering while we were with the professor. They've been using the docs and their herbal bloody medicines as a front to keep the transcorps off the main game. Well, one of them has finally sussed it out. Their entire technology base will be useless after this. It'll take them years to build it back up. And they'll have to move somewhere else to do it."

There was no gunfire, no laser-guided bombs or missiles, no explosions, none of the hand-to-hand combat and street fighting that always appeared in The Market. There was simply the low ominous throb of the hovering helicopters and, occasionally, a frantic figure running from one in-ground entrance or above-ground dwelling to another. Judging by the pieces of netface hardware and other electronic equipment tucked under their arms, they were desperately trying to save some of their valuable resources. But after a few minutes, about a dozen of them gathered in the centre of the compound and looked up from one helicopter to another, their clothes flapping uselessly in the wind kicked up by the rotor blades overhead.

Then it seemed to be over. The helicopters rose in unison, turned together and headed off east, back the way they had come. The men and, it could now be seen, women in the middle of the compound variously swore at the sky, stamped the ground, or smacked their fists into their own hands. Then they began remonstrating with each other, looking for someone to blame. Two of them started to cry, and were comforted by others.

Nihils turned on his portable bypass unit once more, but did not reboot his netface.

"We need to get out of here," said Howard at last. "We must be into downtime by now. We need to get back to the accommodation."

"Worse than that," said Nihils. For the reservationists gathered in the compound were starting to point to the tear in the cyclone fence through which Howard and Nihils had made their escape. One man came to the gap itself and stared through into the blackness, looking straight at them but, hopefully, not seeing them. Yet.

The professor joined the group. He seemed to be arguing on Howard and Nihils' behalf, but some of the others were waving their hands dismissively at him. One even pushed him away, so that he staggered and fell into a sitting position on the ground.

"They think it's us," Nihils said unnecessarily.

"But the professor's telling them it's not."

"Maybe. But he's not winning. If they come this way, Howard, we're stuffed."

"You don't think I can get out and introduce myself as the Member for Canberra, here on a fact-finding mission, what can I do to help them and, by the way, is this the right way to Old Melbourne?" Howard suggested.

Nihils just looked at him.

"Do you still have the speed control blocked?" Howard asked. He was contemplating making a run for it through the compound.

"No. We're back on the CCC bypass. Our chips will be registering extraordinary anxiety levels by now, Howard, and if either of us have a Transglobal chip they'll know exactly where we are. Even if not, another CCC service provider might alert them because we're on a known reservation. We have to remain where the bypass is saying we are, and that is back at our accommodation. We just have to be patient."

One of the men – it could have been Brad – produced a torch and began to walk towards the tear in the fence to join the other. He shone the torch into the distance. There was no mistaking its weak transition across the bonnet of their car, nor its immediate return there. Brad turned and called to his colleagues. Some began to run to join him. Brad began to step over the mangled fencing, his light trained firmly on the hired car.

"On the other hand..." Nihils continued. "Use the front wheel drive, and a low, low gear. Remember the rear wheels are most likely bogged. Edge forward. Make it look like we don't have 4WD. Just edge through them as if we're looking for a firm surface. I'll have to risk looking for a satellite view to find a way out. Hope the choppers are far enough away now not to pick me up."

Howard switched on the ignition and the engine quietly stirred. He made sure the windows and doors were secure, slipped into frontwheel drive, and started to pull the car ever-so-gradually forward. Brad in turn started to run towards them, so Howard turned their headlights onto full beam. He could now see that some of the men running towards the broken fence had gathered implements – spades, maybe rakes, a wrench – enough to damage their windscreen at least. Perhaps even break it. It would be hard enough to explain damage to the vehicle, let alone personal injury or, worse, capture, now that they were so evidently committed to flight.

145

Luckily when their and Brad's forward trajectories met, Brad merely tried to stop the car, uselessly clamping his hands on the bonnet and bracing his own body against the vehicle's forward motion, as if his strength alone would somehow suffice. The weapon-wielding reservationists were now crossing the fenceline, running after Brad. But the professor was back on his feet and running after them. He grabbed one of the would-be assailants and tried to wrest the implement from them. He failed, but Howard thought he could hear the professor shouting after them: "We're not like that! We're not like that!"

"Have you got a grip? On the sand?" Nihils asked.

"Think so," Howard said. He was not feeling any wheel-spin. The car was moving forward despite the pressure and thumping from Brad and, now, at least one other reservationist.

"Okay. Don't go into 4WD until they are upon us. It looks like there's a firm surface right at the fenceline which goes around the compound. We need to make that. Then I'm going to take a risk and throw on the jammer, just for the second or two it will take us to accelerate out of here. Do you understand? Keep the 4WD in reserve as long as possible. Element of surprise etcetera."

Howard nodded and started to veer the car to the left, approaching the fenceline at an angle that would enable them to get a faster grip on the firm surface once they found it. Brad and three or four of his fellows were now trying to push and bang the car at its front and righthandside. The weapon-wielders had arrived but were vying for a good gap through which to get in a good blow. They did not want to hurt their fellows.

"Just gun it Howie. Gun it! Four wheel drive NOW!" Nihils commanded.

They were within twenty metres of the fenceline. Howard changed gear ratio obediently and tried a gradual acceleration, which would keep the frontrunners running with him and, hopefully, the weapons

146

bearers still at bay. Suddenly Nihils shouted, "Gun it, fuck you!" and threw the car back into rear-wheel drive.

Startled by the action, Howard did as commanded and flattened the accelerator. Nihils grabbed the wheel and spun it madly to the left. The back wheels started to fly wildly in the sand and, at the same time, the car turned, seemingly on the spot, spewing out sand behind it.

Howard was totally out of control. The car span in slow motion through three hundred and sixty degrees, sending the entire pack of assailants into a confusion of assault and, at the same time, attempts to shield their eyes and mouths from the spray of biting sand. Weapons were either raised in defence or dropped altogether, just for a moment. Long enough for Nihils to, as the car came to the end of its three-sixty degree slide, throw the vehicle into four wheel drive. The vehicle leapt forward and, in a further spray of sand, gained the firmer roadway around the perimeter.

The car then accelerated rapidly. Although the reservationists tried to run after, or run across the compound to intercept, the hire car sped through a sharp dog leg to the right around the perimeter fence, followed quickly by another before jarring a left onto the access road by which they had arrived at the compound less than half an hour beforehand.

Even as they accelerated away from the compound, figures wielding metal implements were running through the front gate after them. But Howard and Nihils were well away. Their final dash was achieved in less than thirty seconds. Howard was staggered by the acceleration of which the car was capable. But the moment Nihils switched the jammer back to cyber bypass, the vehicle was gripped as if by a giant mechanical grab and hauled back to regulation speed, regardless of how flat Howard plunged the accelerator to the floor.

But it did not matter. They were away, and they were unscathed. And if they wanted it, Mick Turition and his Shadow had a scoop which would last, oh, at least thirty seconds on the front page of The Market, according to Nihils, before Transglobal had it pulled.

Chapter Eighteen

"That was just amazing," Howard was still marvelling as he and Nihils grabbed a quick fuck during downtime back in Warrnambool. "I still can't believe Transglobal can just fly in and wipe out the competition like that."

"It's probably their CCC that's copping most of the false data," Nihils ventured. "And they're not getting any of the other business to offset the damage."

"Where did you learn to drive like that?" Howard asked again.

"Well, you were doing the driving, Howard."

"Yes I know but you did, you know, all of the tricksy bits."

"Alright, if you must know, I've seen it done on old action vision from the last century."

"You mean like movies?"

"Yeh, you know, Europacific stuff, from the Americas. With bloody great fossil-guzzling cars that bash and crash into each other all over old New York or San Francisco."

Howard laughed as he puffed.

"I used to watch them as a kid," he said.

"So the LAN they use is sort of like an electronic shield?" Howard asked again.

"Through which they feed out false CCC data for the regional population, yes."

"But it's a made-up population."

"No, it was for the local population. They were jamming the CCC feed of the local population. But yes, it looked like they'd co-opted a number of MID's over the years to add to the mix. Maybe that's how Transglobal got onto them."

"And who was the Eliot the professor was talking about?"

"Which Eliot?"

"The professor. It sounded like he was talking about some sort of machine. As in, the Eliot machine. I couldn't get it."

"Jeez, that Brad was a bit of a bronco but, wasn't he?"

And Howard came inside Nihils' unbearably cute little arse with a whimper at the mere thought of the footballer's moistened cock parting his own waiting buttocks.

The following day at their breakfast briefing, Bishop surprised them with not only a comprehensive revision of the power generation component of their proposal but also an instruction from the Leader of the Chamber to simply drop the water component and reduce the price accordingly, if that would clinch the deal. The team made the concession by cybermail before leaving for the drive west along the Great Ocean Road which, on receiving a cell card call from transglobal about half an hour in, they foreshortened by an inland route to make a lunchtime meeting in Transglobal's old office tower in the Old Melbourne CBD. This looked 'official'.

Katharine O'Brien herself was at the meeting, and she announced at its outset that, given the VIC Government's prompt revision of their proposal, and pending a few minor details, it looked like they had a deal. She produced yet another bottle of Krug, some crystal champagne flutes were brought in, and she popped the cork.

While Bishop and the rest of Transglobal team huddled with their glasses of bubbly to finalise the details, O'Brien took Howard aside to admire the view from their top floor window. It was not so much of a view these days. The elegant "Ballerina" spire on the former

Arts Centre had been taken down before it fell down. The multiple glass exteriors of the high office towers were increasingly dowdy and poorly kept. The streets were empty and uncleaned.

It was only inside the buildings that the complex and expansive hardware and labour force of the cybernet was massively at work along with, Howard already knew, the equally extensive conglomerate of courts and appeals tribunals that no appellant attended anymore because there was no space, and the outcomes were a foregone conclusion anyway - more debt of one form or another: lawdebt, educationdebt, healthdebt, Social Safety pre-payment. The entire hidden workforce of the old state capital's CBD, Howard had learned from Nihils, came and went by secret underground tunnels to ensure security; whose, it was not entirely clear.

Up on the surface, in the streets, Old Melbourne and Old Sydney, Old Adelaide and Old Brisbane were like ghost towns. Only Perth and Darwin survived as healthy business hubs due to their proximity to South Asia. And of course Hobart, for its vital eco-monitoring access to the Antarctic, the global eco-barometer of the twenty-first century.

"What changes we've seen in out lifetimes," O'Brien offered, reflecting his thoughts.

"But for the better," Howard replied, sporting the party line. "The emerging primacy of nation states from the old Australia has seen a strengthening of the old inter-state competition that produces results exactly like the one we have achieved here, don't you agree? The region, and its ecology, is better for it. The economy, and its vitality, is better for it. Let's face it, without the changes you and I have seen over the last twenty years, the old federal Australia would have lost its place in fourth phase progress entirely. Particularly in VIC."

"And you believe there is a strategic centre to that? That there is an intellectual and decision-making force that determines its direction and energy, its power. What you keep referring to as Real Truth."

Howard found himself being drawn back reluctantly to the other side of the scales in his conceptual opposition around what constituted real truth. The Tie-cutters had, after all, been working towards a surprise raid on the market place with a carefully planned niche product, not to right any social injustice but to make their fortunes. So where was the Real Truth movement amongst the underclass?

"It's a hypothesis, yes. How else does it happen?"

"Well, market forces I would suggest."

"Isn't that twentieth century economics? Isn't the way transcorps move their production sites around the globe a way of managing market forces, so that they contribute to the capital growth spiral?"

"That sounds a little like a conspiracy theory, Mr Johns."

"Not at all. You are all in competition with each other. It's business. How can you have consumer choice without the business to produce the goods and services from which the consumer can choose?"

"You certainly have a point there. Why don't you come round tonight? To my place. We can have a little celebratory meal."

It sounded to Howard as if there was a covert invitation locked inside the surface formality of O'Brien's offer. He glanced involuntarily at Nihils, whose eyes flickered momentarily in acknowledgement from their guarded fixation on the netface at which he sat, alone, on the far side of the negotiating table.

"You can bring your colleagues," O'Brien added with continuing pleasantry, "Although I suspect Mr Bishop may better enjoy the company of those on the Transglobal team who share a similar professional interest. I think there may be an invitation transpiring at this very moment."

And indeed, Bishop was looking guiltily in Nihils' and Howard's directions, and nodding enthusiastically to his fellow negotiators, who were all standing now, their business complete. The foursome clinked glasses with mutual coyishness and drank.

*

That evening, Howard joined Nihils in the chauffeured hybrid limousine that had been ferrying them around the former city for the past three and a half weeks. It glided out east of the CBD, past the former Arts Centre and War Memorial, beyond the now deserted residential apartment blocks and high office towers to the leafy suburb of Toorak. Even in this obviously once-wealthy residential zone, every second house appeared to be dark, its gardens untended, its gates closed and driveway empty.

One orange electric lantern lit the front porch, however, of the residence to which the limo delivered them. It was a wide, deep, double-storeyed house with mock-tudor exterior, including criss-cross leadlighting on the windows. A wisteria threw a bedraggled mess of vegetation across the top of the porch, casting shadow over the front door even at night. There was a vestigial fleur-de-lys iron knocker on the front door that looked so functional Howard automatically stretched out his hand to physically alert those in residence to their arrival. He need not have bothered, however. The door opened electronically, from remote operation deep within the house, and Katharine O'Brien strolled leisurely to meet them in the front hallway as they stepped inside.

She extended a more feminine hand that her usual executive greeting, and invited them to follow her into the drawing room for drinks. Dinner was almost ready.

In a tight-fitting, full length deep maroon dress, with low back and shoulder slung, the proportions of Katharine O'Brien's exquisite body were more evident than ever. An aide emerged from an ante room to take their coats. The same aide then appeared in the drawing room to assemble their pre-dinner beverage.

The walls of the room were rather like a photograph exhibition, with shots of a much younger Katharine O'Brien with others in a range of South Asian locations, showing machinery to local indigenous people, or standing with them to present cheques or awards. Over the chimney to the unused open fire grate was the centrepiece to the display: a citation for the prestigious Power of Choice over Poverty campaign instituted by the New World Order on its formation in 2038.

Over drinks, and on into dinner, O'Brien talked of her involvement in the corporate campaign against poverty during the 2020s and 2030s that led the New World Order to declare in 2038 that the 2018 global poverty remission targets had finally been met. She could tell a story about each of the photographs in the drawing room, and how each mission had resulted in one ethnic group or another developing the means to pull themselves out of the poverty trap through the judicious application of third phase progress principles.

She was never boasting. It was impossible to doubt the sincerity of her belief in her efforts. She was unstintingly committed to the power of capital as the solution to economic disadvantage in the world. By comparison, Howard found himself touching on quite dull stories of the intrigues and betrayals of political life, and Nihils said nothing at all.

It was not until the main course had been cleared, and the second bottle of wine opened, that O'Brien turned to the reason for their meeting.

"So you want to know about Real Truth?" she said as she placed her knife and fork neatly together with barely a clink of silver on china.

She saw Howard and Nihils glance nervously at the aide who was clearing the table.

"It's alright, you can trust him. There's little that passes through this house that he doesn't know about. He has my complete confidence."

"So there is such a thing then," said Nihils. It was almost the first time for the evening that he had spoken.

O'Brien turned to him without affectation.

"Truth is such a matter of perception and interpretation, isn't it," she replied. "But your colleague, Mr Johns here, has a number of times referred to the Real Truth movement. He believes it exists at the centre of transnational capital, and drives the strategic development of the economy and, therefore, the world. I imagine he even expects to find Smithson Adams himself at the strategic centre of it all, planning the future. Is that about it, Howard?"

Howard nodded. Although in reality he had never imagined Smithson Adams as continuing to exist anywhere other than on the giant vision screens during the Two Minute Vision. He would be surprised to find Smithson Adams still alive, given the age he was when he was reborn into New Prosperity. If anything, Howard imagined visionaries like Adams were more used as figureheads and consultants. Never CEOs or company directors. Let alone key strategists.

"Rather than in some counter-revolutionary underworld?" O'Brien sought confirmation.

Howard nodded again. Although he was still not convinced that this was entirely obviated as an option either. Mick and Shadow had still not made contact with any real MFEs that would admit to the status (apart, he reflected, from his own mother). On the other hand, while the market objective of the one Tie-cutters reservation they had penetrated was not proof that all such reservations were equally pro-choice, Nihils' experience remained evidential.

"But you are sceptical, Mr Nihils?" O'Brien was continuing, with that uncanny knack she had of echoing Howard's thoughts.

Nihils just shrugged.

"It's just Nihils," he said.

"But if I told you I was aware of your presence at Transglobal's raid on a certain competitor's research and development facility yesterday evening, you wouldn't be surprised."

Nihils looked impassive, but Howard knew him well enough to sense he was uncomfortable.

"My bypass unit was down for a moment."

155

"And it's only designed to be a CCC and cybernet bypass unit really, isn't it. You would hardly be surprised that our security forces had equipment and technology that was far more advanced. It's probably software you'd love to get your hands on."

Nihils nodded with a cross between a grimace and a grin.

"But you don't think that means there is a central intelligence to the development of such technology, or the activity of such security forces."

Though a statement, it implied a question.

Nihils shook his head.

"Why not?"

"I don't think I should be going down this line in Howard's presence. He really is interested in this Real Truth stuff. He likes meaning."

"Admirable loyalty. You don't want to spoil his chances."

"Exactly."

"But you think…" O'Brien left the sentence for Nihils to complete.

"I don't think we'll be finding Smithson Adams in an office at Transnational Headquarters masterminding global capitalism. I think the action of chaos is a better explanation for the outcome of competition. In reality competition, like combat and other forms of direct action, for all the planning in the world, takes on a life of its own and turns and twists in unexpected ways. It's as creative as painting a canvass or throwing a pot or writing a cybernet program. It's as endlessly inventive in its interiority as the inside of an atom. Capital has theorised this for a long time, Ms O'Brien."

Nihils knew it, and O'Brien seemed to know it. But Howard didn't. His understanding of economics and corporate theory fell wildly short here. It also alarmed him greatly just how much a transcorp like Transglobal knew about his activities, despite measures he had thought protected him. So much for the anonymity of Mick Turition. He suddenly felt dreadfully out of his depth.

O'Brien held Nihils' gaze for some time without emotion, nodding so very slightly. Then she turned to Howard with a sizeable intake of breath.

"So, Mr Johns, there is no Real Truth movement after all, it seems," she said.

"I don't believe that's possible," he said with courage. "I think perhaps my friend here has spent too long inside systems, working them from within. I tend to look at them from the outside, and while I'm not a determinist – as you know, I don't believe in an omnipotent or divine force that designs the future and fashions fate – there is too much in the self-evident and unfolding history of capital for it to be attributable to mere chance. There has to be strategy, and it has to be well organised."

For once, he almost convinced himself.

There was a pause, as O'Brien looked from one to another.

"And it didn't surprise you, Howard, to discover that Transglobal has its own security forces active in your own Nation State? It's not the sort of thing we generally make known to local governments," she said finally.

"Yes," said Howard after a pause. There was no point in hiding the truth. "It did. But as my good friend here pointed out to me, it's more than the average nation state has at its disposal to resource and finance a winnable border war. Again, this points to the centrality of strategy, and transcorps as the likely locus of it."

"But not a conspiracy." Again, it was a question rather than a statement.

"Strategy is a better explanation. Conspiracy is just a cheap sensationalisation of strategy we fear."

157

There was a further pause in which O'Brien seemed to consider her options. When she spoke, it was on the basis of a decision.

"I'm going to give you both an infochip," she said, extending her hand to her aide, who stepped forward and placed a small velvet pouch in it. "I want you to take it, read it together, and tell me if you continue to be interested. It's an introduction to the real Real Truth movement."

Katharine O'Brien placed the pouch on the long dining table in front of her, and stood up. Howard and Nihils politely followed her example.

"Your limousine is waiting. I shan't see you out, if you don't mind. Everything out there has vision and audio. We can see round corners and into shadows several times over. As you have so aptly observed, Mr Johns, you purchase your satellite intelligence from us."

Chapter Nineteen

That day, having completed their business with Transglobal, the VIC Government team had moved into hotel accommodation paid for by their own side. After they were dropped off there by O'Brien's limousine, Howard and Nihils lost no time in scurrying back across town, by a series of narrow back streets Nihils had identified on satellite positioning, to spend a final night together in their room above Cross Antiques.

Howard was surprised at how, after just three weeks, he had become immured to pro-choice violence. The first time he and Nihils had hot-footed it through the dingier back streets of Melbourne's dockside suburbs, the violence of roaming gangs of consumers shocked him to the core. It was one thing to know such violence existed, thanks to the privilege of a position in government, but another to be actually confronted with it on the streets. The unadulterated pent-up and unruly anger of these Caucasian consumers, who could not understand how their birthright had been denied them, how a century of genocidal behaviour toward the country's indigenous population, followed by another century of patronising immigrants from old Italy and Greece, the Slavs and the Balts, Asia in its entirety, had resulted only in their economic disempowerment. What had they done that was so wrong?

So much easier, than deal with their disabusement, to throw it at the smaller, manageable manifestations of the perceived cause of their relegation to the social scrap heap. In the service industries of the northern half of the main Australasian continent, such 'manifestations' were the majority; indistinguishable from the rich and powerful in ethnic appearance, due to the business migration resurgence in the 2020s followed by the guestworker schemes of the 2030s. But down here … the first time Howard had witnessed a mob of failing-to-thrive white supremacists physically pick up a shopkeeper of obviously Chinese ethnic origin and shake him by his

159

neck, flaying him with verbal abuse about 'so-called customer service', Howard hid in the shadows and was physically sick. It was Nihils who watched the entire spectacle – one which resulted in the asphyxiated shop owner dropping ignominiously to the floor, dead – with keen but familiar interest.

The next time, *en route* to Cross Antiques, they came to pass the window of a South Asian grocer in which the vendor was surrounded by a menacing band of local denizens assailing him with questions about the right by which he practised here, when there were *real* VICtorians looking for work, and what right did he have to the fridges and houses government handed out to his kind when they, the *Australians*, were here *first* – conveniently forgetting that they too were once migrants - Howard managed to swallow his guilt and with Nihils sweep swiftly past, shadows in the night.

Tonight, Howard and Nihils slipped without a second thought past half a dozen vigilante-style bullyings and beatings of convenient ethnic scapegoats, each and every one the perpetrators characterising themselves as victims as they rained down blows. For this was their last night together in the little love nest above the old antique shop in the shadow of the giant, but increasingly deserted, South Melbourne shopping world. It was to have been a simple night of sex and sleep, before returning to their hotel at dawn to check out and meet up with Bishop for the ride out to the airport. As a result of their dinner with O'Brien, however, they had an infochip to read.

Sitting up together in their bedsheet after sex, cups of tea in hand, they poured over the opening sections of the text. It outlined the emerging primacy of capital, and its economy, as the key drivers of human activity around the globe. Howard had seen snippets of this text before, in his early searches of the cybernet as Mick Turition, before his cyber champion had taken to throwing sheaves of uncovered text at him with disdain, cajoling "You're not really interested in this stuff, are you *boss*?".

After the Third Phase of Progress and the collapse of the two Super Governments in 2020 after the Oil Wars, constraints on accelerated industrialisation disappeared. The transnational corporations realised that the dependence on larger and larger national governments or coalitions of government to match larger and larger transnational corporations was not the key to ensuring standardisation of infrastructure and services to finesse corporate objectives.

All larger government did was to use infrastructure and bureaucracy to build its own power base, depending on war economies to drive large fiscal policy that enabled government to match the financial leverage of even the largest investors. Whereas corporate experience with the smaller dictatorships helped them to understand how much more quickly capital could be developed if one smaller country was pitched against another to develop competitive advantage. Capital could control infrastructure services and standards anyway, through demand. This was, in the longer run, more efficient. Who needed governmental democracy, when capital itself could become democracy?

It was the Australian economist, Smithson Adams, who coined the syllogism that was adopted as the brandgrab of what became known around the world as New Prosperity:

> *Democracy is Freedom*
>
> *Freedom is Choice*
>
> *Choice is the Consumers.*

The syllogistic feint, in supplanting the Consumer for Democracy, was lost on everyone. By focussing the action of the economy on the individual consumer, and reducing human rights and sentience to the choices of the consumer, in time capital would be able to remove the 'middle man', government, altogether.

161

So the transnationals covertly underwrote the nationalisation movements in the smaller countries and ethnic topographies of Europe, Russia, India, China and North America as they had in the Africas and South Americas, and the transnationals themselves took on the commercialisation of alternative power sources to fossil fuels. In so doing, they marginalised the OPEC states rather than using Super Governments to level the playing field with them. Alternative power sources such as thermal, solar, wind and water, along with the development of trans-oceanic power supply technologies, opened up expanding smaller nations to consumer choice.

It was the transnationals who called this policy New Prosperity, opening the poorer nations up to capital growth. The formation of the New World Order in 2038 was a necessary construct, to maintain a sense in the emerging nation states that government still had global leverage and legitimacy. In reality, however, from 2038 on, local policy would always be determined by economic interest, and economic interest would always be the domain of transcorp strategists. There would be truth, and there would be real truth. And only the transcorp strategist has access to the latter.

There was much more. It all placed the transcorp at the centre of global politics.

"We could make a killing in The Market with this, if we could get someone to publish," said Nihils.

"Which, of course, as we've found too many times already, we won't be able to," Howard rejoined.

"So if you can't beat them, join them?"

"Well, if it means being able to operate at a level of truth, a level of authenticity and closeness to real meaning..." Howard was struggling with his attitude to this – opportunity, was it? Or threat.

162

"And you think this is how they recruit their top strategists?"

"Well, how else do they do it? They have to have *some* way of finding people they can trust."

"You're such a sentimentalist, Howard. Hooked on the idea that there is always a better way to be a better human being. Howard, if they can penetrate my CCC and cybernet bypass, they will also know what Mick Turition and his Shadow have been up to. Surely you don't think *they* think that tracking down money free exchangers and reservationists with a view to blasting *their* stories all over the front page is activity they might even remotely associate with trustworthiness?"

"Well, yes, in a perverse sort of way. I mean, what does it matter to them? They will have any such material blocked anyway. And our activity shows a sort of determination and inventiveness they might value. We haven't actually done anything wrong or illegal, have we? Simply exercised freedom of choice. They would respect that. Perhaps even admire it."

Nihils was literally beside himself with laughter, rolling around the bed, his little willy wiggling around in its tufty nest of light brown pubic hair.

"H-Howard!" he struggled to contain his mirth. "Howard! Th- the way they sh-showed th-their respect – respect for me was to t-torture me!"

"But that's ..." he wanted to say 'ridiculous' or 'just you', but that did not make sense.

"I mean they wouldn't..." but even as he spoke he knew they might. He remembered the reservationists uncovered by Transglobal the night before. Part of him still felt he should champion the oppressed and dispossessed. Another part of him questioned whether they really existed, except in the interests of The Market. And yet there was Nihils' own experience.

"Surely..." there were just too many possible endings to this sentence for any of them to be plausibly the right one.

The awful possibility of the situation he had drawn around himself began to solidify in Howard's mind. It was a solid, dense, dark object of foreboding that sucked all thought of a hopeful nature into it. Even plans, the what-I'll-do-nexts of routine mental life, clung only momentarily to the outer surface of this solidifying awareness before being whisked away deep into its growing horror.

"Shit," Howard said simply. "So this is the way the world ends."

"This is the way the world ends?" repeated Nihils, still laughing.

"Not with a bang but a whimper."

It was not Howard who spoke. Nor was it Nihils.

Both men froze, Howard with his little finger neatly cocked above his tea cup, Nihils naked with his arms and legs in the air, like a dead cockroach. Their heads ranged around the room, looking for the source of the voice.

"This is the way the world ends," Howard said to the room.

"This is the way the world ends," repeated Nihils, rolling over onto all fours.

The voice seemed to boom from the four walls:

"NOT WITH A BANG BUT A WHIMPER!"

It was so loud the room seemed to shake. Nihils and Howard had to cover their ears. The cross above the bed fell onto Howard's head. The candelabra on the table fell over, knocking Howard'd precious Tibetan Prayer Bell – which he had placed ceremoniously in front of it on their first visit – onto the floor. The three religious pictures on the three walls all suddenly scrambled into live vision, and the face of Mr Cross appeared.

"We are the hollow men," Cross's voice boomed.

"We are the stuffed men

164

Leaning together
Headpiece filled with straw. Alas!
Our dried voices, when
We whisper together
Are quiet and meaningless
As wind in dry grass
Or rats' feet over broken glass
In our dry cellar
Shape without form, shade without colour,
Paralysed force, gesture without motion,
Welcome, my hollow men! Welcome to the world of choice!"

At that, six women entered the room, each dressed in the livery of one of the region's international air carriers. They formed a circle around Howard and Nihils' bed and struck poses like models, gazing dispassionately down at the two men.

"Choose!" commanded Cross from the vision screens. "Which airline will you travel with? The fare is pre-debited to your accounts. Our only condition is that you travel separately."

Six men then entered the room, each one taking up a pose to one side of an airline stewardess. Each man was dressed in a smart concierge's outfit, each bearing the brand of one of the six major hotel chains found throughout VIC, NSW and QLD.

"Choose!" commanded Cross from the vision screens. "With which hotel will you stay on arrival. The tariff is pre-debited. Our only condition is that you stay in separate venues."

Six chauffeurs then entered the room. They all wore the same ill-fitting chauffeur's jackets, were all too fat to properly fit behind the wheel, and all carried those large name tags that helped arriving passengers identify them in airport arrival halls. Each name tag bore a different name.

"Choose!" commanded Cross from the vision screens. "Which name will you adopt upon arrival, once you have signed your mandatory identity displacement order at reception? You are the consumer, and choice is yours'. Choose!"

And with that, six armed security operatives entered the room, and stood between the stewardess-concierge-chauffeur threesomes, their guns pointed at Howard and Nihils, their faces concealed by large protective helmets and darkened visors.

"Choice is yours!" Cross repeated, and himself strolled casually into the room.

He picked up the Tibetan Prayer Bell. Its hammer had broken loose. Cross held the two broken pieces in the palm of each hand and looked at them.

"Consumer choice," he said, offering the two pieces up to Howard and Nihils, "Is always with you."

So, thought Howard Smithson Johns ruefully, it was a fake after all. Meanwhile Nihils, who had scrambled into bed and covered his modesty with the sheet, turned to Howard Smithson Johns and said, in a high voice that betrayed a certain absence of hope, "I don't suppose this is some sort of bizarre last night treat, is it?"

Chapter Twenty

It was just before dawn. Howard could make out the straw inlay in the six-panelled conical ceiling of the losman in which he had spent the night. A large, metal fan redolent of the Colonial era hung above him, casually circulating air. The louvered windows that formed three sides at the front of the losman must have been open, because he could clearly hear the sea lazily lapping its way up a smooth, white sand beach nearby. He had noted the beach, separated from the resort by its orderly line of tall, bowed palms, when he arrived the night before. He had wanted immediately to walk along it, to feel the sand cool between his toes and beneath his bare feet. But he had been barely able to keep his eyes open, he was so tired.

The louvres must also have been protected by fine fly screening, because his losman was free of mosquitoes. Unless, of course, they had been genetically eradicated in this region, as they had in many tourist destinations these days.

Allowing his head to loll to the left on the accommodatingly soft pillow, he could see that the losman also had an air conditioning unit, but it was not in operation. It was still cool enough outside to serve the needs of body temperature without being cold. Humidity laid a thin film of moisture across his skin. As if he had dreamt all night of moving through water. The room smelled of damp bamboo, palm and straw.

His head was still slightly steel-wool from a surfeit of gin. The one litre bottle had been sitting on the round, glass-topped bamboo table upon his arrival, and the tonic in generous supply in the bar fridge. A note leaning against it yielded an elegant card which read: With the compliments of the manager. But below this was written, in slightly hurried ink pen, "Welcome, and sleep well – Katharine O'Brien."

Exhausted though he was from a day of travelling, he had sat down on the veranda provided by the overhang of his losman's generous

167

straw roof, in the cushioned bamboo armchairs provided by the resort, inhaled the still-warm sea air and drank several tumblers of gin and tonic with an emphasis on the gin rather than the tonic. He intended to engage with O'Brien's entreaty to the letter.

The day had, after all, been confusing. Even though the invasion of their flat had taken place at the end of a working day, it was of course early daylight outside. He and Nihils had been taken outside dressed as they had arrived and, without any opportunity to retrieve their luggage from the hotel, had been driven off in separate vehicles.

He had no idea where Nihils was now. All he knew was that he had been driven to Old Melbourne airport to a private air park, where he had boarded one of the new executive sail planes. Rather than using the conventional runways, these aircraft were slingshot into the air, whereupon giant sail-like wings unfolded and bore them up into the stratosphere under the silent power of solar micro-cells, which pattina'd the surface of the sails.

In flight, the sail plane looked like a giant, swept-wing kite, slipping across the outer surface of the earth's atmosphere. It was a beautiful experience, enhanced by the luxurious interior of the long, slim cabin, and first class in-flight service. He was the only passenger, and was expertly plied with modest quantities of very expensive food and the best beverages.

Although it felt like they were travelling at speed, the continent seemed to pass slowly below them. It was easy to see the east coast pass gradually south beneath, but as daylight disappeared they still had not escaped the northernmost confines of QLD. When they finally slid down to land, he had no idea where they were. Only that it was balmy and tropical once he stepped out of the railpod from the airport.

Because he had responded to the travel, rather than the usual routines that regulated a working day, he had now lost his sense of where he was in the 36-hour day. There was no illuminated timesignal in the

168

losman, and he had discovered quickly that his cell card had no reception here and was, as a result, useless.

He had been too stunned, he reflected now, by the nature of their 'arrest' to contemplate his situation in much depth the day before. He thought they had been 'discovered' and were in some way to be 'punished' for 'subversive activity'. Although in reality he could not see how what they had done was, in the world of consumer choice, actually subversive. It was only his own sense of guilt that attached to his thoughts the negative concept. He knew that some doughty, recalcitrant nugget of cognition at the back of his mind that did not 'buy' the dominant ideology. For it was just that: a system of ideas, loosely connected and with the logical and, more pertinently, philosophical flaws of all ideology.

Ironically, however, it seemed that it was in the dominant ideology itself that he had finally come to suspect 'real truth' lay, in the strategy that drove consumer choice, and the economic system that serviced it – not only the transcorps themselves, but also the governments upon which they were dependent for infrastructure and the mechanisms by which capital growth was maintained in a world devoid of new resources, new sources of commercial value, genuine disparities in labour costs which could fuel natural competition and purchasing power.

Spirituality had failed him early on in his quest for some explanation for the ennui that had so clearly led him to attempt suicide. And after even the briefest of forays into it, the notion of some counter-revolutionary proletariat subsisting in an underclass of MFEs and Tie-cutters appeared to be something altogether too woolly and disparate to be likely; even enough to prove the logical positivist null hypothesis the logic of which now eluded him.

But there remained something inherently confounding in his current choice for Howard Johns. On one hand he was looking outside the hermetic seal of an ideological system, but on the other he was seeking the same enlightenment from its very centre, deep inside it. He wondered whether he had always thought so poorly. Perhaps he had finally been found out: a poor thinker, a fraud, not the man of potential and competence he had always managed to seem to those he worked with.

But then, Katharine O'Brien had seemed genuine in her offer to invite him into her world – the inner life of a transcorp. And she had personally welcomed him here, with a bottle of spirit. And this was no prison, no re-education camp or rehabilitation centre. It was a luxury resort in the tropical north. And even when, at reception, he had refused to choose a new identity, as Cross had told him would be required, the duty manager simply smiled and said "Of course, Mr Johns. Your room access has been coded to your Consumer Choice Chip. Your bags have been delivered to your room already."

And sure enough, there in his losman, neatly stacked alongside the table on which stood the gin, had been his luggage from the Old Melbourne hotel to which he and Nihils had never made it back. The only item missing from it, a quick search revealed, was his netface. And there was not another to be seen in the room to which he had been allocated.

So what was he doing here? For his 'choice' had certainly been no choice. There was no suggestion that he was going to ignore Cross, walk out of the flat in which he and Nihils had spent so many joyous hours of unchecked buggery and carry on with life as usual. The entire event had been constructed to use the term 'choice' to indicate that choice had its limits, and Cross was in control of how those parameters were constituted.

Beyond this, Howard knew no more. He assumed hopefully that, as he appeared to be in a narrative constructed by an intelligence beyond him, signposts would emerge in good time. But as the first rays of sunlight were slung across the surface of the sea to light up the underfringe of the palms and be parted by the louvres of his losman into dancing fragments on the rattan walls, the one reality he had discovered here so far, sleep, had definitely deserted him.

Twenty Forty-Eight

The bamboo bedframe creaked appreciatively as he rolled off the all-too-comfortable mattress in search of shower and a shave.

Chapter Twenty-One

Outside it was warm but moist, as if it had rained heavily the night before. The sun was climbing the sky on the other side of the resort from its beachfront. Ibis casually punctured the ultra-green lawns as Howard followed the winding, loosely paved path from his losman to the restaurant in the main resort complex. The grounds were littered with individual losmans like his, each with its own veranda and louvred glass on three sides facing the sea. He could see large, brightly coloured tropical birds perching in the palms that lined the beachfront. Equally large black birds, like outsized Currawongs or Magpies, flew between the lawns and scattered tropical trees in lazy pendulous curves.

Two and a half sides of the capacious restaurant were completely open to the elements, except for a colonial, wooden balustrade with posts to mark its boundary. It was clear that thick, polythene blinds could be rapidly unrolled to form transparent 'walls' in the event of inclement weather, but these looked as if they were rarely used.

Simple square tables for four, in dark uncomplicated wood, with equally simple but comfortable dining chairs, gave the restaurant and its tiled flooring of subdued tropical colours a work-a-day feel. As if customers could come and go at their leisure any time of the day, and someone would always be there to attend to their culinary or beverage needs. He looked forward, for instance, to an evening cognac here by oil lamp, or a cold beer at dusk with canapés. Over near the bar, to one side of the high-ceilinged, wooden-beamed structure, were comfortable bamboo lounge chairs with floral designs on their cushioning.

He was surprisingly hungry. Breakfast was not usually his meal, and he had been well fed and watered during the journey the day before. But after a good night's uninterrupted sleep he felt ravenous. He quickly cobbled together a blend of cereals around a muesli base, which he drowned in cold milk and wolfed down with an orange and pineapple juice. The cool chrome around the base of the large, bell-like juice dispensers was lipped with condensation from the balmy air.

He then went to the chef on duty at the frying pan and gas ring for an omelette with ham and chives, which he delighted to watch in the making. He loved the expert hands whisking the ingredients in a light stainless steel bowl, pouring them from an increasing height into the hot oil of the pan. The egg sloshed around the ham and chives like water panning for gold. Then the omelette was flipped over half, flipped again and emptied onto a warmed plate, lusciously soft and moist in the middle. Mouth-watering to consume, delicate yet satisfying, accompanied by grilled tomatoes and lightly garlic mushrooms from the hot buffet.

A fresh coffee appeared in the cup at his table without his even asking, poured deeply from a round metal serving jug by a waiter dressed in a white kurta. The milk he joined with it from the compact steel jug on his table added a rich and creamy texture to the beverage. A touch of fresh ground pepper to spice up the tomatoes. He was enjoying this.

So it was understandable that he did not notice O'Brien stride into the restaurant after a steady stroll across the compound's lawns from the opposite direction to Howard's losman. She helped herself to a grapefruit, an apple juice, and a coffee from the waiter as she glided between the tables to slide into the chair opposite him. He looked up into her beautiful dark eyes and full, unadorned lips and could not help smiling, despite a mouthful of succulent omelette and tomato.

"Surprised?" she asked archly, and with uncharacteristic coquetry.

Howard shook his head, still enjoying his mouthful.

"Not at all," he swashed out of one side of his mouth, and swallowed. "I got your note."

She accepted his unspoken thanks with a demure downcast of the eyes.

"I certainly wasn't expecting Cross," he said, reaching for his coffee.

"No, he's with Nihils," O'Brien rejoined, inserting a polite teaspoon into her pre-scored grapefruit half. The bonhomie left Howard's smile as the delicious coffee slipped down his throat.

"How come everything tastes so good in the tropics?" he asked rhetorically, gazing appreciatively at his raised coffee cup as if such analysis would yield a collective answer.

"Do you know where you are?" Katharine O'Brien persisted.

"Not really," Howard admitted. "Somewhere up north, obviously. Could be Queensland or NT, even though the staff are from Asia."

"Guestworkers."

"Exactly. But we could equally be in Malaysia or Java or Timor, couldn't we? Or Thailand, or one of the Philippine states."

"Any one of the island nations in the Asia Pacific region."

"Any one."

"Do you feel safe?"

"Yes, very. Especially now that you are here. Shouldn't I?"

"I think that's up to you."

Howard gazed out over the lawns towards the sea. It was a pale but rich aquamarine, sparkling in the morning sun. The bay in which the resort was cradled curved out into the water in raised but gentle, unbroken ridges which descended to a point on either side. The backs of these two headlands were covered in dense tropical trees. They gave the bay a protected, secluded temper.

"I feel great," Howard reflected. "Better than I have in a long time. I feel well looked after. Well treated. Almost cared-for."

He looked back at O'Brien.

"Well, that's good," she said, levering a wedge of the pale fruit out of its thick rind and placing it into her mouth in a manner that both pressed and drew the juice.

"I suppose the question is, what am I doing here? I can't imagine this is a routine identity change. If Nihils is with Cross, I suspect that his experience is closer to the norm, whatever that is. I wouldn't know. This is my first time."

"It is?"

She was right. He had been approached once before to change his identity, but he had argued he needed to retain his family name for political reasons, so that his electorate could identify him with a history. That was when Adam became Howard; a minor compromise. But it seemed like a long time ago now and definitely far away from here.

"So you are well-informed," he replied.

"Of course. And you did not believe Cross? What did he say to you, in your flat above his antique shop not twenty four hours ago?"

"Consumer choice is always with you," Howard recalled, somewhat grimly, as he also remembered the broken pieces of the Tibetan prayer bell in Cross's open hands.

"And?"

"Choice is yours. But there were definitely uniformed men with guns to assist in the choosing."

"And…"

"Yes, yes, six airline stewards, six chauffeurs, six concierges, none of them had guns. But six security operatives did. Loaded? No, I didn't think to engage in any action that tested a hypothesis that they were empty of life-threatening ordinance. And Cross was talking gibberish that ended in him calling us his hollow men. Wasn't that threatening? Intimidating? Potentially life-eviscerating? He had been watching us all along."

175

"So?"

"So…" Howard paused before he swallowed more bait, and took another gulp of his coffee, which was going cold. "No, other people think they have privacy in their homes, Katharine. Just because I know what I know about the information-gathering powers of the Consumer Choice Chip doesn't mean that I should not hold the same values. Cross was using surveillance. Opticals concealed in the room."

"And you think there aren't similar surveillance facilities in every home?"

Howard sighed.

"Alright, but why? Why would you bother to do that?"

"Why do we do what we do with the CCC?"

"Market research."

"And not social control? You have a theory that we are into social engineering, don't you? You believe that we work strategically behind the scenes to move finances across borders in order to create labour markets and growth opportunities in order to effect a capitalist growth spiral in what is essentially, in fourth phase progress, a flat global economy."

"Well, it makes sense, doesn't it. Why else does government work so hard to attract your investment?"

"And of course you know the answer to that."

"Ipso facto."

"Ever the scholar."

Another waiter, of the same slight Asian build and features, equally dressed in a cooling kurta, offered more coffee and milk, which Howard gratefully accepted. O'Brien took hers black with a slice of lemon. They both gazed out at their tranquil surrounds.

"So you don't really believe Cross," O'Brien continued after a while, but not looking back at him.

He, however, glanced at her.

"You are sceptical," she said, lingering over her enunciation of the word 'sceptical'.

He nodded. He remembered her using the same word with Nihils during the meal at her house.

"And that is why you are here," she continued, returning to meet his eyes. "To see whether you can be convinced that Cross is correct. That democracy is freedom, freedom is choice, and that choice is the consumer's. That this is the truth, and not just a catch phrase, or a buyline, or-"

"A cheap and exhaustive exercise in ideospeak," said Howard, completing her sentence for her. "And you want me to believe that?"

"I want you to know it. I want you to experience it. I want you to understand it to be true, to discover its truth."

"That I can have everything. Anything."

"Choose. You can choose anything. Obviously you have to invest the appropriate effort in attaining it. Nothing is free. Not even good will."

"Not even free will."

"Ah, a philosopher. So your scepticism is bedded deep, Howard. You lead the life you do, in government, but yet you suspect it to a fundamental level. You don't believe you have choice at all."

Again Howard chose not to take the bait. Instead, he retrieved control of the conversation.

"But why now?" he said. "Why me? Or are there lots of me here? All here for the persuading."

"You thought you were going to be punished, didn't you? You thought you had been discovered, that what you and Nihils were

177

doing was wrong, and that your time had come." O'Brien was not to be diverted. "But why should you be? What had you done but exercise choice – or free will, as you call it? Even your forays into the cybernet as Mick Turition, what was wrong with them? The cybernet remains free space – even government fails to regulate it, as you well know. There are rooms and rooms full of authorised counter-hackers in the otherwise deserted CBDs of the old coastal cities trying to keep the cybernet virus-free, let alone ethically or ideologically clean. So Mick Turition gets to look behind the facades, into a few grimy corners. So what?"

"I'm obviously not as clever as I thought I was. And neither is Nihils, I suspect."

"Nihils rarely is. You need to know about him."

Howard said nothing. He looked out across the lawn. He did not say what was in his mind: "I need to know more immediately what I am doing here." But he might have well.

"There's no second agenda, Howard. I want you to believe you have choice. If you could choose something you wanted, right now, what would it be?"

Howard tried not to look into Katharine O'Brien's irresistibly beautiful brown eyes. He tried to keep his mouth from salivating at the thought of what she might look like unclothed, and what it might be like to make love with her.

"Can I go anywhere here?" he asked her instead, still looking out at his surrounds.

She laughed, easily, generously.

"I'm not your gaoler, Howard. How do you know I'm not just here for a holiday myself?"

"Because you know that Nihils is with Cross. And I doubt they are here."

178

"Why don't we meet later in the day, and we can talk some more? Go anywhere you like. Relax. Have a good time. My choice is a swim. Hence just the grapefruit. The chef's on duty here for another two hours yet."

She smiled at him and rose from the table, swished her wrist across the CCC scanner at the restaurant's bookings desk and strode out across the lawn without looking back.

Chapter Twenty-Two

Howard looked at the nape of Katharine O'Brien's neck, amazed to find that she was still there. He could smell her sweat, so different from his. And whatever it was she washed her hair in now mingled with other bodily odours. If he shifted slightly, he could detect the intense acrid stench of their sex, wafting up from beneath the sheets. It made him want to make love with her again, and he could feel his penis stiffening.

He had thought there would be some lengthy intellectual foreplay before they had sex. If, indeed, they ever had sex at all. But that afternoon, Katharine O'Brien knocked on the door of his losman and entered. "Do you want to make love?" she asked plainly.

"Of course," Howard replied clumsily, feeling uncovered.

"Of course you do. Why wouldn't you? I'm told I am a very attractive woman. I find myself attractive too. When I masturbate, I imagine myself having sex with someone like myself."

She undid the sarong she had tied around her neck in a halter and let it fall to the floor. Underneath it, she was completely naked except for her scuffs, which she let slip first from one foot then another. She stepped across and lay on her side on the bed, facing him.

"So am I?"

Howard could not think what to say.

"Will I go?"

"No. No, please."

"So what will you do?"

She was looking Howard up and down.

"Sorry," he apologised, trying to remove his clothes without fumbling. When his underpants came off, his penis was

180

embarrassingly erect. But she continued to smile at him, and opened her arms when he approached the bed.

Sex with Katharine O'Brien was of the sort he had dreamt of with a woman for most of his adult life. She had no hesitation in taking his penis into her mouth after their first languorous kiss. And he revelled in sinking his tongue as deeply into her delicious vagina as he could. The more she drew on his sex, the more he plunged his tongue into hers. Moving his lips back up her lithe body, he found her breasts dropping elegantly with age, long and rounding into the most inviting aureoles, the teat in the centre of which he teased with his tongue and drew deep into his mouth.

Her long legs eased across his and he was inside her before he knew it, warm and sliding as if drawn into her womb itself. He was losing himself in the rhythm of their lovemaking and the exhaustiveness of their entwining tongues. Her buttocks were long and slender, and he loved the feel of the muscles in them working her hips against his. As their rhythm intensified, she brought her knees up to sit astride him and bore down upon his penis. He gripped her buttocks even harder and she presented a breast for his mouth to engorge. She began to vocalise. It was a downy, dark moan. As he drew and drew upon her breast, the other nipple brushed across his chest. He was moist with sweat. They both were.

At the last minute, she switched breasts, and guided one hand into the cleft between her taut cheeks. He allowed his middle finger to slide in and gently depress her anus. As she climaxed, he found his own gasps caught in his throat, waves of yelping forcing themselves against the breast full in his mouth. He panted free, the breast dropping to his chest. His prostate seemed to surge and surge again. He was sure he would disappear inside her forever.

Finally their heaving subsided. Their breathing returned to mere sighs. She let her legs slide back down along the length of his and relaxed onto his still throbbing frame. He kissed her tenderly on the cheeks. He wanted to tell her he loved her. He caressed her buttocks, and the small of her back. And then he drifted into a deep, deep sleep.

Now that he was awake, he found she had covered them both loosely with a sheet, and fallen asleep herself. It was still light outside, but light was fading. He could hear voices passing. Sounded like people on their way to the bar for a drink. He wondered whether he would like a drink himself. But the smell of Katharine O'Brien's rich, salty vagina drew his penis to her back.

"So you're awake then?"

She spoke, but did not move.

He kissed the nape of her neck and pressed his erection into her buttocks.

"Evidently," he said.

She turned to face him, kissed him, and they made love once more.

*

"So you see," she said to him finally, "It is possible to choose something you want, and have it easily."

He was disappointed for a moment. They were sitting in bathrobes on the veranda of his losman, having showered and fixed themselves a gin and tonic. The sun had set as they watched, and now the reddened sky above the horizon was deepening into a burnt umber. Howard could still see its glow burnishing O'Brien's face. A light breeze came up from the sea as waves lapped the shore.

"You mean me?" he said, fishing defensively.

But she smiled and threw back her head with a half laugh.

"And me, don't you think?"

182

"But it was a lesson."

"It was instructive. And it was enjoyable."

"Do you do it often?"

"As often as I want to. But probably not as often as your friend Nihils."

There was still laughter in her voice. But the implication did not escape Howard. He looked down into his drink.

"Yes, I hadn't thought…"

"Oh don't worry about me, silly. I'm not perturbed by the fact that you'd fuck a little runt like him. He usually is, as I'm sure he told you the first time, very clean. But I'm afraid he does make a bit of a habit of discovering people like you and – how shall I put it? – attaching himself to them."

"You make me sound gullible."

"I think 'transparent' is probably a better term. You come across as an honest man, Howard. A man of integrity. Vulnerable. It's endearing. Even during negotiation – at which, by the way, you *are* very good – your authenticity is disarming. Endearing even."

"So you fancied me."

"Probably not as much as you fancied me. It was terribly obvious, I'm afraid. But nevertheless, yes. I fancied you. Not that I need to, of course."

"What do you mean?"

She looked at him for a long and steady moment.

"You don't quite get it, do you?" she said after a while. "I'm not in love with you Howard. We're not having an affair. We just had a fuck. I enjoyed it. But I can enjoy it as I choose to. I may be an attractive woman, but I'm also a reasonably powerful one."

Howard felt uncomfortable. Like a puppy.

"Don't get me wrong. I don't have tickets on myself. I just have a good idea of who I am, and what I'm capable of, and what I need to do to get what I want. Please don't be disappointed."

Nevertheless, disappointment was what Howard found himself sinking deeper into.

"Didn't you want it too?" she asked him rhetorically.

"Yes. You know I did."

"So why such a long face?"

"I don't know. I just … I guess I expected it …"

"To mean something."

Howard nodded, and sipped his gin for comfort.

"And it didn't?"

"Well, it did to me." He was almost sulking now. He couldn't bear himself.

"And it didn't to me? Didn't I just say that I chose it, wanted it, enjoyed it? Why does there need to be more, Howard? Why does there need to be attachment? Cathexis?"

Cathexis. Now there was a word he had not heard in a long time.

O'Brien breathed in the evening air.

"Isn't this just beautiful?" she said, closing her eyes.

And Howard noticed again the fabulous gloaming sky, and palms now silhouetting against the sea, the smell of soft salty air and, now, the aromas of barbecuing meat and seafood wafting from the restaurant. A large black bird swung across the sunset.

"Yes," he said with honesty, "Yes it is."

"See?" said O' Brien. "It doesn't need to matter."

"No," Howard agreed, and smiled at his sentiments. "No it doesn't."

"Hungry?" she asked.

"Ravenous," he nodded.

And they re-entered his losman to dress for dinner.

Chapter Twenty-Three

Katharine O'Brien actually had to return to her own losman to dress for dinner. For obvious reasons, neither the bath robe supplied in the room nor the sarong in which she had arrived that afternoon seemed sufficient. For Howard, shorts and a holiday shirt would have been fine, but he made an effort and donned slacks and a more business-like, if still short-sleeved shirt. He drew the line at shoes and socks. There was a rather comfortable pair of leather sandals he chose instead. An entire wardrobe of clothes had been supplied which, miraculously, matched both his taste and his various sizes.

"You chose them yourself over the years," O' Brien explained over dinner. "Most of your reactions to goods when shopping are monitored."

She noticed Howard's eyes involuntarily flick around for internal vision.

"And by CCC," she qualified, following his eyes. "We just bought in the information we didn't have and threw together a quick wardrobe you would never buy for yourself, because you thought it was just beyond your price range."

Howard had to admit that, with just a cursory rifle through the wardrobe during the day, he was pleasantly surprised at the quality of the material.

"Just to show you that you can," O'Brien concluded.

"I'm paying for this?" For the first time, Howard was alarmed as well as surprised.

"Well, not yet. But you will. When you can afford it."

"And when will that be?"

"When you make the kind of decisions about your future I think you know you are here to make."

Howard sipped his soup from a spoon in order to digest this information.

"I don't really know, you know. The conversations have been arcane. You haven't spelt out to me what I am here for. What the decisions are."

"What you mean is that I haven't offered you the job."

"Or even outlined what job that might be."

"That's because we're not sure yet. Either about the job, or about your suitability for it. We don't trust you, Howard; surely that's obvious. Of course we're interested in the man who invented VIVO, but that was a while ago. Do you want to achieve or not? Do you want to succeed or not? Do you want to make the step up or not? What do you want to do? The choice is yours."

He sipped more soup uncomfortably.

O'Brien sighed with barely concealed irritation.

"So there would be an increase in salary," he ventured, trying to re-enter the conversation at a level he could control. But O' Brien lost patience and threw her napkin onto the table in anger.

"Of course there'll be a bloody increase in salary! What the fuck do you think we're talking about? At the moment, Howard, you're like everybody else. You're up to your ears in lawdebt from your stupid bloody speeding fines. You have an education debt from three higher education qualifications dragging along strapped to your heels. And you've been moonlighting as a cyber journalist. If we wanted, we could have you arrested for bankruptcy and money knows what else a hundred times over by your own authorities, by the very nation state you represent and supposedly occupy a leadership role in. You'd never see the light of day, and we'd have your mother inside to because the debt would be passed up the line, and your two previous wives because the debt would be passed horizontally. That's the world you live in. That's the world everybody lives in."

"But you don't," he shot back quietly after the briefest of pauses.

187

O'Brien folded her arms with an exasperated expulsion of breath and looked left and right as if seeking some less pathetic object for her attention. Finally she looked down into her own meal.

"No, actually I share the same sorts of debts," she admitted. "But at least I understand where they come from, how they are managed, and am on a plan that will ensure I trade beyond them into my future."

This was beyond Howard.

"It's difficult to explain in one night, Howard, over one meal. But as you suspect, there is an inner working to capital, there are strategies at work within it that enable you to have hope, to have a future, to understand freedom in a way that transcends the institutionalising naturecreep of debt and credit."

Naturecreep – another concept he had not heard from for a while.

"You wanted to understand the strategic nature of capital at its centre, didn't you?"

"Yes," said Howard, but still with some ambivalence.

"Then you have to make choices. But they have to be choices that are in your interest."

As she had in a previous conversation, she paused slightly before the final word of the sentence and enunciated the full syllabic structure of 'interest' cryptically.

This was starting to sound like a conundrum.

"What sort of choices?" he asked nevertheless.

"About the attachments you have to sentiments and ways of thinking that restrain you, that hold you back."

At this point, luckily more wine arrived, and their main meals. They ate in silence for a while, but Howard was frantically thinking: Where to go next? How not to make any further a fool of himself.

"So what are the choices I have to make Katharine?" he ventured finally

"Well," she commenced, "You already seem to have made one."

She left a pregnant pause but, try as he might, Howard couldn't second-guess the right answer. As usual, there were just too many possibilities for the rational mind. His decision to agree to the final deal with Transcorp? His questions about the inner strategies of capital? His decision not to resist his non-arrest? His decision to make love with her? His decision to order the duck instead of the steak? So finally, yet again, he gave in to the prescribed rhetoric.

"So what was that? I'm sorry, but I make so many decisions."

"True," she conceded. "I was thinking about Nihils."

She left a moment for the topic to sink in. As indeed it did. He did not need her to say what she said next.

"You haven't even missed him, have you?"

"Well I've had ... other interests." He tried to sound coy.

"I'm not sure I appreciate the comparison."

"I worry about him."

"Because you think he is being tortured."

"The evidence of my own experience here would mitigate against that."

"One of the most intelligent observations you've made to date, Howard."

"Nevertheless yes, I know he's not had a good time in the past in such circumstances. So why would things change?"

"Fatalism. You see? You are cathected with fatalism as a personal ideology. You believe people are tied neo-genetically into life pathways that afflict them with negative outcomes regardless of the choices they make. Pre-determined almost. Teleology. Creation by design. The god who knows your future, because he – and sadly it still usually *is* a he – fashioned the pathway. And it is, for the most part, bound in with the fall from grace. Doom. Sin. Hell. You're a Christian, Howard. By default."

"I didn't think we referred to those religions these days," he quipped before he could check himself.

"Yes, that's right, you heard yourself even as you spoke, didn't you? The ideological dogma of the day. You are emotionally bound to your critique of ideology. You have never accepted the Society Standards Sects. You remember the religion of your youth and automatically believe it has greater veracity. Atavistic authenticity.

"And yet you don't believe, do you? You don't believe even in that Christian God. Or the Hindu God – or rather, the full and astounding range of Hindu Gods. Let alone the plethora of Old China deities, and where will we go next in the world? Comparative religion. You'd have a sociological or ethnographic view of it, wouldn't you? Cultural relativist? Or even post-modernist – counter psychological, the decentering of the subject. That would still have been popular when you went to university. The last vestige of social sciences that were by then passé. Humanity's last call in the face of economic rationalism. Have I found you?"

Howard smiled sheepishly.

"But you don't feel sinful for having sex with Nihils. For feeling the way you did about him?"

And it was true. He didn't.

"No, I mean I miss him. I really enjoyed sex with him. It blew my mind – to have the freedom to finally give in to it."
"More teleology? You really ARE homosexual?"

"Of course not," he was not pretending now. "I really enjoyed my time with Nihils. I mean yes, it was a revelation, to be able to finally explore that part of myself. I did *love* it in that sense. But I enjoyed the cups of tea afterwards too. The laughter. We got on well. He has a great sense of humour, sees the funny side of most things. And I found him a great asset. His understanding of the underside, the other world, and of cyberspace - it was better than mine-"

"Ah, pride."

"Yes, bugger it. I know cyberspace, Katharine. I'm one of this nation state's - "

"Yes, yes, I know. But you were in love with him, weren't you."

"No, that's what I'm saying. He was really cute. I loved his little tail curling up out of the base of his spine, and parting so neatly into his pert little cheeks. I genuinely liked him and found him really attractive. I'm getting an erection just thinking about him. But I didn't love him."

"Just as you didn't love me."

"Well ... "

"You think you would," she completed his sentence. She had caught him again. He sighed and smiled at the same time, shaking his head slightly.

"It's what I'm used to," he simpered, trying to sound adult.

"Heterosexual emotional interdependence."

"And sexual," he qualified.

"The dominant paradigm. After all of these years of selling multiple marriages and inter-gender sex. Have we failed so miserably?"

"So I need to give that up?"

"You don't need to give anything up, Howard. You need to make choices that are in your best interest. You've already done that with Nihils, haven't you?"

The Mersault was getting the better of him. He couldn't remember enough of his brief relationship with Nihils to remember its emotional history in its entirety.

"The first time you had sex you told him you loved him," O'Brien prompted.

Howard couldn't believe the reach of their surveillance. He visibly shook his head in disbelief, but quickly recovered.

"It was just the magic of it, Katharine. Of discovering that in myself. Just as it was with you this afternoon. Honestly, that *was* the best."

And he could feel her floating out from the mooring, a boat to sea.

"And I should feel flattered."

He shook his head again, laughing in disbelief at his own clarity.

"I don't give a fuck what you feel. Really. Sorry."

Ironically, she smiled.

"Please don't be sorry. That's perfect."

He still shook his head, trying to clear his mind for whatever might come next. This entire conversation was confounding.

"Two profound sexual discoveries, by your account. And yet you have already overcome the need to cathect them as love; as emotional experiences that automatically bind you into a meta-analysis of symbolic proportions, to fix them in time with moral obligation towards the objects of your desire. You see how easy it is, Howard? To exercise choice?"

"Sure," he said, slightly drunk and nodding. "So that's what this is about? Separating myself from my emotions?"

"No, of course you've done that for years. You do that every day in your professional life. But love, Howard. Is that something you would choose to de-prioritise in the face of other pressing imperatives?"

Howard was back on the shifting sand again.

"Well, I suppose … " he said, without finding anywhere to go.

"Two wives. You didn't love them?"

"Well yes. But after a while ... and no, the second marriage was political. I haven't known love in a long while, Katharine."

"Much though you have wanted to. You don't think that was a contributory factor in your suicide attempt?"

Mother of Money, thought Howard with internal alarm, they know everything. He couldn't let his naivety show any further.

"Yes alright, I've missed it. I think it should be a part of my life. I think – or hope – it's never too late. I buy the mythology." As if confession would deflect her.

"And you think most other people don't? You think that most lovers, when they think about their partners, are more concerned about what present will satisfy them next birthday? Next Christmas? Next Mother's Day? Next Father's Day? Next Caregiver's Weekend? Next Dogweh Feast? Next Yahlah Eve? Next Braal Breakfast Day? Next Almah Fall? You think they don't understand love in the way you do, Howard?"

He shook his head.

"I wouldn't know," he said, wishing the evening were over so that he could sleep.

"No, it's a long time since we have subscribed that calibre of qualitative research, isn't it? So is there something essential here we are missing about the human condition?"

"Well of course you would question the centrality of a concept like the human condition, wouldn't you? I mean, it's naturecreep, isn't it? A reductionist concept that, if allowed dominance in an ascendant discourse, is accorded a pre-eminence of its own, the value of an absolute principle the action of which is in fact purely cultural."

Katharine O'Brien smiled at Howard, as if he had got the joke at last. It was a smile so generous, she could have been applauding him.

"So is it a concept you could choose to think beyond, Howard? To operate beyond? Could you gain control of your seemingly ineluctable will towards cathexis in order to separate your emotions out from your intellectual experience, and from your personhood, at the same time as allowing your feeling intelligence free play to serve the interests of personal choice – free, that is, from the imperative of cathexis?"

It was too late for Howard. He was tired. The wine had mulled his brain. What was left of his duck had congealed in the fat of its sauce. He needed a strong black coffee.

"I'm sorry," he said perhaps too easily. "It's late. I'm tired."

He could hear the wine-induced slur entering his speech.

"Well that's a shame," replied Katharine O'Brien, "Because there is another important choice before you. You see, one of you has to take a mandatory identity change, either you or your mother. And I think you might understand that it's probably in both of your interests for it to not be you. Isn't that right?"

Howard Johns looked across the table at Katharine O'Brien in mild disbelief for just a moment.

"We've known about her MFE activities for a long time, Howard," O'Brien said clinically, but with that familiar half-smile. "Surely you understand it would only have been a matter of time."

Chapter Twenty-Four

Needless to say, Katharine O'Brien did not sleep with Howard that night. Nor did Howard sleep with himself much. It was a fitful night punctuated by disturbing dreams which a psychologist would have little difficulty tracing to his relationship with his mother.

After bidding O'Brien goodnight, he took his mandatory cognac for a walk along the beach. It was a full moon. The fringes of the trees that lined the two headlands arcing out into the sea to form the resort's cove glinted unashamedly in the silver light. The sea itself glistened like quicksilver, shifting oleaginously in subtle but contrary currents in the balmy evening. He could not believe that he was even considering O'Brien's proposition that he should sacrifice his mother in order to secure his own future.

All of the precepts fell into place. His mother would be nothing without him, and if he had to change his identity she would undoubtedly lose him. The misery and sorrow, along with the ultimate alienation from the present entailed in losing the last of her surviving family to, it would seem to her, politics, would break her will as well as her heart.

Of course if she took the fall instead, and Nihils was even halfway right about the fate of MIDOs, they may kill her. For she was surely too old to be re-assigned to a new labour opportunity. She would become one of the New Disappeared, as they were called in counter-ideospeak accessible only to the likes of Mick Turition. Or at least they would be, if only Mick could turn a trick and place a story.

But equally, Howard was himself a relatively powerful man. He could intervene, seek evidence of her continued good health and well being. And she might still enjoy what life she had, knowing that he was also alive and thriving. But how could she sustain identity displacement at her age? She was so tied to her community, her memories, her history, her values and beliefs, her family, her money-free exchange network. She would never accept it. And even if she agreed to the displacement, she would never adapt. He couldn't do it to her.

So what was the deciding principle here? Eventually he lay down on the soft sand and looked up at the moon overhead, listening to the waves lap some metres below his feet, his brain tired with the effort of it. It was, of course, an assumption on his part that identity displacement entailed a death of some sort, not the simple transfer of persons in place and material disposition portrayed in consumerspeak. To surrender one's identity was to die. That was his belief. Katharine O'Brien would ask him what evidence there was for this logic. And all he could offer was the logic of opposition, of questioning the received wisdom, distrust of the propagandist lucidity of ideology with its freedom from grounded theory or pure logic, its disconnection from the persuasive balance of evidence.

Ironically, ineluctably, his fundamental cathexis was with scepticism, with absolute distrust of the emotionality that made ideology so attractive, so emblematic of truth rather than truth itself. He was embedded in the emotional infidelity of ideology. O'Brien's fundamental proposition was, he knew, intellectual rubbish. There had to be a rational way around the bureaucratic dice she had thrown before him. Him or his mother? Who said? Why? A due process could be re-processed. And hadn't she talked so much about the strategies at the centre of capital that could achieve solutions beyond the received morality, the perceived inevitability of 'law' and 'debt' and 'credit'? So couldn't that intelligence just re-arrange the choices with a click of its metaphorical global fingers?

It was all too clever by half, and it astounded him that he was even thinking about committing his mother to an uncertain future or, indeed, end. And *in* the end, his mind could find no place to settle. He returned to his losman, too tired to stay awake. But when he slept, it was in a relentless travail from one dream to the next. By dawn, he was exhausted, but unable to remain in bed any longer. He went for a swim beyond the palms in the cool, lazy waters of the

196

bay. When he emerged, the sun was full above the horizon, its rays already warm on his back.

He showered, drank tea on his veranda and allowed the early bird life to find the tenor of the day. Once dressed, he sauntered across to the main restaurant for breakfast. And noted, with unreasonable jealousy, O'Brien perambulating across the lawn to the beach with another man on her arm. Laughing coquettishly, or as one who had come from a night of love. I mean, of course I didn't expect, he prevaricated with himself; but so soon?

It was not until, after a full buffet breakfast, including tastes from the impressive array of hot bahasa dishes on offer, that Howard recognised the man now entering the dining area with O'Brien. O'Brien spotted him immediately, and brought her companion over.

"Howard, good morning. Isn't it beautiful? You remember Bishop, of course."

"Of course," Howard said, narrowing his eyes. Bishop was, like himself, dressed in a calibre of style just beyond his usual financial reach and vision. And, it took Howard a couple of beats to work it out, he had permed his hair. The once fairly buoyant but kempt crop was now a tousled mop of rather gay curls. "A bit far from home, eh Bishop?"

Howard Johns extended his hand without rising.

"Bruce, please," Bishop said, taking it in a firm but relaxed handshake.

"Bruce?" Katharine echoed to Bishop with an amused smile.

"Howard insisted on first names. Unlike Cedric Simpkins," Bishop smiled back. It was the first time Howard had seen the loyal legislative data analyst exhibit anything resembling a sense of humour, let along wry irony. He was almost winking at her.

Katharine O'Brien responded by raising her eyebrows at him in askance.

197

"Shall I, er ...?"

"Yes, of course," Bishop replied with assurance. And O'Brien strode off, her shift flowing from her shoulder as she went.

"Mind if join you?" Bishop gestured the vacant chair in front of Howard. "I'm not eating."

"Of course," Howard conceded urbanely. "I'm almost done anyway."

Bishop sat down and looked out over the lawns towards the palm-fringed beach with an ease Howard did not readily identify with him. It could have been a completely different person to the man who, just days before, had been locked with him in the final stages of a negotiation with Transcorp.

"I expect you're surprised to see me here," said Bishop finally, without actually looking at Howard.

"Yes. Especially in your ... present company."

"You're my present company, Howard," said Bishop smoothly, cleanly, smiling at him wryly. "Katharine and I are just good friends. I don't suppose you noticed her approach to me, did you?"

"On the launch? To Warrnambool?"

Bishop shook his curly locks with a smile.

"All the time, Howard. I noticed her approaches to you. All the time."

Howard was embarrassed at his ego. But said nevertheless,

"So you haven't slept with her."

"We talked about it. About whether each of us wanted to. I admitted that I did. Katharine was frank about the fact that she didn't. And I was equally frank about the fact that I actually wouldn't anyway. Because I love my wife, Howard. Despite yours and Cedric's jibing about second marriages. I love my wife, and I love my children."

"So are you avoiding selling them off for an identity displacement order? What's she offering?"

"It's not like that, Howard. There is no subterfuge, no twisting of the arm, no ideological cat and mouse. I've been offered a choice, and I'm taking it. Because I find I have services people want to pay for. Have you finished your coffee? Shall we walk?"

*

When they reached the beach, both men in shorts, they removed their sandals and sauntered first to one end of the beach and then to the other. Then they sat under the shade of a palm. It was nearly lunchtime by the time their conversation petered out. Howard Smithson Johns learnt some surprising and unsettling things about his former bureaucratic colleague. That his new identity was, for instance, to be John Howard Smithson. "I did it in honour of you, Howard. You have been a real role model for me."

He also learnt that Bishop was here with his new team, a Transglobal employee now, planning for the water project he had just secured the legislative passage for, and also for a bold new move into geothermal for Tranglobal in SA.

"So it's a sort of planning retreat?" Howard tried to understand their presence at a five star resort.

"No, it's just routine. Transglobal project teams work anywhere, Howard. They have, after all, the whole globe to choose from."

Another thing Howard learnt about Bishop was that he was prepared to leave his family in order to take up the new identity.

"As you probably knew long before I did, Howard, it is perfectly possible from within capital to monitor just about anything. I have been guaranteed access to all of the CCC and other data on my wife and children whenever I choose. I will make sure they are well taken care of, one way or another."

"But you love them!"

199

"Exactly."

Bishop – or Smithson, as he was in the process of becoming – actually smiled at him without artifice or affect. It was a genuine, unashamed smile, full of love.

"I don't need to be with them physically to continue loving them, Howard," he explained. "It is enough for me to know that, through my future efforts and choices, I can continue to ensure they are well provided for, and have the choices they need to make an enjoyable and fruitful life."

"But don't you worry that they will miss you? They will be heartbroken, surely, full of loss and grief at your disappearance?"

"They will be informed I have undertaken an identity displacement. They will be pleased for me. They will know I am safe, and that so are they. We have faith in the system, Howard. Unlike Simpkins, who had no faith at all."

Howard shook his head in disbelief.

"I think you never got to know me very well, Howard. I suspect I am not like you. I am no 'high flyer'. I have skills, and knowledge, and the intelligence to use both to good effect. But I have no great aspirations. Under Transglobal, my sons can access an education that involves face-to-face teaching, with a real teacher live there in front of them. I know such values are passé these days, but I happen to believe in them. With money, I can choose for them the sort of education I believe to be in their best interests.

"They will learn real history – the rise of capital, the four phases of progress, the history of the global economy, economic migration, mathematics, cyberskills. At the moment my children are subjected to mindless hours of ideobrief, Howard, about the rights of guestworkers and the social enrichment to be had from transborder cultures, and why it was so useful for VIC's handful of remaining indigenous people to have a treaty with the rest of us. It's all such irrelevant rubbish, when they could be learning values and skills that prepare them for the world as it is. Family values. Work values. I can buy that for them now, Howard."

"Sleeping with Katharine O'Brien is inconsequential compared to such benefits. I cannot tell you how happy I am with the choice I have made. I am not a leader like you Howard. I am grateful for my opportunities."

One part of Howard's mind was certain Bishop was a plant, to try and persuade him to the virtues of Katharine O'Brien's freedom from cathexis. Here was Bishop, the model convert, the ideal acolyte. If only Howard could be more like him, the script ran. But if he was a contrivance, Bishop certainly seemed innocent of the fact. He revealed more about himself to Howard in their walk on the beach than he did in the entire period they worked together in VIC Parliament. The man was authentic.

"Anyway," he said after a while, "I should get back. Need my sleep for tomorrow. Katharine said I could have time off if I wanted to spend more time with you, but I'm part of a new team now. Hope you're not offended Howard. You're a lucky man."

As he stood up to shake hands with the new John Howard Smithson, Howard's mind was befuddled with conflicting thoughts. On one hand, he was reminded he had dropped out of the 36 hour day in which Bishop – Smithson – was clearly still operating. On another hand, he was confused about why he was 'lucky' in Bishop Smithson's eyes. The inference that Bishop was referring to O'Brien seemed all too easy. Or did Bishop know something about what was planned for Howard's future that he as yet did not? And then there was the artless formality of Bishop's apology. So unnecessary, so lacking in guile, such well-considered communication skills – it made Howard want to cry at the simplicity of it.

But all he did was shake Bishop's hand and smile.

"Take care Bishop. Or is it Smithson now?"

"Well, the team know me as Smithson. So I guess…"

John Howard Smithson smiled the smile of a man who had recently found Dogweh (or Yahlah, or Braal, or Ahlma), turned, and ambled off through the palms towards the low main resort buildings with an unaffected gait, and a casual wave that did not look back.

Chapter Twenty-Five

After traversing the length of it twenty four times, the beach along the resort's foreshore became very short. And with each lap, Howard's demeanour became more and more intense. Why was it so easy for Bishop – now Smithson – to believe? Why had he no sense of history? Why did he not remember the last position presented by ideospeak and compare it to the one before that? Put two and two together and see the internal inconsistencies? It was understandable for the majority, the consumers. They were given no alternative. Their world of information was strictly controlled and guided by the collusion of commerce and government to ensure the economic system that brought them well being and prosperity continued.

But even as he slipped into such thinking he knew he was succumbing to conspiracy theory. He sought a centre of meaning to everything. To become the meta-analyst O'Brien seemed to want of him, to de-cathect himself from the need to make every aspect of his existence meaningful to some conceptual core, to separate the meaningful from the decision, he would need to deracinate that core driver to his thinking being: his desire to intellectually reduce experience to essence. Surrender his centring of self, his ontology. It was impossible to imagine.

But then the O'Brien in his mind would recall the issue: he was not being asked to change fundamentally; just decide whether it was better that he or his mother should undertake the identity displacement. And he would be caught up afresh in the pro's and cons of this debate, which would lead him once more to his sceptical position that the premise itself was false: the inner workings of capital could find a way round the either/or proposition, as they found a way around everything else. Which in turn led him back to what it would take to make the quantum jump into O'Brien's headspace, the deracination of his own essentialism. And round he would go again.

203

The more he paced the beach, the more his mind became locked in a cycle of thought he could not break out of. And the more immersed in the cycle he became, the more it occurred to him that both he and his mother were in danger. Why else would they have been thrown together in this logical vice? How did O'Brien know of an identity displacement imperative that was normally the preserve of government? What did it have to do with Transcorp? Yet O'Brien came armed with it, as a threat. Clearly the choice was an artifice, an impossible conundrum. In fact, neither mother nor son was intended to thrive. Neither would win by the choice.

He needed to know more, desperately. But there was no netface in his losman. He touched his pocket. His cell card was still with him. But there had been no reception in his losman. He flipped out the slim strip of polymer anyway and found, to his good fortune, a signal. If he could log on to Mick Turition, he might be able to penetrate MIDO security barriers to find out what was intended for his mother.

But Mick was not in the mood for instructions. He was slashing his way through a jungle, sweating both from exertion and the humidity. The land was riven with small, steep ravines, and it was easy to become disorientated. But Mick's firm satellite fix had brought him over a ridge to view a brand spanking new mega-mine right in the heart of the jungle.

Where are we? Howard asked Mick, risking VIVO. "New Java," the cyber champion replied breathlessly. "I've found him, Howie. I've found him." Mick kept on repeating the statement as he thrashed his way down the incline and breached the perimeter of the mine compound. There was infrared vision everywhere. He was sure to be seen. Here in this gaping bleached cut in the jungle, the glare of alloy pipe, emission stacks, storage facilities and machinery made sight difficult. And there was no protection from the ozone-free sun. Workers trudged around like automatons, bowed under the oppression of the atmosphere as much as their work demands. They looked like ants between the large trucks and earth movers that dominated the site. But Mick quickly made his way to a low, long facility that looked like a portable meeting room or bunkhouse.

Mick took Howard up to the window, and then through the white grime that obscured it. It was a workers' cafeteria. Exhausted men and women ate in silent rows, mouths too tired almost to chew. Their clothing and hands were ingrained with a fine white dust. Their eyes red-rimmed and lifeless. They all wore cloth caps with short peaks, which also looked battered and the worse for wear. The food on the plastic plates on the bench before them looked unappetising.

"See?" Mick said, pointing into their midst. "See? There he is?"

"Who, for money's sake?" asked Howard irritably. He had other urgent business.

"There! It's him?"

"Who!"

But even as he shouted at his cell card, he could see the face Mick was focussing. If it wasn't for the familiar hawk-like nose, and his obvious height above the rest even while seated, Howard wouldn't have recognised Simpkins. He looked older, tauter in features than before, haggard almost. So it was true. This was the fate of the MIDOs. Nihils has been right.

Mick turned to see two shadows materialise not five metres away. They immediately turned towards him.

"Gotta go!" he said, and the vision faded. But Howard needed to know no more. He now understood well enough what would be planned for his mother if she undertook the MIDO. And it would not be the positive alternative facing the pro-choice, compliant Bishop.

He knew now that he needed to reach his mother, urgently. If the two of them were together, they were a dialectic solution to the false bi-polar proposition. There need be no either/or, because together they could defend their interdependent identities as a new state, a state beyond the either/or.

During his successive passages along the beach, he had noticed the occasional gunboat traversing the horizon. The place to which O'Brien had brought him was clearly associated with military operations. But that also meant there would be sea as well as airborne means of escape. He had to get back home, fast. But it was also important he avoided detection. If he left via the airport by which he had presumably arrived, his movements would be known. But if he headed around the arm of the bay from which direction the gunboats came, he might find his way to some alternative form of transport.

Before he knew it, Howard had left the beach and was making his way up into the tropical vegetation foresting the high-ridged promontory encircling one side of the bay. His mind was now planning ways in which he might argue his way through border control if he was, indeed, outside Australia – for he had certainly entered through no border control on his way in, and so would be a suspicious presence to another nation state. But O'Brien and Transcorp had access to the intimate details of his life. Even his sex life with Nihils, which he had gone to such lengths to conceal. They would be alerted to his departure the minute he registered his CCC on a ticketing machine or at a border point or to make a purchase anywhere in the world. They would be able to track his exertions at this very moment through his CCC transmissions.

For Howard realised he was experiencing considerable physical distress. The vegetation was far denser than he had expected. The easy path he had taken up off the beach soon disappeared into the large flanges of giant tropical trees, which dropped creepers every which way. Then the creepers themselves became the text of the scrub. They thrust in long, horizontal branches, criss-crossed at angles, falling over each other, wrapping around each other. Before long, Howard was climbing through the horizontal and vertical scrub itself. Great hands of green foliage prised their way between the sinewy spars of creeper. Both creeper and giant leaves wrapped themselves around grey and silver trunks of giant trees slithering through space and furry trunks of tree-ferns that seemed to defy gravity. He soon had no idea where the actual ground was. And the dense canopy of deep green tropical trees that clamped this world upon the hillside prevented him from being able to tell where the sun was, or even if the sun was still there at all. Was the growing darkness due to his penetration of the forest, or the waning day? And was he even going in the right direction?

He tried to make his way up, in the hope of finding the top of the ridge to gain a view and thence his bearings, but it was impossible to tell even which way was up. At one point he fell through a layer of scrub only to find himself landing on another layer. He was losing all certainty of where he was in space at all. Running on nervous energy, he knew that if he stopped he would find himself too hungry and tired to continue. His clothes were filthy and torn. Why hadn't he noticed them tearing? His mother would never forgive him.

Howard started to sob, like a boy. He wanted his mum. He was afraid she would be dead before he reached her. Perhaps she was already dying, naturally. Perhaps that was the intelligence O'Brien had over him: that the choice she had placed before him was futile because his mother was actually dying. Yes, that made much more sense. In which case, all the more reason for him to reach her. He would phone her now to warn her. He reached for his cell card, only to find the pocket torn away, his only source of communication gone. He tore at his clothing in case the card had snagged or caught or somehow impossibly stayed with him. But it was nowhere. He was nowhere – nowhere he could grasp with any kind of physical or mental mastery. The sobbing retreated to a chill, still panic of fear.

Why was he doing this? O'Brien had said he was free to go where he wanted. Why didn't he just return to his losman, phone for transport and leave with a packed bag? He would be tracked whatever he did. But what if he were now unable to find his way out of here? What if, by the time they found him, he was himself dead of exhaustion and hunger? If he could not find his way through this entangling terrain of multi-layered scrub, how would anybody else make it through to find him? Why would they even bother? He was readily showing himself to be an irrational thinker and poor manager. Not much meta-analysis here.

Soon Howard started to laugh at himself. He found himself extraordinarily funny: the predicament into which he had worked himself. But at the same time he was crying once more, because he could not imagine how he would find his way out of this place. His skin was lashed with scratches and grazes, his clothes would not see him through a cold night, it could rain and leave him totally exposed. And he had not even begun to entertain the range of possible dangers to which he had exposed himself from the local population of animals, insects and reptiles.

Luckily, night was falling, and Howard began to make out the lights of the resort through the scrub. They moved, and were slight, or in fractions. But as he began to scramble and clamber his way back towards them, creeper by creeper, they gradually became more distinct and the calibration of a compass for him. Even though he imagined venomous snakes writhing around each bough around him, deadly scorpions scuttling between the straps of what was left of his sandals, paralysing spiders scurrying to his neck across the webs through which he found himself floundering blindly, he had a constellation of lights to work towards. He had hope. And all the while, he made sure his mother clung fiercely to his back, her arms around his throat. Hang on, mum, we can make it, he thought to himself. Hang on, mum. Hang on.

By the time he stumbled back onto the beach he had left hours before, he was exhausted beyond care. The beach was deserted. The moon had gone. Yet there was activity in the resort. And of course, Howard reminded himself, Bishop/Smithson and his team would probably still be working somewhere in there.

He dare not sit down on the beach to catch his breath. He was simply too tired to stop. So he pushed on to his losman, which had been immaculately made up in his absence. Effortlessly he found the netface he should have expected to be an automatic service offered in such a room, tucked away in a now obviously inconspicuous native wood cupboard. He quickly logged on and dialled his mother's number. Heard her voice, slightly croaky, disoriented. Had they got to her already?

"Mum?"

"Is that you Adam?"

"I just needed to talk to you."

"At this time in the morning?"

"To check you were alright."

"Well, I was alright until you woke me up. It's still dark outside, you know. Isn't it dark in Canberra?"

"Yes. Well, I'm not in Canberra. I'm – well, I'm at a resort."

"Oh, on holiday are you? Or is it work, Adam?"

"Bit of both I guess."

"But you're alright."

"Yes, sure. Sorry, I didn't realise how late it was."

"You sound worried, son."

He was too tired to think.

"Well, a bit, yes. I just wanted to check you were alright, that's all."

"So you've said, Adam. Why wouldn't I be alright?"

"I'll call you in the morning, mum."

"But you've called me now. And I've woken up. If something's the matter, Adam, you might as well talk about it now if you're going to talk about it at all. I'll just worry about it if you hang up now, you know that."

"Sorry. It's just, there's talk of an identity displacement."

"Who? Who's talking? Have you had a notification? It needs to be a formal notification."

"Only if you don't have cybernet. Look, maybe we should talk about this in the-"

"Mine was formal. It came as a letter. Who's talking?"
"Someone here. Someone influential, who would know. What do you mean, a letter?"

"I've had notification that I'm up for an identity displacement."

"But ..." Despair emptied his voice of words. He felt he had lost the argument before he had even formulated it in his mind. "What are you going to do?"

"Well, what can I do? It's mandatory. I've avoided enough of them, Adam. I can't keep it up forever."

"But ... I could do it for you, Mum. I could pull a few strings..."

"You've already done that, Adam."

"Say I'll take the change instead."

"Don't be silly, son. It would ruin your career. No-one would know who you were any more. You'd need to make your political name all over again. Anyway, what do I care about a name? No-one's saying I have to move, are they?"

"Well, usually, but ... I mean, if they're not saying at this stage..."

Even as he spoke, Howard suspected he had enough influence to ensure she could remain where she was if she took the MIDO.

"You make too much out of things sometimes, Adam, do you know that? It's just a name son. I've already changed one when I married your father."

Of course she had. Why didn't he think of that?

"It was always you that worried about these identity displacements, son. I learnt long ago that the system was crook. You just avoid it as

210

long as you can, but when it finally catches up with you, what does it matter really? If it makes the bureaucrats happy. They must find it so hard to understand the world, poor souls. Like I said, Adam, I've had a good run."

"But you always sounded ... You always said..."

"Of course they made me angry, son. You resist injustice and insensibility as long as you can. But there's a limit, isn't there? You have to think about what's most important for your well being each time. Look at your father. I saw it kill him, trying to defend principle. It was never worth that, Adam. He was lost to us both then, wasn't he?"

Howard was silenced. He had never heard his mother talk this way before. Probably because he had never asked the right question.

"Okay Mum," was all he said finally; "Sorry to have bothered you. I was just worried, I guess."

"Well, you shouldn't be. I'm fine. Now go back to bed. Then I can do the same."

"Thanks Mum. Will do. Love you."

"I love you too son. Now go back to bed."

Howard released the connection and closed down the netface. Back to bed. What a joke. He fixed himself a substantial gin and tonic, and went and sat on the verandah of his losman. Light was just beginning to show on the horizon. He began to sob once more. Big, gulping, uncontrollable sobs. Horrible, little-boy's sobs with grown-man's hollering wallowing around behind them. Sob, sob, sob. Until it made his ribs hurt. Slobbering on mouthfuls of gin. Fixing himself another, his nose running with sobs. Sobbing into the sunrise. Poor, sad Howard Winston Johns. She knew, he sobbed. She knew. You bastard. You knew.

He was exhausted.

Chapter Twenty-Six

"You look wrecked," Katharine O'Brien said to him as she stepped on to his veranda the following afternoon. "I told you you could leave. I said: you could go anywhere, do anything."

For a moment, Howard thought he even detected a note of genuine compassion in her voice.

"I didn't believe you."

"And you found the netface so easily."

Howard nodded, and looked disconsolately into the remnants of the bowl of cold coffee he was nursing in his lap.

"You could die in that scrub, you know. It's not designed for tourists."

"So, you believe in design then."

She laughed lightly and shook her head in disbelief.

He smiled, for the first time that day.

He had, ironically, slept like a log. Not awoken until the sun was well up and the breakfast service long gone. But he was so hungry he couldn't eat anyway. Took some yoghurt and a bowl of latte back to his losman, and logged on to the cybernet once more.

"What were you hoping to find, Howard?" Katharine O'Brien asked enigmatically, but with a firm edge of anger.

"I was worried about my mum."

"And now you're not?"

"You know full well." Now it was his turn to barely conceal his anger.

"So she's fine, isn't she Howard. You didn't know her as well as you thought you did. You could've just called her, and found out. You made a more complex and personally costly choice, when a much simpler one would have solved the problem for you. Guilt. Self-focus. Ego. Love, even. Where did it get you?   Believing that you were the author of your future as well as your present, that you were responsible enough for others to need to protect them despite themselves. Isn't that paternalism, Howard? You think you can escape your own ideological imprinting just because you're smart, but you're just as cathected to it as anyone else."

He didn't need this.

"Family isn't ideological," he protested. He actually wanted to cry again, but held on to himself. He was, he realised, still emotionally weak from his ordeal the day before.

"So it's based on something more than a construction of ideas?"

"It's about love, and relationship," he struggled on.

"It's about identity, Howard; one in which you are happy to embed yourself – or rather, allow yourself to be embedded. It's comfortable for you to sit in the woolly insulation of your emotional self, eyes and ears locked on to the need for love and approval into which you were born. You call it family on the promise that it will protect you forever from the need to love yourself, to feel unloved. Whereas in reality it's just a system of obligation and role ascription.

"You have to love your*self*, Howard. You have to know love and understand that it doesn't have to drive you and dominate you. That you can love and still do other things with your mind, with your self. You know that's true, don't you. Think about your previous marriages. Think about Nihils."

She was right. He had believed his first marriage, to Yvonne, was 'the one', true love that would last forever. But the divergent pull of respective careers and the failure to produce progeny teased it apart in a matter of years. Love just got left around the place like pieces of torn cloth. They lost the centre of their relationship, drifted apart. And he learnt to place her in a part of his heart that he didn't need to visit.

His second marriage was far more one of companionship and convenience. They both understood how their association benefitted their respective careers, and when it ceased doing so, they parted. He told himself all along that he loved her, but when they parted she was too easy to tuck away in another part of himself, but this time one that simply needed no further attention.

As for Nihils; yes, he had found it easy to forget Nihils in the immediate days past. He felt guilty about that, it was true. But he didn't miss Nihils at all. Nihils had let him down.

"And what did you find out about me?" asked Katharine O'Brien, drawing him back to the present, and his foray into the cybernet as Mick Turition not half-an-hour before. For he had indeed been searching not for news of his mother on this most recent foray into the electronic ether he so prized.

"That you're a relatively small player in the corporate scheme of things, even though you're a hot shot executive in VIC and the Australasian region right now."

He said no more. Howard had actually found information about O'Brien whilst looking for Mick, who he eventually uncovered in an ice-bare, tiled room, being interrogated – of sorts – by a man much older than Katharine O'Brien but who also bore her surname. Mick was emaciated and sickly, half-starved, as if he had suffered deprivation for a long time. His clothes were rank and dishevelled. His eyes were sunken, hair dank and dripping with cold sweat. His nose ran. His O'Brien was holding a bamboo-like cage which seemed shaped to fit a man's face. It had straps at its curved ends, as if it would be tied around the back of the head. Large, ugly rats worried desperately from side to side, baring their teeth at shadows.

"Take Julia!" Mick was bellowing at his O'Brien. "Take Julia!"

Now that Howard looked, he could see the red welts along Mick's cheekbones, where the cage had in fact already been fastened to his face.

"Who's Julia?" Howard asked. O'Brien looked up, but not with surprise.

"I've got no fucking idea," Mick cried. "They keep wanting me to talk about her. Keep saying I'm hiding her. I've never heard of her!"

"It's okay," said a familiar voice behind Howard. Mick's O'Brien was looking beyond Howard's virtual shoulder to the source of the voice.

"He can go now," the voice said. It was Katharine's.

"And then you found…" Katharine O'Brien prompted.

"That you were watching me."

"Exactly. So why don't we log on again, Howard, and I'll take Mick a little further."

*

All the while Katharine O'Brien was taking a suddenly restored and smartly dressed Mick Turition by the hand through one level of the corporate hierarchy of Transglobal after another, from one sandwich war to another, through records of economy shifts and labour market transfers and the entire conspiracy of transcorporate manipulation of labour markets across nation state borders that Howard had always suspected was the basis of the modern economy, she was talking.

"What did you think you would find, Howard? Some strategic epicentre to the global economy? A place where the pattern of competition between the big four transcorporations became a methodical, macroscopic dance around the tactical centre of Fourth Phase of Progress? Look at it, Howard. Do you think Transglobal creates these cross-border conflicts? Do you really think we work with governments to target them and generate them on the basis of

215

some grand plan, in order to be able to transfer wholesale cohorts of identity displacement into newly deflated labour markets, generate a new source of production and supply in artificially depressed 'currency', until the newly invigorated nation state reaches global parity; whereupon we simply move to the next border conflict we have generated to start again? Is that what you expected to find?

"Look at it, Howard. Where is the grand planning? Look at the number of them. Look where they are in the world? Think about shipping lanes and the cost of air travel and the provision of infrastructure and money knows what else. For choice's sake, Howard, does it look that organised? Isn't it more likely that we go in when we see the sandwich wars emerging and capitalise upon them, pardon the pun? Isn't it more likely that we make the most of our opportunities as they arise? Make the best choices available to us from the options we find there?"

"So Nihils is wrong: you don't finance them?" Howard interrupted.

"Of course we fund them. How would your average nation state find the wherewithal to finance a major cross-border military campaign? Let alone a Third Phase country. Whereas we can have state-of-the-art military equipment transported around the world at will. For a price."

"Or a debt."

"More to the point, yes. But often, Howard, it's much easier just to manufacture such skirmishes artificially. They are just as effective infovision on The Market as they are action vision on netface entertainment."

The penny dropped.

"The action vision in the shopping world."

"You've seen one in the making then?"

He nodded.

"Of course. I apologise. It's not uncommon, especially in the older shopping worlds like the one behind your Mr Cross's establishment.

"So are you beginning to see, Howard? Think about the deal you and Bishop have just brokered with us, while you and Nihils enjoyed the now-dubious privacy of Mr Cross's upstairs bedsit. Think about the marginal advantage the deal with VIC Government gives us over Pancontinental in NSW. Where is the mega-plan? Where are the huge profits? What makes you think an organisation of the size of Transglobal or Pancontinental has the logistical capacity to work to a single strategy?

"They depend on the work of the small players like me, Howard, who look for and exploit local opportunities, make the most apposite regional choices, are where we need to be at the right time, talk to the right people. They depend on us marshalling order out of the chaos of local economies and market forces, so that the macroscopic patterns of observable capitalism can appear to remain the stable forces of economy in the world.

"Why do you think we encourage governments to marginalise the Money Free Exchange movement? It's one more element of chaos in the market place we just don't need, Howard, at the level where we need to be the most effective – the local."

"Do you remember what happened to the small investors? No, no-one does. They simply disappeared into the chaos, unable to make enough of a return to insulate themselves against the meteorological scale of market forces.

"And what happened to the larger investors, Howard? Why don't we have a stock market any more? Because it became irrelevant once money became irrelevant, once the transcorps became large enough to have no need of other competitors' money. In Fourth Phase Progress, economy is sealed. I know you understand this already, Howard. Yes, the growth spiral is an illusion based on the harnessing of minor fluctuations in labour cost and corresponding shifts in production geography. But for any real fuel, Howard, the economy depends on the essential micro-generational nature of chaos at the local level. Do you understand?

"Think logically. Think back in history. From the moment big government offered an open cheque book to underwrite the banks, both were useless. Money was dead from that moment. The power of investment was lost. Debt became currency. We just call it credit."

She was right. He knew all of this. But Howard couldn't help wondering what he was hanging on to. Subterfuge? Underground? Counter-revolution? Class? It all seemed so irrelevant in Katharine O'Brien's world order – or world of disorder. He loved his mum. There was no getting round it. Giving her up was simply something he thought he could never do. Even though he knew now he did not need to. For she had given up herself. Or rather, someone he didn't know had emerged from part of the mother he loved without question. Love could be teased apart and compartmentalised. He could work with it, rather than be immersed in it.

But still he found it hard to let go of what he had held onto for so long as his sense of her, and all she was. So would he dissemble? Would Katharine O'Brien have sex with him again if she thought he could surrender his mother? She had once before. She had seen him in the flesh. They had been joined. Intimacy had an imperative of its own. It carried the presumption of interior knowledge – but did sex reveal that much about the mind? The emotions? He knew this was untrue, despite his desire that it be so. Katharine O'Brien had already shown him that the relationship between sex and interpersonal dependence was a choice, and one she chose not to make.

He felt so alone in his sense of emotional attachment to things. Ideas. Beliefs.

"So what is the role of government in all of this?" he interrupted irritably. "You make us sound irrelevant."

"Don't get petulant with me, Howard. Look at the history again. It's what you're good at, remember?

"Capital has always depended on governments to provide local infrastructure. It's never been either profitable or logistically sustainable for capital to provide its own. How could we have the transglobal flexibility we need if we had to rip up transport highways and systems and haul them around the world with us whenever we made a move from one site of production to another?

"We've always depended on governments to wage the wars for us too, to draw on the public's identification with their sense of nationhood, tap into that need to belong in order to fling one nation's bellicosity of resources at those of another. Governments keep us at one remove from the dirty stuff, Howard, so that we still look clean and legit as the economy. You know this. Government is essential.

"But they don't create the choices, Howard. Not for real economic action. Look what happened to carbon credits back in the twenties. Government once thought they would provide an eternal regulatory purpose for the legislature, but as soon as the transcorps began to see the profit in energy alternatives, they simply became another form of currency. Government is irrelevant in the larger scheme of world affairs. We have a New World Order that was powerless from its point of creation."

"I don't understand."

He genuinely didn't. He knew the creation of the New World Order. Had studied it closely. It represented a change in the global environment that his government knew would yield great benefits for the emerging Nation States in Australasia.

"It was a global response to climate change, in the wake of the Oil Wars of the 20s," he offered, as if this was some kind of defence. Remembering, even as he did, the document O'Brien has given him and Nihils to read on the night of their 'arrest'. But O'Brien was now powering in another direction.

219

"And it was the tombstone on the grave of the superpowers. Don't you remember London, Brussels, those grand initiatives of hope in the first two decades of the century, the campaigns to encourage local action, household heat recovery and solar power credits, high office tower-based heat and water recovery systems – they thought local solutions would solve the power and emission problems of major conurbations. Even the supergovernments, Howard, realised that the solutions lay at the level of local chaos, and marshalling order from it. But the result? Massive maintenance failures within ten years. Ironically, government has never been able to manage the local, Howard. It just locks itself into the inward micro-management spiral of bureaucratic accountability.

"But capital can. We are totally dependent on doing everything in our power to yield the most capital-friendly outcome from that most local of all market phenomena: the decision that emerges from the chaos in the consumer's mind at the point of purchase. Don't you see? It's vital we assist the macroscopic patterns that lead to a stable economy, functioning under the illusion of growth, to continue to emerge from the force of chaos represented by the individual's propensity to choose. That's why ideospeak and brandgrab are so essential. Choice is all, Howard, and choice is the consumer's. That's the only real freedom we have. The continuing action of humanity depends upon it."

She paused, but stared at him intently still, as if allowing the magnitude of her logic sink in with even herself.

"Look, Howard, you have a decision to make here. You can either remain forever embedded in a level of social order that depends on its mistaken self-perception of a power to yield order from chaos, remain wedded to a web of emotionally validated ideas that you call values and beliefs, or you can choose to make your emotions, and the values, beliefs and ideas that they bind together, work for you. You can take the step up, Howard, and marshal your self to make choices that are in the best interests of capital," O'Brien concluded.

Howard felt confused and defeated.

220

"But surely," he began, trying one more time to summon a failing intellect to his defence, "Surely there has to be something … some meaning. Surely."

"Don't you realise you're just pissing in the wind, Howard?" O'Brien was remorseless. "And it keeps coming back at you. And will continue to do so. Until you make the choice. You're like a man with incontinence, dripping this addiction to cathexis. Each drip, you hope some new meaning will emerge from the space into which it's fallen. Something else to keep your mind here, bound to the hope that your investment in your cathexis will somehow reward you, that there is a pay-off at the toilet's end.

"But there isn't, Howard. There's just you, your thoughts, your desires, and choice. And a lot of stuff that needs flushing away. You're not at the centre of anything. You're not the author of anything, or the origin of anything but action, ideas and decisions. The only capacity you have that makes any difference whatsoever is choice. Choice is All. It's just a question of at which level of human organisation you choose to exercise it."

He was too beaten even to sigh. He just sat there, impassive, immobile, barely breathing. Or so he thought.

"Why *did* you try to commit suicide, Howard?" O'Brien asked after a pause. It was a thoughtful question, not an aggressive imperative. He had not expected to return here. He had thought that topic dealt with already and filed under 'love'. But he suspected Katharine O'Brien now had another answer for him.

"I don't know," he replied honestly.

"You don't think it's because you simply thought there should be something more to life?"

He nodded. It was obvious.

"And perhaps there is. It's just not where you think it is."

O'Brien sounded once more almost compassionate in tone.

"We don't need people to feel too deeply about things, Howard. We don't need them to hang on to things too much. We need them to want change, to enjoy the new, to embrace the next thing. We need them to make the right choices more regularly. Our future depends upon it. But you – you could do something differently in relation to your capacity for feeling."

She paused again. He sighed again. New World Order. Government. Capital. Demonised underclasses in The Market. It was beginning to sink in.

"So the infochip, that you gave Nihils and me, that was all bullshit?"

"Completely and utterly."

"Simpkins?"

O'Brien flipped out her cell card and summoned up an image. It was Simpkins, with her, smiling for the vision, at the very same table at which she had joined Howard on their first day here.

"He was here less than a month ago, Howard. He chose not to choose choice, but that's not to say he is where your cyber journalist found him."

"So why ... I mean why ... me?" was all he could think of to say.

"Because you have curiosity, Howard. And that is a skill you could use more in your own interests, and in the interests of capital. And you are capable of doing more with your propensity to cathexis than simply depend on it, and feed off it emotionally."

Then they were both silent.

"Why don't you give yourself a break, Howard?" Katharine O'Brien suggested eventually. It was like a verbal touch on the thigh. "There is so much to enjoy here. There is so much enjoyment to be had in the world out there. I bet you haven't even noticed the name of this place, have you?"

Chapter Twenty-Seven

Once he started to look for it, the name of the resort was everywhere. It was on the meal menus, it was on the signs directing patrons around the grounds, it was even on the napkins. Paradise 101. He had to smile. The number of the room in which he had found Mick Turition. But the resort was so different.

"Why 101?" he would ask O'Brien later. "Why not?" she would reply. "It's actually one in a chain of Paradise resorts, from 1 to 150. It was a singularly unimaginative piece of marketing by whoever was responsible for it at the time. But we now have loyal consumers who actually try to visit every Paradise resort in the chain – an ambition which, as I'm sure you can imagine Howard, the length of a lifetime never quite enables them to achieve on a once-a-year holiday budget."

He took O'Brien's advice. Went for a swim in the clear, azure water. Booked one of the resort's jet skis and went out bounding across the bay's surface, terrorising swimmers, sailors and undersea life alike. Played table tennis with whoever turned up in the air-conditioned sports room to match him. Even did some working out in the gym. Although not too much. He really *was* out of condition.

He perused the cybernet to find out more about the resort at which he was staying. It was actually on an island just off the coast of Malaysia. The gunboats were Malaysian, from a naval station on the island. Fishing was the other local economy. Small fish called blinis were the industry. They looked like what he knew as 'whitebait' back home.

He took a taxi into the local fishing village, expecting foolishly to encounter some culturally original artisan existence, with bronzed, wizened fishermen in battered old fishing boats fingering out nets in long lengths as they putt-putted away from the dilapidated wharves with a trail of diesel plumes.

But of course what he found was a well-resourced dockland with the latest in fishing vessels, run by economically neat crews, coming and going from beneath a giant shopping world. Well and truly towards the fourth phase end of third phase progress. And obviously owned by Transglobal – why would they build a resort on an island on which they didn't also own the major industry and shopping world?

Beyond the main centre, he did find what they called these days a 'model village', where tourists could stay in losman-style accommodation built on wood-a-like piers and be served by guestworkers in folk dress, using quaint baskets and coconut shells and various other bowls and cutlery to intimate a First Phase village custom that no longer existed. Just around the corner, on the other side of the ridge descending to the southern tip of the island, was the naval base: modern, fortress-like, grey, inviolable. Owned by Transglobal too? Probably not. As O'Brien had so cogently pointed out. Just supplied by, more likely.

Back at the resort, though he rarely 'shopped' as such, he took the time to wander through Paradise 101's merchandising centre. Some odd, quirky commodities caught his eye. Another (clearly imitation, this time) prayer bell. And an audiofile of church bells he was sure he didn't have.

In his losman he relaxed to gin and tonic, and the sound of church bells from around the world, and idly sent a chastened Mick Turition, now back in a clean white mackintosh and seemingly unmindful of his recent experience in Room 101, off to into cyberspace to find out what he could about them. Reluctantly, it seemed, as Mick was still pining for Cold War Tatania, who had knocked him back when she learnt about the pregnant Hanianese cyber-hacker from the virtual bar in Shanghai.

Despite some of his obvious logistical failures with Mick Turition's narrative programming, Howard felt renewed somehow. The more he thought about it, the more what O'Brien had put to him made sense. He had bogged himself down for far too long in guilt and ego and the rest of it. He could so easily trace his depression and mental instability of recent years to an unnatural and unnecessary obsession with his sexuality, his desire for love, and his need for affection and comfort. But when he reviewed this history of thought in a more balanced way, he really didn't care that much about love. It only caused him pain in the end. And it was more the expectation of what it would bring him than the emotion itself that so beset him with the plethora of guilts and fears of obligation and disappointment that mired the whole prospect of relationship in misery.

Whereas the more he entertained the prospect of all he could have, his self seemed like a small price to pay, especially since he got to keep it anyway. It was not a question of surrendering his identity. More a matter of making it work better for him. And for capital, of course.

The thought made him mentally lighter in step. Intellectually, he began to develop a saunter and a swagger in his manner. Identity, self and love were, like all other features of human existence, commodities to utilised, facilities to be maximised, potentials to be fulfilled. He had hung onto them as some essential ontology for too long. And wasted a lot of mental and emotional energy in so doing.

A begrudging Mick Turition, resentful of being sent in search of church bells, flung him the English philosophers Bentham and Mill from the darkest annals of the cybernet, and told him to "cop that!". But of course Howard remembered the utilitarians from his second degree in political science. The very principle on which democratic government was founded was the same as generated the culture of individualism: enlightened self-interest. And this was, of course, the very foundation of Smithson Adams' New Prosperity:

Democracy is Freedom

Freedom is Choice

Choice is the Consumer's

He proudly shared his findings with O'Brien on what was becoming a regular 'sundowner' G&T on the veranda of his losman. And he was somewhat disconcerted when she rejected his assertion that consumer choice was built on self-interest.

"Is it self-interest or self-deception?" the corporate executive rejoined. "As you know, the consumer has only the choices capital places before them. And capital manipulates the choices they make through the control it exercises over the market, through ideospeak and brandgrab. It is essential capital does this, in order to minimise the risk and maximise the chance that the individual decision will result in a choice that is constructive for the majority.

"Journalese controls the very information available to the sensory powers of the consumer. Interpretation is futile. The consumer believes they have perfect choice, but in so doing they are perfectly deceived. How can there be Real Truth in deception, Howard?"

He was, as usual, completely flummoxed by the ineluctability of her logic.

O'Brien's attention turned to the bells, which accompanied Howard's time in his losman almost night and day now.

"You like them?"

It seemed an innocent question.

"Massively. I thought I had every audiochip of religious or spiritual bells in the known world, but…"

"Paradise has yielded more."

"Exactly."

She listened intently for a while.

"What's the attraction?"

"I don't know. It's the churches really. I find such peace inside a church. Not when anyone else is there but – maybe it's the wood and

226

the stone and the stained glass, the hard-seated pews and the high-vaulted ceilings. You can hear a pin drop in them.

"But it's also the spirit that created them. I don't mean God. As you well know, I'm not a theist. But, especially in those smaller country towns, every one has a church. Some, two or three. And they are all built by the community in the very act of the community building itself. It's as if they embody all that is positive about community, what people can achieve if they commit to a consensus. Community at work. It's very powerful."

"It certainly is."

Howard found O'Brien was staring at him intently. There was a flat, toneless reflection in her voice that turned his thoughts around to face him.

"A very deeply held belief," she said, further pressing the reflection home.

He held her gaze for a moment, and then allowed his eyes to drop into the empty space between them.

Chapter Twenty-Eight

"Welcome back, sir," said Greaves, admitting Howard through the various screening devices of the Member's Entrance. "It's been a while. I hope you're fully recovered."

"Yes, fully," replied Howard without emotion.

VIC Parliament had not changed, as he walked through its timber-veneered columns and marbled floors and the pervading transparency afforded by Transglobal's solar-powered roof. But then, why should they? He could only have been away for about a month, including the period it took to broker the Transglobal deal.

Indeed, it was as if he had never been away. The party whip, the Speaker of the Chamber and the party leader all separately greeted him warmly as he crossed the Seventh Hall on the way to his office. They all welcomed him back, but not with a sense that his absence had been anything unusual.

The party leader actually congratulated him on sealing the Transglobal outcome, and commented on what good reports he had heard from their side. Informed him he had arrived back just in time for the final passage of the amended bill, and was sorry he had come down with such a nasty virus at the end of so fruitful a negotiation.

So he had been in Paradise barely a week.

His office was pretty much as he had left it. Spotlessly neat. Except for the small envelope on his desk. He knew what it would contain. His netface had been riddled with shadows the night before. A shadow rifled through his backlog of e-messages, and a flash appeared on the opening of every second one, saying "Do You Want Sex?". And sure enough, inside the little envelope was a card bearing a graphic and unashamed rendition of a human penis, inside of which was the same question, with "Welcome back!" scrawled in small handwriting in the bottom right hand corner.

228

Using his office netface, he buzzed Nihils' cell card immediately, and arranged to meet him in the VICCaf.

*

"This is very public," was Nihils' first comment, rising slightly from his seat in deference to Howard's arrival.

"I have nothing to hide," Howard responded without attitude.

"Of course not," Nihils responded quickly.

"You look well," Howard said almost immediately.

"I didn't last long."

"You didn't like it?"

"Well, it wasn't exactly paradise."

"Mine was. It was even called Paradise."

"It's unlikely they gave you the same opportunities they extended to me. I could show you the burn marks if you like. They're in a convenient place. If you want to have sex, that is."

Howard paused and sipped his coffee. He noticed for the first time that Nihils didn't have anything.

"I'm sorry," he said, gesturing the empty place on the table in front of the genomporph. "Can I get you something?"

"Of course not. I'm off most things except water and fluids. Until I recover. Aversion therapy is fast and furious, but not necessarily long-lasting."

There was another pause.

"I'd love to make an honest man of you Nihils," Howard said at last. "But I'm afraid you are not in my long term interests."

"Not the sort of marriage for a politician," Nihils empathised.

"Or a businessman," Howard added. Nihils raised an eyebrow.

"They've made you an offer?"

"Not yet. But if it's in their interests, they know it's in mine. But yes, I would find the burn marks alluring."

"I wondered whether you would."

"But not just yet. I'm still not fully myself either. And we would need to be discrete."

"Of course," said Nihils. "That's in my interest too."

Howard sipped his coffee again.

"I can't authenticate you forever, you know," he said after a while. But he already knew Nihils' answer.

"There's no need to feel guilty, Howard. You know we're beyond that."

Howard remembered what he learnt about Nihils during his brief stay in Paradise, and nodded with resignation.

"I notice Mick has gone," Nihils ventured after a pause.

Howard barely grimaced, and drained his coffee.

*

Back in his office, he found a largish parcel on his desk: one that had come by what remained in VIC of a regular postal service. He unwrapped the thick brown paper carefully, although he was certain the object would have been screened down in Dispatch. It revealed a carton heavily bound with clear sticky tape, in which he recognised the handiwork of his mother.

He felt nothing as he worked away at the tape with a metal letter opener inadequate for the job. But he was not surprised to find, upon unravelling the protective wrapping, the old wooden clock that had sat on his mother's mantelpiece in whichever home they had lived for as much of his youth as he could remember.

There was more wrapping to remove from the innards of the wooden casing, and the key was taped to the inside of the rear door. Once he had ensured that the mechanism was free to work, and the hammer free to strike the spiralled gong, he carefully placed the old clock on his wooden display shelves, amongst the various official gifts he had been presented on official visits. He wound the clock's inner spring through the small aperture in its face, and replaced the key in the body of the clock by its rear door. Then he set the hands of the clockface by the timesignal in his office and sat back behind his desk.

He downloaded a range of e-messages relevant to the passage of the revised legislation through the house, and forwarded these with the revised legislation through to his netface console in the Chamber. The mechanism in the clock on his display shelves whirred into life, and the hammer struck the inner gong eleven times. Outside in the corridors, the bells swiftly followed, announcing the call in the chamber for a division on a bill. This would be his water bill.

He was dispassionate about the success of his negotiations, unmoved by the passage of his bill. All he knew was that he had made his choices to the best of his ability, and choice was everything.

For a moment, however, the image of Nihils' cute little tail and pert buttocks drifted across his mind. And he realised what had been different about the genomorph. He had lost his horns. His hair had been styled forward over the scars. There must be a devil of a joke in there somewhere, Howard thought to himself without smiling. Deadpan. Back-us-up. On a satyrical note.

He picked up his cell card and digital notepad, made a mental note to initiate the search for his first wife, Yvonne, as he had promised his mother, straightened his desk, and left.

THE END

www.ingramcontent.com/pod-product-compliance
Lightning Source LLC
Chambersburg PA
CBHW061139170626

46809CB00003B/912